SWEET
SIXTEEN

SWEET SIXTEEN

Michael Molloy

SINCLAIR-STEVENSON LIMITED

First published in Great Britain by
Sinclair-Stevenson Limited
7/8 Kendrick Mews
London SW7 3HG, England

Copyright © 1992 by Michael Molloy

British Library Cataloguing in Publication Data
A CIP catalogue record for this book is available
from the British Library.

ISBN: 1 85619 158 3

Typeset by Rowland Phototypesetting Limited
Bury St Edmunds, Suffolk

Printed and bound in Great Britain by
Clays Ltd, St Ives plc

CHAPTER
ONE

SARAH KEANE would not acknowledge that her husband was dead. When the news had come the previous February, the branches were bare and snowdrops had edged the lawn. More than a year passed, and there was now blossom on the fruit trees, but she continued as before: caring for her children's needs, attending the long high-walled garden and cleaning the house she had lived in since her marriage, seventeen years before.

At first, friends tried to offer their sympathies, but Sarah would not take part in any conversation on the subject of Jack's death. After a few awkward sentences they would fall silent and she would begin discussing her domestic problems. Gradually they stopped calling. Sarah seemed happy enough with her self-imposed isolation.

She had always been reserved and that aspect of her character had been encouraged at her boarding school, where the Sisters of Charity considered any display of flamboyance sinful, in addition to being unladylike.

Sarah was the only child of a doctor with a country practice. Her mother had been a loving parent but ill-health had caused her to

1

seem remote and her frailty made her unable to provide enough of the companionship her daughter needed. So Sarah was forced by circumstances to rely on her own resources, and she accepted loneliness as a normal state of existence.

When she eventually got a job on a newspaper her abilities and dedication were highly regarded, but her shyness and careful manners gave her the reputation of being superior and aloof. Then she met Jack Keane, and her life changed like a rose opening in the sun.

Everybody loved Jack: messengers, editors, secretaries. He was a big man, powerful and handsome, but it wasn't his looks that attracted people. It was the joyful quality that he possessed which caused others to seek his company and claim his friendship. Like all good raconteurs he listened to others, regardless of their importance or station and by his attentions enhanced their self-esteem.

She knew of his success with women from the conversations that took place around her in the newsroom, and was secretly shocked that those of her female colleagues who had bestowed their favours on him treated the matter as a triumph.

Sarah was involved with another man when Jack first asked her to go out with him so she refused his invitation. Then a few days later an envelope appeared on her desk that contained only a single ticket to a performance of *The Nutcracker Suite* at Covent Garden. Sarah dearly loved the ballet and when she took her seat the following evening she found Jack Keane seated next to her.

A year later they were married, and within a month Sarah was pregnant. She did not miss work; life with Jack was a full vessel that brimmed with pleasure. He introduced her to his friends and she learned to accommodate the eccentricities of his behaviour because he was exciting. Originally, she had intended to return to work after the birth of her daughter, but soon she was expecting again and the birth of twin sons kept her at home. The house in Hampstead became the centre of Sarah's universe, but to Jack it was more like a club that provided his every comfort, and a location where he could entertain the retinue of friends who accompanied him through life.

When he moved from the newspaper to television his work took him away more often but Sarah was happy enough with the children for company and in truth she enjoyed the relative calm brought about by the absence of her husband's cronies.

And so the years passed, the time alternating between frantic celebrations when Jack was home and the gentle peace of his long departures.

It had not been difficult to put the reality of his death away from her. There had been no funeral because his body had never been recovered. Reliable witnesses had sworn affidavits that they had seen the Land Rover carrying his television crew hit by rocket fire somewhere on the Saudi border. There had been nothing to mark their graves. It was a big desert. Sarah's father came up from Suffolk to take care of the necessary administration. With a distant obedience she had signed the forms he presented to her and returned to the housework that had now become her obsession.

When Jack was alive, her special attention had been reserved for the garden, but now she turned to the rest of the house with equal devotion. Each room was scrubbed, scoured and polished with a continuous ferocity that had caused her cleaning woman to resign.

'You don't need me these days, Mrs Keane,' she had said when she gave in her notice, her tone somehow implying that Sarah's efforts were a mute criticism of her own standards. Sarah accepted her departure with the same distant serenity with which she greeted any tribulation that had arisen since that cold day in February.

Slowly, her appearance changed. She was of average height, and had been a good athlete at school, winning prizes for swimming and middle-distance running, but during the years of her marriage, contentment had caused her to grow heavier. She'd carried the weight well, it had not coarsened her features, and she had worn her dark glossy hair long, the way Jack liked it. He had not seemed to mind her loose clothes and thickening body. But now the regime of punishing work she'd imposed upon herself in the past year had altered the shape of her frame just as surely as if she had attended a gymnasium every day.

Each morning she got up before seven to make breakfast and prepare the children for school, and when they'd departed the assault on the house would begin.

Increasing quantities of scalding water, bleach, soda crystals, cleaning fluids, wax and polish were consumed in her relentless drive to hold off reality. It was as if she were responding to the original demands of the Victorian house, when two maids had tended the rambling rooms. Gradually, she returned to more basic ways of performing her formidable duties. She began to boil clothes in the copper basin and use the cast-iron mangle that had lain, long neglected in the kitchen outhouse. She no longer visited the supermarket, but bought instead from the thin scattering of local

3

tradesmen who still kept shops of the kind her grandmother had known. The work filled her days and nights completely. She had no time to read newspapers or watch television; nor did she listen to the radio. Weekends were devoted to the garden, which she approached with the same relentless application. When she stopped each night, it was for the dull, heavy sleep which finally came to blot out her misty existence. Of her three children, only Emily, the eldest, who was nearing sixteen, realised there was anything odd in her mother's behaviour. Occasionally she would telephone her grandfather, to reassure him of the family's wellbeing, but in her private thoughts she worried that things were not as they ought to be.

When Henry Linton received these calls it was sometimes difficult for him to remember how young Emily was: fine boned and slender with light, chestnut-coloured hair and a complexion as clear as spring water, she was one of those rare girls who had seemed to pass gracefully from childhood into adolescence without the usual turbulence.

Her brothers were quite different. Paul and Martin were cast in their father's image: long athletic bodies with apple-red skin and hair that looked as if it had been chipped from coal. Both had flaring tempers, but they took life casually, as if it were an enjoyable game that had been devised for their pleasure. Others indulged their carefree attitude, as if hoping they might share the secret of such blissful unconcern. Even the sternest masters at their school sometimes overlooked their transgressions because their smiles came from the heart and their regrets from a genuine sense of remorse. Happiness was their normal state.

But Emily knew that life was a serious business. Where the boys saw their mother's devotion to housework as the normal order of things, Emily realised that the state of mind controlling Sarah's emotions could eventually blow away, and with it the seeming peace of her existence. Where the boys saw an unruffled surface of self-control, Emily knew there were deeper tides waiting to release their forces. Logic told her so as much as intuition, and she trusted knowledge more than her emotions. From the time she'd learned to talk Emily had sought to understand the meaning of everything she'd encountered. Nothing could be accepted at face value; she wanted to know why the sun shone, what made the rain and where all past years had gone. In childhood, Sarah had taken refuge in a world of imagination. Books had been her way of escape, but for Emily they

4

were a means of answering the questions that teemed through her mind.

Although the love Sarah felt for her daughter was absolute, she knew there was an aspect of Emily that they would never share, and it was that very element that made her close to Sarah's father. It was clear from their earliest conversations that Emily was also going to be a doctor. When they visited their grandfather the boys would be instructed in the use of fishing rods and shotguns, but his real pleasure came when he sat with Emily and showed her his medical books. Watching them together brought back the loneliness of Sarah's childhood more sharply than any memory.

The past year had caused Emily more pain than anyone could suspect because all the resources of her intelligence could not provide a solution to her mother's grief.

Things changed on the May Bank Holiday: but not in the way Emily expected.

Martin and Paul had gone to France, on a holiday organised by their school, and Emily spent the day working in the garden with Sarah. By early evening, Emily was tired and went into the house to bathe. She lingered for a long time, until the water cooled, and then, dressed in a bathrobe, came to stand at the french windows while she towelled her hair. At first she felt happy enough; there was a pleasant hush to the house and the scent of freshly cut grass reminded her of other days.

Then she noticed that Sarah was still kneeling before the same flowerbed at the end of the lawn, in the same position as when Emily had first gone into the house. Puzzled, she watched her mother's still form; a growing anxiety made her hurry barefooted to stand beside the bowed figure. She could see that Sarah was moving very gently, but no sound came from her. Hesitantly she reached out to touch her shoulder and Sarah slowly turned, her eyes blinded by tears. Sinking down beside her, Emily reached out and took her mother in her arms.

'Oh, Jack,' Sarah said after a time. They were the only words she spoke, but they were the saddest her daughter had ever heard.

After a time, Emily brought her back to the house. It was like leading a sleepwalker. Her mother obeyed her instructions without protest. She sat patiently while a bath was run and afterwards Emily handed her a nightgown. She put it on and slipped beneath the turned-back sheets of her bed. She seemed to fall asleep immediately but Emily sat with her until twilight came. Then she left the room to ring her grandfather. She could tell that he had been drinking a bit; his voice was not slurred, but his speech was altered enough for her to know.

He listened patiently to her description of Sarah's behaviour, and then said, 'You've done the right thing. She's still suffering from shock you know, sleep is the best thing for her now.'

'Should I call the doctor?'

'You have called a doctor.'

She hesitated. 'I mean, is her mind all right . . . should she see a psychiatrist?'

He took time to consider the question. 'I don't think so. Grief affects people in different ways. You'll see a lot of it if you're going to be a doctor.'

They talked for a while, and when Emily had said goodnight she returned to her mother's room. It was dark now, but for the light from a street lamp across the tree-lined street. The headlights from a slowly passing car reflected across the ceiling and Sarah's breathing was soft and regular.

Emily drew the heavy curtains and got into bed beside her. For a moment she remembered the times when she and the boys had played on the bed and her father tickled their squirming bodies into helpless laughter, and Christmas mornings when the counterpane and floor were strewn with bright wrapping paper. Sadness engulfed her and she shifted closer to Sarah. There was a moment of stillness and then her mother's arms encircled her and she felt the familiar warmth and the scent of coal-tar soap.

After a long silence Sarah spoke in a low voice:

'Daddy is dead, Emily.'

'I know,' she replied, and then, slowly, sleep came like a blanket of soft black velvet.

When Sarah woke the following morning it seemed that the mist that had clouded her existence during the past months had drifted away, leaving the reality that she had avoided for so long clearly set in the forefront of her mind. There was pain: as sharp and hard as a knife blade, but she knew, in those first waking moments, that now she could cope with the knowledge that Jack would never return to them.

Because his work as a television reporter had taken him away for months at a time during their marriage, it had been easy for her to believe he was on a long journey that would end with another reunion. Now she knew she must put that excuse aside. Her thoughts drifted to a time in her childhood when she was at her convent and she was told that her mother had died. Sister Veronica had taken her to light a candle. The memory of the hushed chapel and the cold, gritty stone beneath her knees came back in a moment of clarity. She realised it had been a long time since she had been to church. Like her mother, she had married an agnostic, and over the years had gradually drifted into her husband's ways.

She looked up at the ceiling, and in the gloom noticed a fine crack that ran from the cornice across the length of the room. Jack had always said he would repair it one day. Now it would be up to her.

Her eyes followed the crack and she thought of other promises Jack had made. Usually he tried to keep his word, but his compulsion to make people happy often caused him to give assurances that were impracticable. He would suggest day trips and holidays to the children, dinner parties and lunches with friends that would never have a hope of taking place; and it was always Sarah who would make the excuses and smooth over disappointments.

She knew that some of Jack's friends thought she was a dulling influence in their marriage; it was always Sarah who had to say no to the suggestion of one more bottle of wine. She did not resent the role he had unconsciously created for her because, like others, she loved his company. The necessity to set the boundaries of his transgressions did not seem too high a price to pay for the happiness he brought. In the clarity that had now come to her, Sarah knew how much her life had begun to drift along, even before Jack's death, like a boat on a wide, tranquil river.

There had only been one, brief storm in the marriage. In the autumn of the year following the birth of the boys, Jack went missing for a few days: Sarah thought nothing of it, until calls from the office made her realise that his absence was nothing to do with work. She had closed up the house and took the children to Brittany, where they remained for more than a week until Jack tracked them down by tracing the payments on her credit card. It took him two days to persuade her to return home and he was shaken by her resolve. It was not her anger but the depth of her hurt that convinced him there was a limit to her tolerance.

Sarah made a conscious decision that she would raise her sons with an appreciation of the pain they could cause to others. So when the time came to make a choice of schools, she turned to the Jesuits. She had never regretted the commitment; it became clear with each passing year that the twins possessed Jack's strengths and weaknesses in full measure. Emily was quite different. The only evident inheritance from her father was a love of music, which was as necessary to her existence as her need to seek wisdom.

Sarah moved again. Her body felt taut and lean beneath the nightgown; when she ran her hands over her flat stomach and small breasts she suddenly felt the roughness of her calloused hands.

There was a stirring and she saw that Emily lay beside her with her tousled hair spread across the pillow. Sarah got up, drew the curtains and examined her face in the mirror on the dressing table. Instead of the soft familiar contours she'd expected, she saw that her features were straight and angular, as if they had been shaped with a sharp instrument, making prominent bones and hollows beneath her cheeks. There were fans of fine lines about her eyes but her complexion was clear and windburnt. Her hair was as rough as a bramble bush and silvered with grey, like the coat of an Irish wolfhound. She brushed it vigorously and tied it up with a ribbon behind her head.

When she had bathed and dressed, she went down to the living room. Emily had also got up and was now eating a bowl of muesli and watching an early morning television programme.

Sarah sat on the arm of a chair and looked at the screen. A line of men were walking across open parkland, examining the ground before them.

'What's this?' she asked.

Emily glanced up at her. 'They're looking for clues, it's about the murders,' she answered.

'What murders?'

Emily looked back at the screen while she answered. 'Two girls have been killed, one at Harrow and one at Stanmore.'

Sarah knew nothing of the events. She found it slightly disturbing.

She went into the kitchen and sat thinking for a few minutes, then, calling to tell Emily that she would not be long, she found her purse and left the house.

The walk to the local High Street surprised her. She felt quite different. It was as if her legs contained powerful springs and if called upon, she would be able to run swiftly and without effort. The surrounding gardens were bathed in a clearer light, colours were better defined, and edges of objects hard and sharply focused.

In the newsagent's there was a line of people waiting to be served. She glanced along the rack beside her and pulled several glossy magazines from the shelves. She bought all the daily newspapers and returned home with the same energetic stride.

For the rest of the morning Sarah remained in the living room, absorbing the contents of the magazines and newspapers with the intensity she had previously devoted to housework.

Just after midday there was a sharp knock on the front door. When Sarah answered she found her father on the step. As always, he seemed to bristle with impatience. Sarah was surprised to see him; he hated visiting London, even the suburbs. He seemed shorter when he leaned forward and gave her a perfunctory, grazing kiss on the cheek. Then he strode past without speaking, and embraced Emily, who had appeared from her bedroom.

'This is a surprise, dad,' Sarah said.

He turned and thrust his hands into the jacket pockets of his tweed suit. 'I'm just passing through on the way to visit your Aunt Victoria.' Sarah remembered: Victoria was a sister with whom he was barely on speaking terms.

'She lives in Guildford, doesn't she?'

'Guildford,' he repeated with a nod.

'Come into the living room,' Sarah urged. 'Would you like a cup of tea? Something to eat?'

Doctor Linton glanced at his watch. 'I wouldn't mind a beer.'

'Oh, dear,' Sarah said softly, 'I'm not sure if we have any.'

'I think there's some in the kitchen cupboard,' Emily said. 'I'll just go and look.'

When she left the room father and daughter gazed at each other in silence. Sarah saw that he looked older. His hair and moustache were quite white. But his colour was good and, as always, he looked fit. It was clear that he still walked a good deal.

'So, how are you?' he asked finally.

'Better,' she replied. He glanced through the french windows into the garden.

'I thought I'd stop to discuss financial matters.' He paused. 'If you feel up to it?'

Sarah nodded.

He drummed his fingers on the side of the chair for a moment, then cleared his throat. 'The fact is, the insurance money is running out. You still have the income from what your mother left you, but it isn't much. Not enough to go on living here at any rate.' He leaned further forward in his chair. 'I thought I'd put an idea to you.'

Sarah folded her hands. For the first time in her life she did not feel awkward in his presence. The yearning to please him or seek his approval was no longer there.

He went on, 'The upkeep on this place must be pretty high, but it's worth quite a bit. Why don't you sell it and put the money into trust for the children?'

'Where would we live?'

'I was coming to that. There would be room enough at the cottage if we built an extension at the back. It wouldn't cost too much.'

He got up and stood before the fireplace as if to warm himself at the cold grate.

Sarah blinked back a prickle of tears but she did not cry.

'Oh, dad. Would you swap your rose garden for us?'

'Of course.'

Sarah shook her head. 'Don't worry – I've got other plans.'

Just then Emily entered the room carrying a brimming glass and handed it to her grandfather.

'Where are the boys?' he asked suddenly.

'France, on a school trip,' Emily answered.

He sipped some of the beer and nodded. 'I thought the place was quiet.' Then he turned to Emily. 'So, how is your school work coming on, young lady?'

She brought her briefcase from the hallway and they quickly became immersed in her textbooks. Sarah watched for a few minutes, then returned to the newspapers.

After an hour or so Doctor Linton stood up.

'On to Guildford?' Sarah said.

He nodded. 'Remember what I said.'

'I will,' Sarah replied as they walked to the door.

He turned stiffly and said, 'You always meant more to me than the roses.'

Sarah waved as he drove away – just as she had when he took her to her boarding school at the end of the holidays.

Emily sat with her for some time. Eventually realising that her mother was not going to stop reading to cook the customary meal, she made some scrambled eggs. Sarah ate the food without taking her eyes from the page. Occasionally she would pause and ask her daughter questions about certain people or some aspect of current affairs, then she would return to the printed words. When the papers and magazines were discarded, Sarah turned to the television, which she watched with equal attention. Finally, late in the evening, Emily bid her goodnight and went to bed.

Sarah continued the same routine for the next three days. House-work was neglected and dishes allowed to dry on the kitchen sink, a practice that Emily knew her mother had previously considered sluttish.

On the morning of the day the boys were due back from their holiday, Sarah finished the papers by nine o'clock. Then she told Emily they were going shopping in the West End.

They took taxis between department stores and shops. It was a well-planned journey, with a purpose. Sarah knew exactly what she wanted to buy at each stop; she had even clipped a file of cuttings from the various newspapers and magazines she had studied so carefully. Their final call was at a smart hairdresser's salon in New Cavendish Street. They left at ten minutes to six and Sarah's transformation was so complete that Emily hardly recognised her. The baggy clothes had gone and Sarah was dressed in a dark blue suit and a white silk shirt. The grey had been rinsed from her hair, which had been cut short and shaped around the contours of her face. Make-up softened her aquiline features. She looks like a stranger, Emily thought, and quite glamorous. But when they arrived at Victoria Station the boys hardly noticed the change although Emily saw one of the masters give Sarah an appreciative glance.

'What's for supper?' Martin asked when they shuffled for space among the many packages in the back of the taxi.

'I hadn't thought,' Sarah replied. 'How about a takeaway?' The boys exchanged glances. They were puzzled and slightly disconcerted. Sarah's new appearance had not bothered them, but for her to offer them a meal that she had not prepared herself suddenly made her seem like a stranger. However, the prospect of Chinese food drove away their doubts, and within minutes they were recounting events of the holiday, as if Sarah was exactly the same woman they had left behind them.

But Emily still found the developments disturbing, although she managed to hide her misgivings. The changes brought a sense of disquiet because she sensed there was something bigger to come. She watched Sarah carefully throughout the journey to Hampstead as if expecting that another metamorphosis might take place, causing her to emerge from the taxi with a different personality again.

The driver was friendly and quite willing to drive to the local Chinese restaurant. While the boys crashed and stumbled about the house dumping gear at the far points of their domain, Emily took the clothes Sarah had bought for her and carefully hung them in her wardrobe.

When she came downstairs she found her mother on the sofa with a cup of coffee, and a small writing pad open on her lap. She was listening to a woman on the television who was speaking about subsidies for the arts. Emily watched her mother cover a page with spidery symbols.

'I didn't know you could write shorthand,' she said.

'More than a hundred words a minute when I get my speed back,' Sarah replied without looking up. This unknown talent added to Emily's unease.

The food was delivered and Sarah called the boys. They assembled in the breakfast room next to the kitchen. When the meal was served, Sarah told them she was going to get a job.

'What kind of job? What can you do?' the boys asked.

'Reporting.' Sarah replied. 'They told me I was quite good at it once upon a time.'

There was a long silence and then Paul spoke. 'Dad always used to say that reporting was a young man's game.'

'I'm sorry,' Sarah replied lightly. 'It's all I know. I'm getting on a bit to start training for a new career.'

Paul drummed for a moment with his chopsticks. 'Maybe they'll let you do the easy stuff,' he said.

'Why do you want to work?' Emily asked in a quiet voice. 'Don't you like it at home any more?'

'Yes, I do like it at home,' Sarah said, 'but we need the money.'

'Aren't we rich now?' Martin asked with all the care he might use to enquire if his tea had been sugared.

'We never were rich,' Sarah replied, 'but your father earned a good salary. There's still money from the insurance, but that won't last for ever, so it's up to me.'

The boys nodded, unconcerned. The food commanded the greater part of their attention, but Sarah could see that Emily was not happy. The slightest upset caused her to lose her appetite. Now the small portion of food on her plate remained untouched.

My darling daughter. Sarah thought. So burdened by the trials of life. If only you had been granted some of the boys' blithe spirit. There'll be plenty of time to worry later on – all the time in the world.

Sarah wanted to reach out and offer her comfort, but she knew it would be wrong. This was not the time for consoling gestures; she must show that their circumstances demanded resolution.

A sudden thought came to Paul. 'Who's going to cook for us if you're at work?'

'You're going to have to help me a bit,' Sarah said. 'I won't be here to prepare every meal.'

Martin shrugged. 'That's all right, I quite like takeaways.'

Sarah shook her head. 'I'm afraid not, darling. Takeaways are going to be an occasional luxury from now on. We can't afford to go on living at these prices.'

'Supposing we gave up lunches at school?' Paul suggested. 'Then we could put the money towards takeaways.'

Sarah shook her head again. 'Sorry, it doesn't work out like that. School meals are cheap. Junk food is expensive.'

The boys contemplated this information in silence for a time and then returned to the subject of their trip to France.

When Sarah had cleared away she took her notebook to a small room at the end of the hallway. For more than a year, while she concentrated on the rest of the house, this door had remained locked. Originally it had been a cloakroom, but Jack had used it as a study. Just before she entered, Sarah hesitated and took a deep breath. Of all the rooms in the house this was the one that most completely retained Jack's presence. Inside, she stood motionless for a few moments, feeling like a swimmer ascending from deep waters, then she looked around the narrow space.

One wall of shelves was filled with reference books, the other covered with framed photographs: teams of boys from Jack's school-days, a group of young men in dinner jackets accompanied by girls in ball gowns. There were newsroom photographs, first in Manchester, then in London at the *Gazette*, showing people gathered for fare-wells, anniversaries and parties. Then they switched to television crews taken in more exotic surroundings. At the end of the wall there was a blank space. Sarah reached out to touch it, knowing that now it would never be filled.

For a moment she thought her resolve might break under the wave of memories, but she shut the door firmly behind her and sat down at the battered desk under the window. Removing the dusty cover from a portable typewriter, she began transcribing the notes she had taken earlier. At first it was slow work; she found it difficult to decipher her shorthand and her hands felt awkward and clumsy on the little keyboard. But as she became more absorbed in the task she forgot that she was surrounded by so many memories of Jack.

After more than two hours she paused and suddenly realised she was very thirsty. There was a sharp ache at the base of her skull where concentration had made her tense the muscles of her neck. Covering the typewriter, she switched off the light and went to the living room.

Emily was reading one of the magazines from the coffee table and the boys were sprawled on the carpet in front of the fireplace, competing to see who could build a larger house of cards. The television blared out, although no one appeared to be watching. She glanced at the screen just as the newsreader began her opening sentence: 'Information has just reached us that the body of another murdered girl has been found in the north London suburb of Finchley. . . .'

CHAPTER
TWO

NEXT morning Sarah got up at her usual time, but preparations for breakfast were completed with a much greater speed than usual. No oranges were squeezed or different orders solicited; everyone was presented with boiled eggs, and before any protests could be made she had left the house and gone to buy the morning papers.

In the newsagent's she glanced at the headlines and saw that the latest murder was page-one news in every national, although the broadsheets gave it less prominence than the tabloids.

When she returned to the house it still reverberated with the noise of the boys getting ready for school. There were no sounds from Emily; she managed most things more calmly. When all of them were ready to leave, Sarah called them and told the boys that she wanted them all to come home together that afternoon. The boys groaned. Being in the lower school, they finished half an hour earlier than Emily. Sarah insisted.

'Is it because of the murders?' Emily asked.

Sarah nodded. 'Don't worry. Nothing will happen to you,' she said, making her voice sound confident.

'You'll be all right with us,' the boys added in reassuring tones, happy now to be delegated the role of bodyguards. After they left, Sarah sat at the breakfast table with a cup of coffee and began to go through the papers. This old skill came easier than the shorthand and typing. It was still a question of discarding the nonessential, she told herself.

Although she took no notes, by the time a couple of hours had passed, Sarah had read and retained all of the day's important news stories. She also had a grasp of the major political developments, and knew what the leading articles of each newspaper proclaimed. If questioned, she would be able to remember where she had read a particular piece and on what page, and which individual report on any subject was the best written, or contained the most facts, which was not necessarily the same thing. Most of the information would lie on the surface of her memory and would fade completely in a matter of days. Only a few of the facts she'd absorbed would be retained for ever.

The story of the murdered girl preoccupied her most. She supposed it was because all of the victims were about the same age as Emily. Information was sparse. The police admitted there were similarities to the previous murders, but they would not be specific, other than to say that all of the girls had come from wealthy families. Sarah sat thinking about the three cases, and suddenly she wanted a cigarette. It was a curious desire. She had stopped smoking when she was expecting Emily and had never wanted to resume the habit until this moment. She glanced at the clock on the wall. It was 9.22; still a few more minutes to go before George Conway would be at his desk.

She had last spoken to George some time in the cloudy period following the news of Jack's death, but she had no recollection of the conversation. Even so, she knew he would not have changed. There was an immutable quality about George Conway that resisted time and fashions, like a thoroughbred shire horse, and Sarah knew that beneath his toughened manner he had a soft spot for her. Jack had always said George was the best news editor in the business and their friendship had continued when Jack moved from the newspaper to television. Although it had never been stated, Sarah suspected that George cared for her just as deeply.

She took the cups and plates to the sink and looked through the window into the garden while the hot water ran. Two magpies strutted on the lawn. Mystical birds, she thought, feared and respected by country people. The old saying 'Two for joy' came to her and a sudden, powerful desire for Jack made her stomach flutter. The realisation that such fulfilment was impossible struck her like a physical blow. She sat down at the table again and gripped her hands into tight fists until the spasm of pain passed.

It had been nearly a year and a half since she had made love, and it had not bothered her until this moment. In fact, the very absence of desire sometimes made Sarah wonder if she possessed a low sex drive. She had a friend called Philippa Stone who worked in television as a producer's assistant, and once, when they were alone in the kitchen after a dinner party, Philippa described the intricacies of her sex life. The stories made Sarah laugh aloud, but at the same time they filled her with a certain amount of awe.

If Philippa was to be believed, she had taken part in sexual encounters that tested the extremities of imagination: in cinemas, the backs of cars, parks, rooftops, the public conveniences of both ladies and gentlemen, and once under the stage of a school hall, after a children's concert. Every surface, flat, horizontal or undulating, she saw as a challenge, and one that must ultimately be explored. After the graphic description of a coupling that was supposed to have taken place in the linen cupboard of a London hotel, Sarah had said, 'I don't know how Patrick manages.' Patrick was Philippa's husband. Philippa snorted with laughter as she put the dishes they were loading into the washing machine.

'Who said anything about Patrick? He's only interested in doing it in bed.'

Sarah had been about to question her further but Jack had entered the kitchen in search of more drink and Sarah had never had the opportunity to find out who Philippa's other partners had been.

Sometimes, after the conversation, Sarah had wondered if it were she or Philippa who was normal. When Jack went away for long periods abroad she missed him, but the need for his physical presence had never been much of a problem. It was wonderful when they were together; that was enough for her.

Although she had grown up in the time known as the permissive era, Sarah had not followed fashion with the enthusiasm shown by so many of her contemporaries. She had lost her virginity to a young man called Frank Ashby with whom she had been involved when she met Jack Keane. The experience had not caused her to wish for a wider circle of partners.

Frank had seemed a glittering prize when she was first introduced

17

to him, excessively handsome with beautiful manners and already successful in the city brokerage house where he worked. Everyone agreed they made a well-matched pair. She continued to live in the flat she shared with two other girls in Holland Park, but three nights a week Sarah stayed with Frank in his mews house in Marylebone. He collected pottery, and all of the walls were lined with showcases. He would make love to her with textbook proficiency, and then get up, shower, remake the bed and fall asleep quickly, leaving Sarah still awake in the semi-darkness, gazed upon by rows of grinning jugs and pop-eyed China dogs.

When she eventually made love with Jack it was an entirely different experience, and one for which she was not prepared. They had bathed together before reaching the bedroom, where Sarah found that it was possible for sex to consume the five senses and all of her emotions.

She looked at her watch again: 9.45. Time to ring. She got through to the news desk of the *Gazette* immediately and an unfamiliar voice answered the call.

'May I speak to George Conway?' she asked. 'My name is Sarah Keane.'

'He's not here just yet,' the voice answered. Then, 'Oh, just a minute, I see him approaching with weary steps.'

She could hear a muttered exchange and then George Conway spoke.

'Sarah?'

'Hello, George, how are you?'

'Fine.' She heard the caution in his voice, and remembered that he had been one of the friends who had contacted her when the news about Jack first came through. Vaguely she recollected brushing his sympathy aside.

'How are you?' he asked.

'Better now. I'm sorry about the last time you called, I wasn't at my best.'

Conway laughed briefly. 'I'm like that most mornings.'

'Who was the person who answered the phone?'

Conway laughed again. 'A little fellow who'd like to take my place. He's called Alan Stiles.'

'Things don't change.'

'Some things, never. What can I do for you?'

'I need a job, George.'

There was a moment of hesitation and Sarah held her breath. Suddenly she could hear the blood pulsing in her temple.

'Things are very tight just now,' George said. 'The best I can offer you is some casual shifts.'

'That's fine,' she answered, hoping that the need did not show too much in her voice.

'Why don't you come in tomorrow then, about ten?' He hung up before she could answer.

Alan Stiles, who was seated opposite George Conway on the news desk, pretended that he was engrossed in preparing the morning's conference schedule instead of eavesdropping on the conversation. George ignored him and tapped a set of instructions into his computer terminal. The reporters' rota for the following day flooded on to the screen and he typed in the name 'Sarah Linton'. After a moment, he obliterated the last name and wrote 'Keane' in its place.

Alan Stiles glanced up at him, unblinking eyes filled with hostility and took another mint from the bag he always kept on his desk. The quality of his breath and the thinness of his hair were Stiles's constant preoccupations, only exceeded by his ambition to usurp George Conway's position as news editor of the *Gazette*.

It wasn't the first time Conway had endured the ambitions of envious deputies during his eighteen years on the paper, but of all the men who had filled the role, Alan Stiles was the first he had absolutely loathed. Conway was not alone in this; Stiles was disliked by most people in the office, but he seemed to have the knack of pleasing the editor, and because of that he was not short of allies. Conway thought he was more than just unpleasant; he also considered the man dangerous. Whenever there was difficulty with a story, when pursed-lipped lawyers and grave executives questioned the judgement of a reporter, Stiles always somehow managed to slip on to the side of those seeking to apportion blame.

Conway pretended to study the screen of his terminal, but was actually watching his deputy from the edge of his vision. Stiles made audible sucking sounds and began to stroke the strands of hair that he had arranged over the dome of his freckled head. The action reminded George Conway of a cat; not a decent tabby, but some vicious ginger menace that prowled about seeking to cause harm. Conway was determined to limit his power. Stiles, given the power, would treat people like captured mice.

After a few more minutes of sucking, Stiles got up and went over to make conversation with Shirley, the secretary on the picture desk.

It was a daily ritual: Shirley was one of the beacons of gossip that studded the office. In a few minutes, Stiles would be bloated with harmful information, which he would spread like droppings throughout the office for the rest of the day.

When Stiles was far enough away, George Conway drew his wallet from the jacket that was draped over the back of his chair and searched for a small black-and-white snapshot. It was a passport photograph of Sarah, taken when she had first joined the paper. George looked at the serious young face for a few moments, then carefully replaced it in his wallet and turned back to his computer screen.

Now that she had made arrangements for the following morning, Sarah felt suddenly without purpose. The rest of the day seemed to stretch endlessly before her, flat and empty, without definition or feature. For a long time she had existed in a half-world. Now, her head clear, she was restless, wanting to bring her attention to bear but unable to find a subject on which to concentrate.

Because of the harsh physical demands she had imposed on herself every day for the past year, her body craved exercise, so she decided to take a hard walk. After driving to Hampstead Heath, she parked near the pond and set off on a long walk down Parliament Hill. It was a cold, shadowless day. The sky was clay-white and flickered with darting birds. She passed the dead flat surface of the bathing pond, and then skirted Kenwood House before setting off across East Heath to return to her point of departure.

The exercise satisfied her body but something still nagged in her mind. She drove down Hampstead High Street and double parked long enough to buy an early edition of the *Evening Standard*. As she had expected, it gave the murdered girl's address. She looked it up in the street guide she kept in her glove compartment. It was no distance at all.

When she arrived at her destination, the road she entered was so like her own the effect was disquieting: lime trees stood each side of the street and the handsome Victorian houses lay well back, behind carefully tended gardens, their fronts dark-red brick and trimmed with frostings of white stone. A police van was parked by the gateway of Number 27.

Sarah was unsure of her reasons for coming; she did not stop the car, but drove slowly past the house and then headed off. Still

20

wondering how to fill the rest of her day, she parked a few streets away while she thought. The solution occurred to her: as it was to be her last day at home she would cook a special dinner for the children. The selection was not difficult, roast turkey was their constant choice. Filled with determination, she drove back towards Hampstead High Street.

Later that evening they sat down at the dining table, which glowed with candlelight.

'Do you know what I really like about turkey?' Paul asked as he helped himself to vegetables. 'The turkey stew we have the next day.' He looked towards Sarah with sudden anxiety. 'We will have it tomorrow night, won't we?'

Sarah nodded. 'I'll prepare it later. You'll have to put the oven on when you get home from school.'

Martin looked down at his drumstick. 'Is turkey kosher?' he asked.

Sarah thought for a moment. She was used to the erratic directions conversations with the boys would suddenly take.

'Yes, I think so,' she answered. 'Not the bacon and sausages, though. Why do you ask?'

Martin reached for the gravy and said, 'Father Robson lived on a kibbutz for a year once, he said the food was all kosher.'

Paul nodded. 'He lived with a tribe of Indians in South America as well. He ate a snake then.'

'Father Robson seems to get about. Which one is he?'

'The one who was standing with the art master when you came to pick us up at the station.'

'Which one is the art master?'

'The one who fancied you.'

'You mustn't say that about a priest,' Sarah said.

Martin shook his head. 'Mr Collins isn't a priest. He used to draw women without any clothes.'

'I wouldn't mind being a Jesuit,' Paul interrupted.

'Don't you want to get married?' Sarah said quickly.

He shrugged. 'Priests will probably be able to get married by the time I'm old enough.'

'I don't think the Jesuits will change that much,' put in Emily.

'Would you like to marry a priest, mum, or would you prefer an artist?' Paul asked the question casually but Sarah could see that all of them were waiting to hear her answer.

She paid closer attention to her meal. 'The choice seems a bit

21

extreme,' she answered noncommittally. Then she turned to Emily. 'What about you, darling?'

Her daughter looked up. 'I think I'd like someone who was home more often than dad was.'

Sarah remembered the moment of desire she had experienced earlier and decided to change the subject.

'How is it?' she asked, noticing their enthusiasm.

'Not bad for a last supper,' Martin answered with a smile.

CHAPTER
THREE

SARAH set about her usual tasks with a brisk determination, but her new-found confidence began to ebb when she came to choose the clothes she would wear for her first day back at the *Gazette*. Suddenly all the outfits she'd bought on her recent shopping trip seemed unsuitable and she searched deeper in the wardrobe to discover dresses she'd worn before her weight had become a problem.

Eventually she found a plum-coloured dress she'd bought when Emily was still in a pushchair, Jack had been with her that Saturday morning, they had gone shopping in Kensington High Street: perhaps it was a good omen. Later than she'd intended to be, and slightly flustered, she drove to Gray's Inn Road. The weather was patchy. Hard bright sunlight came in bursts through the rainclouds and sudden slanting showers blew against the windscreen.

She parked on a meter in Doughty Street and walked through a narrow lane to the office. Gray's Inn Road hadn't changed much, she thought. Despite some recent efforts at gentrification and the awkward imposition of a few modern office blocks, the same comforting seediness prevailed. As always, there seemed to be too much traffic for the narrow, shabby street. The smell of diesel fumes and car exhaust mingled in the damp air as lorries, buses and motor cars jammed together, grinding the short distance between Holborn and King's Cross.

The *Gazette* building was almost as she remembered it, a drab, grey stone exterior, its façade dominated by a large sign proclaiming the newspaper's title. When Sarah had first worked there the sign had been made of black tin, the letters shaped in the same Gothic style that had decorated the masthead since the newspaper's foundation in 1861. But in 1983 the *Gazette* had been sold by Lord Burntwood, the last descendant of the founder, to a City conglomerate which had begun to harvest failing businesses in the late 1960's. The parent company, which traded under the deadening name of London and Overseas Communications PLC, placed the *Gazette* in the hands of a young manager called Kershaw, whom they had extracted from the entrails of the head office. His instructions were to do what was necessary to make the newspaper profitable, as long as he was mindful of the friends of the chairman, Sir Robert Hall, a little man whose drab personality was only matched by the gigantic dimensions of his ego. It was rumoured that Sir Robert, sensitive about his stature, had had special furniture constructed for his office, scaled down to give the impression he was of normal height.

Kershaw, uninhibited by more than a century of tradition, set about transforming the *Gazette* from a broadsheet into a 'lively' tabloid. His plans did not work, even though he appointed a succession of brutally ambitious young men as editor. Each one attempted to drive up the circulation by hiring more of the less fastidious members of the profession, but the expected readers failed to materialise, and what was worse, LOC PLC was tarnishing its reputation in the city. Eventually Kershaw was dismissed and Sir Robert Hall, donning the mantle of saviour, announced that he would restore the *Gazette* to its former respectability. The *Gazette* remained a tabloid and new technology brought it back into profit. But now the policy was to produce a 'family newspaper': one that would grace the breakfast tables of the nation without causing further embarrassment to the Board of LOC PLC.

Brian Meadows, a respected journalist from the quality end of Fleet Street, was appointed editor and instructed to drive the recently appointed from the building, as the stoats and weasels had been ejected from Toad Hall. All that now remained from the reckless ventures of recent years was the newly designed tabloid mast-head that had replaced the old Gothic letters.

Now the squat sign, glowing orange outlined with blue, looked to Sarah like the livid sign on a supermarket as she approached the building.

She entered the main door, but instead of being greeted by the old-fashioned commissionaires she remembered from the past, she was confronted by two burly young men, dressed like American policemen, who sat before a bank of surveillance equipment.

'Are you a visitor?' one asked. He made it sound as if he were implying a threat.

'I've come to work.' Sarah wished her voice did sound so defensive.

'Which department?' he asked in the same tone.

'Editorial.'

'Fill this out,' he instructed and pushed a book towards her. Sarah wrote her name and address and was supplied with a plastic ticket that attached to her jacket with a sharp-toothed metal tag.

'Third floor,' the young man said, and returned his gaze to the video screen.

Sarah did not take the lift. Instead she climbed to the wide stair-case and, pausing at the mezzanine floor, she looked through a bank of windows into what had once been the publishing yard. It was filled with parked cars. Once, such an act would have constituted sacrilege. The publishing yard of the *Gazette* had been the main artery in the newspaper's production, but now, she remembered, the paper was printed at some remote site on the Isle of Dogs and the business of transporting papers to the railway stations was no longer part of the nightly ritual in Gray's Inn Road.

She felt a moment of regret at the change. Nothing else in her experience matched the sense of excitement generated in a news-paper office, when raw copy and pictures were manufactured into a newspaper and printed in the same building. She could still recall what it was like to have a story in the paper and be at her desk when a slight tremble told them that the presses had begun to turn below. A memory came to her of the exaltation she had felt when she first stood back in the vanway to watch the lorries filled with freshly printed papers roar from the ramps outside the publishing hall. She turned from the window and continued to the next landing. This floor had housed the composing room; now she could see that the cavernous hall had been converted to open-plan offices. Young men and women in bright clothes sat in the glare of neon lights. She passed on: at least the pale grey marble of the stairwell and the shaped metal handrails were as she remembered.

When she pushed open the large swing-doors that led into the newsroom she was confronted by another transformation. The old, scruffy editorial floor, which had always rung with the chattering noise of a tropical rain forest, was as silent and well ordered as a hospital ward. No messengers moved between the rows of desks distributing proofs and copy and the strident ring of telephones had been muted to gentler tones. The air was clear of tobacco smoke and no footsteps could be heard on the carpeted floors. Beneath the sound-absorbent ceilings, rough voices shouting instructions had taken on the gentle murmurs of a suburban tea room.

Where people had sprawled at their desks in a variety of postures now they sat before their computer terminals, hands occasionally flicking across the gently tapping keyboards. Cream-painted walls that had been patchworked with noticeboards and pasted signs were now a plain quilt of primary colours, chosen to blend with the orange and blue of the carpet, and lines of bright neon lights eliminated the shadows in the long room.

Unsure where to go, Sarah looked about her and became aware that, despite so many changes, the original layout of the floor remained the same. The various departments were still, more or less, where she remembered. Reassured, she walked towards the horseshoe-shaped news desk. George Conway looked up at her approach, and while he spoke on the telephone, gestured her towards the empty seat opposite him.

They had not managed to renovate George, she noticed. He had been in his early thirties when first appointed news editor of the *Gazette*, and even then his heavy, muscular body had always caused his clothes to bag and billow about him like a carelessly wrapped bundle of laundry. His face was the colour and texture of a house brick, and rough salt-and-pepper hair matched heavy eyebrows that jutted from his lined forehead above a nose battered flat by boxing and rugby, the passions of his youth.

Conway sat back in his chair, the telephone cradled against his shoulder, and sighed while he vigorously scratched the lobe of his left ear with a thick finger. He reached into his jacket pocket and took out a packet of untipped cigarettes. He was about to light one when he suddenly glanced up at the NO SMOKING sign, took the cigarette from his mouth and threw it on to the desk where it bounced and rolled under the computer terminal. Then he leaned forward over the desk and the muscles bunched over his shoulders.

'Listen, Sinclair,' he said, in a voice heavy with menace, 'I want to know about everything you write, do you understand? I don't care what Stiles said. I know he's in charge of the investigation, but I'm in charge of Stiles – so don't give me any more of that garbage or I'll put you on nights for so long you'll think you've turned into a milk float.'

A milk float, Sarah thought, what a fine piece of surrealist imagery. She remembered that George rarely swore, but for all that, his insults had always been devastating. When he replaced the receiver, he tore a sheet of paper from the pad before him. Sarah could still see the word 'VISOR' by the indentation left on the paper below. He screwed the paper into a ball and then looked up at a sulky-looking young man who had come in and now stood beside her. It took a moment for Sarah to realise that she must be sitting in his chair.

'I'm sorry,' she apologised, and started to get up, but George gestured for her to remain seated. 'There's someone in the waiting room who says he knows what happened to the crew of the *Marie Celeste*,' George said flatly. 'Take care of it, please.'

Alan Stiles looked towards the reporters' desks. 'I'll get Gates to speak to them.'

George smiled and shook his head. 'No, you do it, Alan.'

Stiles hesitated for just a moment, as if about to speak again, then walked away.

George turned to Sarah once more, and now he smiled. 'I'm a bit tied up now,' he said. 'Let's have a drink at lunchtime.'

Sarah nodded, then reached out and touched his computer terminal. 'Will I be expected to use one of these?'

'Don't worry, they're not that difficult, I'll get someone to explain to you.'

'Claire,' George called out. He waved to a desk nearby. Sarah looked towards a slim woman watering a potted plant that stood on a filing cabinet and felt her heart sink. The woman looked so cool and elegant. Sarah suddenly felt like an ageing dolly bird in the dress she had chosen. Inwardly she cursed herself for not wearing the dark suit that had cost so much.

'Claire,' George called out again, 'for pity's sake stop gardening. I've got some work for you.'

'Give me a few minutes,' the woman replied.

He turned back to Sarah. 'It's all different, isn't it?'

She glanced at the computer screen again and then smiled. 'I'll get used to it.'

George pointed towards an empty seat. 'Take the first one on the aisle.'

'Is there anything you want me to work on?' she asked.

He shook his head. 'When you've cracked the equipment, I'll find something.'

As she walked towards the reporters' desks, she was aware of three curious faces that glanced up to watch her approach. They look so young, Sarah thought, hardly older than Emily, and she had to fight an impulse close to panic that made her want to turn away and walk from the building. Then a newspaper was lowered by a figure that sat in the row behind them and Sarah breathed an almost audible sigh of relief. Cat Abbot! If he had survived the tumultuous years since she had last worked on the *Gazette*, what had she to fear?

'I heard you were trying to make a comeback,' he said, without bothering to conceal the hostility in his voice.

In the first moment that she saw him, time played a curious trick on Sarah; she had been prepared to greet Abbot with the warmth of an old friend, but now an old emnity surfaced like an unbroken thread that stretched across the years.

'Hello, Cat,' she said sweetly, 'I see you're still wearing the same nicotine stains.'

The young faces swivelled with interest at the exchange. Sarah nodded to them, her confidence suddenly restored: 'I'm Sarah Keane.'

'Mick Gates', 'Bob Anderson', 'Pauline Kaznovitch,' they replied in turn. Sarah noticed that the girl sat with the slightly exaggerated posture of a dancer, her pale freckled features made small by the cloud of startling, bright red hair that framed her face. The two youths on each side of her looked – Sarah sought for an apt description – they looked like young reporters, she decided finally: white shirts, loosened ties, shortish hair and nondescript suits, the pockets bagged with diaries, notebooks, pens and over-stuffed wallets. She could remember the time when Cat Abbot had looked the same, but the years had padded his body and jawline with fat and his black knitted tie had been replaced with a carefully arranged bow.

Abbot watched her take the seat, then cast the newspaper aside and slowly walked over to the news desk, where he began a conversation with Alan Stiles. The red-headed girl and Anderson returned their attention to the computer screens, but Mick Gates, who sat next to her, said, 'Are you staff?' Sarah sensed the question was important to him. She shook her head. 'No, I'm doing casual shifts.'

'Me too,' he replied. 'Are you an old friend of Cat Abbot?'

'We've known each other a long time.'

'He's a bit of a legend around here. I suppose you know he's called Cat because he's got nine lives?'

As he spoke, Anderson made a curious flexing motion with his right hand. He saw that Sarah had noticed and opened his palm to reveal a spring-loaded gadget. 'It strengthens my grip,' he said quickly, 'for squash.'

Sarah nodded.

'About Cat,' he continued. 'You should hear some of his stories about the old days.'

To her dismay, Sarah could tell he was about to relate one of them, but his telephone rang and he snatched it from the cradle and began a soft muttering conversation.

Nine lives! Sarah thought, and she smiled: Abbot had earned the nickname in his early days on the *Gazette*. She remembered how he had written a story describing the scene when a lone, round-the-world yachtsman had finally been reunited with his wife. The other reporters sent on the same job had been less successful, and when chastised for their lack of copy they pointed out that the reunion so graphically described had taken place in pitch darkness before dawn, and at the end of a jetty a hundred feet from where Abbot stood with the rest of them. After a severe reprimand, he had only just retained his job. But although for months he had been known to his fellow reporters as 'Cat's-Eyes' Abbot, time had eventually shortened it to Cat.

Sarah's recollections were brought to an end by the slender woman, who had finished watering her plants and now stood beside her. Sarah judged her to be in her late twenties. Her copper-coloured hair was arranged in a tumbling fashion about a narrow face accentuated by heavy make-up. Her blue jacket and pleated skirt were expensive, but with the silk scarf she wore at her throat, the effect reminded Sarah of a uniform worn by an air hostess.

'Hi, I'm Claire Trevor,' she said with an American accent. The smile completed the image. Everything about her seemed so neat and crisp that Sarah was reminded of a doll she had once bought Emily. It was as if Claire had just been taken from the box that morning. She pulled a chair alongside Sarah and sat down.

'Now, do you want the full tuition or just the idiot's guide?' she asked.

'What's the difference?'

Claire Trevor smiled again. 'With the full tuition, I actually tell you how the system works – the idiot's guide is just what buttons to push.'

'I think I'd like to understand, but if it gets beyond me can we switch?'

'Sure,' she said, sounding pleased. 'Let's have a cup of coffee and get started. How do you take it?'

'Just black.'

Claire nodded and walked over to a dispensing machine. When she returned with the polystyrene cups the coffee tasted much better than Sarah had anticipated.

'Marine coffee,' Claire said after a sip. 'My dad used to call it that. He was in the Corps.'

'Whereabouts in the States are you from?'

'All over. I was an army brat,' Claire explained. Then she pointed to the terminal before them. 'OK now, this system is called Textel. It's not the best on the market but the outfit that manufactures it is owned by our parent company so they insist we use their equipment.'

Sarah listened patiently while Claire explained the intricacies of the system: the way copy was stored, retrieved, edited and delivered to the composing floor, where it was finally spewed from the machines as strips of photographic paper. It did not seem too complicated. The only difficulty appeared to be in remembering the correct sequence of key strokes. Claire had presented her with a sheet of printed instructions to use as a crib.

'You're going to be fine,' she said after an hour. 'Why don't you play around with it for a time while I go see the library. They've got some problems I've got to take a look at.'

Sarah watched her walk away, and for a moment felt a small stab of envy at her self-assurance. Although Claire Trevor had been friendly enough, Sarah sensed a certain detachment about her manner, an edge of reserve, as though the warmth she had shown towards her was a professional mantle donned with the elegant clothes and perfectly applied make-up. Perhaps I'm just being sensitive, she told herself with slight irritation, and turned her eyes to the glowing screen. She tapped in the necessary sequence of instructions and watched fascinated as the menu of agency stories appeared. Selecting the one she wanted, she typed in further instructions and the full text of the story flooded on to the screen.

As her confidence grew she found she could test the system with greater efficiency. It seemed quite simple to her and at the same time gave her greater power than she had ever known in the past.

In her previous days on the *Gazette*, it had not been possible for an individual reporter to see all of the copy filed to the newspaper; distribution was limited to senior executives. But now Sarah saw that anyone on the staff could watch the day's production unfold, and judge the decisions taken by the executives. She continued to be absorbed by the intricacies of the machine until she heard Cat Abbot, who had returned to his desk, mutter, 'Her Gracious Majesty approaches.'

Sarah looked up. All eyes were turned to a commanding figure who was striding towards them along the aisle that stretched the length of the newsroom. The woman, who seemed to be bearing down on Sarah, was accompanied by a tubby, harassed-looking man wearing a grey chauffeur's uniform, who struggled with an awkward variety of luggage and large brown envelopes, while she had both arms free to wave greetings to the members of staff who called out good morning. Sarah recognised the regal figure, although she had changed a good deal since they had last met. In those days, Fanny Hunter had walked hesitantly about the office in flat shoes, eyes cast down, her nervous features almost concealed by long brown hair. Although her body had been slender, Sarah recalled, Fanny had always hunched her shoulders and tried to conceal her large breasts by holding her arms folded before her whenever possible.

Now a carefully streaked mane of tousled hair curled about the wide-padded shoulders of her tight silver dress, and the pressure exerted by each four-inch stiletto heel left a clear trail of indentations in the carpet as she moved with the powerful confidence of a showgirl. Hips swaying and bouncing breasts thrust forward, she drew closer and Sarah was engulfed in a cloud of expensive perfume. She could hear a sound that reminded her of the jingle of a horse's harness, as chains and pendants of gold jewellery clashed together.

Fanny Hunter did not actually look at anyone as she waved, so Sarah was able to stare without inhibition. She had to admit that Fanny transformed was impressive; even her tanned features looked stronger, as if the flesh had been remade in some more durable material. Sarah thought of medieval alchemists fruitlessly searching for the secret of how to turn base metal into gold. Fanny seemed to have achieved the objective that had eluded them.

But her long journey to success – which had taken her from a Council flat in Bethnal Green via Cambridge University to her present position as the *Gazette*'s top columnist, might have been judged by some to be unnecessary. For Fanny Hunter had reached the pinnacle of her chosen profession by reverting to the opinions and prose style of her father, who was a porter at Smithfield Meat Market and proud that he voted Tory. A fact that Fanny Hunter proclaimed constantly now, although there had been no mention of it when she first joined the paper.

Just as the pair were about to pass Sarah's desk, a bundle of the large envelopes slipped from the chauffeur's arms and spilled to the floor. Fanny Hunter stopped while he bent down to retrieve them, glanced across to where the reporters sat, shrugged and said: 'Blimey, Raymond, come on. You're about as much fucking use as a eunuch's dick.'

'What would you know about a eunuch's dick, Fanny?' Cat Abbot called out, in a manner that managed to sound cheeky yet at the same time properly servile.

Fanny Hunter grinned to show she could still exchange banter with the workers. 'My readers' letters, Cat, that makes me a bleeding expert on everything,' she replied, and then just for a moment her eyes met Sarah's before she walked on.

'Good old Fanny,' Abbot said, still warmed by the reflected glory of the exchange. 'She swears just like a man.'

'Actually, she swears just like a woman,' Pauline Kaznovitch said drily.

'What's that supposed to mean?' Abbot asked.

The red-headed girl did not bother to turn around when she answered him. 'When men swear they do it to appear more powerful. Women simply denigrate themselves.'

'The voice of Women's Lib pronounces,' he replied, his voice heavy with sarcasm. 'Well, I don't see any chauffeur carrying your bags in the mornings. She's the one at the top, and she got there by remembering she was still one of the boys.'

'I think I should prefer to be remembered as one of the girls,' Pauline answered.

Cat Abbot got up. 'Christ, I can't stand any more of this. I'm going to the Mitre. Are you coming, Mick?'

'Sure,' Gates replied. After glancing at his companions, he followed Abbot, who was now strolling along the newsroom.

When they were well out of earshot, Anderson looked up. 'Well, at least we know we'll be safe from his inane conversation in the Red Lion,' he said. 'I couldn't stand another session of Abbot's reminiscences about the good old days.'

He and the girl stood up and prepared to leave. Then he hesitated and said to Sarah, 'Fancy joining us?'

She glanced towards the news desk. 'Yes, I would,' she replied, 'but George Conway said something about a drink at lunchtime.'

Anderson nodded. 'Well, you know where we are.'

After they had gone Sarah turned her attention to the screen again and decided to call up the copy on the latest murder, but she could not find any staff material. Then she remembered George Conway's conversation with the reporter called Sinclair. She entered his name into the system but found nothing. Recalling the word George had written on the pad, she tried VISOR: it revealed a security file with a limited access code. The word was still on the screen when Claire Trevor returned to her desk. She glanced at the image. 'Why are you interested in VISOR?' she asked.

Sarah shrugged. 'I wanted to read about the murder of the girl. All the staff copy seems to lead here.'

'That's right,' Claire said. 'There's a special team on the story.' She pulled a chair close again. 'Now, show me what you can do.'

Sarah demonstrated her powers and Claire was impressed. 'Well done,' she said finally. 'You're a natural.'

'It doesn't seem so difficult,' Sarah replied, hoping she didn't sound too boastful.

Claire smiled. 'That's what the kid on the high wire said. Believe me, strong men were weeping when we first installed the system. Some people just seize up when they get near a computer screen. Their hands sweat, their throats go dry. One guy's pulse rate went up to one hundred and twenty-two. Just thank the Lord that the computer likes you.'

'Don't you mean I like it?'

Claire shook her head. 'No – they've got to like you, honey, or you're in big trouble. You've heard of the ghost in the machine?'

Sarah nodded.

'Well, this one's loaded with vampires and werewolves, so don't frig about with it or it'll bite your ass.'

They concentrated for a while longer and then George Conway loomed above them. 'I can't make it for lunch,' he said, 'the editor's called a meeting.'

'Don't worry,' Sarah replied. 'I have another invitation.' George shifted from foot to foot like a regretful schoolboy before he departed.

After a few minutes more, Claire Trevor pushed her chair away. 'You seem to be in pretty good shape,' she said. 'If you get into any difficulties give me a shout.' She wrote down a number and left it on the desk. 'This is my bleep contact, so if I'm somewhere else in the building you can track me down.'

When she had gone, Sarah told the news-desk secretary where she was going and followed the young couple to the pub. She found them at a section of counter along the crowded bar next to a window and Anderson bought her a glass of wine. Pauline was eating a sandwich, and suddenly Sarah became aware of her own hands. Pauline's were well shaped, the flesh soft and clean. They made a noticeable contrast to Sarah's, which were red-raw in comparison. Pauline only ate half of her sandwich. She pushed the remaining portion away, stood back with a contented sigh and produced a packet of cigarettes, which she offered to Sarah. Without really thinking, Sarah took one and accepted a light. The first lungful of smoke jolted her system like an undiluted glass of whisky. She looked at the slender white tube for a moment and then stubbed it out. 'I forgot, I gave them up,' she said with an apologetic smile. Pauline nodded and blew out a stream of blue smoke. 'I wish I could,' she said.

'Actually, it gave me up,' Sarah said. 'There was no willpower involved.'

Pauline raised her eyebrows questioningly.

'It was when my daughter was born.' She held up the palms of her hands. 'I just stopped.'

'How many children do you have?' Anderson asked.

'Two boys and a girl.'

'How will you manage working?'

Sarah leaned across the bar and slowly stirred the contents of an ashtray with the remains of the cigarette she had extinguished. 'I'm not sure yet,' she answered.

Pauline pulled the ashtray towards her and stubbed out her own cigarette.

'Having kids must be a pain. I know how my parents worry.'

Her words seemed to open a gulf between them. When Sarah had first entered the pub she had not thought about the age difference, but now it occurred to her how much more she would have in common with Pauline's mother. Certainly they would have plenty to talk about: the universal subject of children. How could this girl know anything about the oceans of concern brought by daughters?

They talked on for a bit until Anderson said, 'Weren't you going to have a drink with Conway?'

'He had to go to a meeting with the editor,' Sarah answered, and she waved to attract the barmaid's attention.

'Oh yes,' Anderson said knowingly. 'Are you sure?' and he smiled at Pauline.

Sarah glanced at them both. 'Why do you say that?'

Anderson shrugged. 'Conway goes to lots of meetings these days. Some of them last all afternoon, but they're not usually with the editor.'

Pauline nodded. 'In fact there's talk that he's about to be kicked out of the Big Club.'

Sarah managed to buy a drink, then turned to Anderson. 'What's the Big Club?'

Pauline flicked a hand dismissively. 'The top cats, head honchos, you know: the executives.'

Sarah nodded. 'Well, it always was a case of Them and Us,' she said, almost adding, even in the old days. She stopped herself in time.

'I could take Them and Us,' Anderson said, 'we all know how good it used to be, but now it's Them, Us and Those.'

Sarah felt she was losing the thread again. 'Who are "Those"?'

'The Chosen Ones,' Anderson said flatly.

'I still don't follow,' Sarah said. She was beginning to be irritated by the oblique nature of the conversation.

Anderson began to speak to her as if she had a learning problem. 'Don't you know there's a special team for the big stories?' he asked.

'Is there?'

He continued, 'Stiles has been put in charge of the so-called high-flyers. The rest of us, the rubbish, are left to your friend Conway, when he's not too pissed. The whole fucking place is run like a third-rate police state. All the information is held at the top. We just do what we're told.' He looked at her with curiosity. 'I don't know why you came back. It's not like the good old days now, you know.'

Sarah felt a moment of weariness. This was a part of journalism she had forgotten until now: the eternal preoccupation with office politics, and the curious conviction that there had been a golden age when justice prevailed and all had laboured at their tasks in an atmosphere of universal brotherhood. She did not know what to say. What would be the point of telling them that newspapers were no different to the rest of life; that everything was in a state of constant change and that fifteen years from now it could be Pauline Kaznovitch jangling through the office accompanied by an outrider – and maybe Anderson playing the part of Cat Abbot. Instead she smiled and said, 'I'm afraid I've got to go.'

As she got up to leave, Sarah looked at a solitary pigeon that had perched on the window ledge beside them. It was a scruffy bird, but it strutted along with a certain independence that she liked. Somehow it reminded her of how the *Gazette* used to be. Perhaps they were right, she suddenly thought, maybe things had been better in the old days.

The afternoon went slowly, broken only by trips to feed her parking meter. George Conway did not reappear on the news desk and she was given nothing to do by Stiles. At 6.30 she logged off duty with the rest of the day staff and made her way home through the last of the evening traffic.

Emily had prepared a salad for her, and was in her room finishing her homework. The boys were caught up in a new craze that had swept through the lower school and were busy at the table in the breakfast room, which was spread with paper, bottles of red and black ink and paste-pots.

Sarah tried to watch television for a time, but could not concentrate. She felt vaguely dissatisfied with the way that the day had gone and the thought irritated her. Eventually she went into the breakfast room to check on the boys. 'What are you doing?' she asked.

'Making papers,' Paul explained.

'Why?'

Paul looked up. 'You know in those old war films, when the Germans say: "Papers" to the escaped prisoners of war?'

Sarah nodded, she remembered the scene well.

'That's what the prefects do to us now,' he said.

'What happens if you don't have any?'

'They beat us up,' Martin said without rancour.

Sarah was surprised by his phlegmatic attitude. 'Don't you mind?' she asked.

Martin shook his head without looking up. 'Not really – they used to beat us up anyway – now they have to have a good reason.'

Sarah thought about the complaints of the young reporters in the Red Lion. Their grievances seemed light in comparison to the oppressions suffered by her sons. 'Can I help?' she asked.

Martin looked at her. 'Do you think you could forge me an identity card in the name of Jean Pierre Lamont, stating that I'm a toolmaker in a German armaments factory?'

'I can have a go.'

Her efforts proved to be more rewarding than she expected,

36

especially when she earned warm plaudits from the boys for her potato-cut of an eagle clutching a swastika in its talons.

'Very good, mum,' Paul said when he examined the results, and Sarah felt an absurd amount of pleasure at the praise. When she eventually went to bed she slept badly, waking at one point after a dream that she was back at her convent, and Fanny Hunter was the Mother Superior.

The following morning George Conway was not in the office again and Gates told her that he had been delegated to perform some special duty by the editor. Stiles sat at his place on the news desk, and by the late afternoon she found that she was the only reporter who had not been sent out on a story. At about five o'clock a nervous girl with a south London accent appeared at her desk. 'Are you Miss Keane?' she asked.

'Mrs Keane,' Sarah replied.

'Sor*eeee*,' she said, making the word sound like the call of a trapped animal. 'Miss Hunter says, will you come to her office.'

The girl began to walk away and then stopped when she realised that Sarah was not accompanying her. She returned to Sarah's desk and said, 'She wants you to come *naowwww*.' This time the cry was even more plaintive.

Sarah smiled. 'Tell Fanny I'll be along when I've told the news desk where I'm going.'

Unsure, the girl rocked from foot to foot for a moment and then hurried away. Sarah took her time about the task, and after seeking directions, strolled to the office at the far end of the newsroom. She knocked briskly, entered and found Fanny Hunter talking on the telephone. Gesturing for Sarah to take a seat, she mouthed a silent 'Hello'.

After a few more minutes Fanny brought the conversation to an end. 'Listen, my old darling,' she said, 'I've got to go, an old mate's just walked in.' She hung up the receiver and shouted, 'Jackie!' The nervous girl reappeared.

'Get Mrs Keane a drink,' she ordered.

'Would you like tea or coffee?' the girl asked.

'Get her a real drink,' Fanny said. 'Christ, she's a journalist, not a bloody secretary.'

'Actually, I would prefer a cup of tea,' Sarah said.

'Ah, balls, let's have a bottle of champagne,' Fanny answered, and Sarah realised that this was to be a battle of wills.

'I'm sorry,' Sarah said, beginning to enjoy the game, 'I'm afraid cheap champagne gives me indigestion.'

Fanny did not hesitate. 'Make it the Dom Perignon, Jackie,' she ordered, not taking her eyes from Sarah's. When the glasses were filled, Fanny gestured around the room. 'Well, what do you think? All done by a top decorator. Not bad for a barefoot girl from Bethnal Green.'

'Very impressive,' Sarah replied, choosing the phrase with care.

'It's vulgar, isn't it?' Fanny said in a softer voice.

'Yes,' Sarah agreed, knowing she would not believe any other answer.

Fanny smiled. 'Jesus, you're the first person to tell me the truth around here in years. Do you know how many editors I've seen off? Seven. They come and go, but the management know I've got what the readers want.' She took a sip of champagne and changed the subject. 'Stiles tells me you're doing casual shifts.'

'That's right.'

She put her glass down on the table. 'Would you like to work for me?'

Sarah did not have to consider. 'Thank you, Fanny, but no. I think I'm better off as a general reporter.'

Fanny waved a hand in disgust. 'Blimey, reporters are just like slices of bread, who can remember the difference? You'd be better off in my department.'

'Why are you offering me this?' Sarah asked.

Fanny shrugged. 'Say it's a favour for an old mate.'

'We were never really friends.'

Fanny paused for a time and looked down into her glass. 'Jack was, once,' she glanced up. 'I always wanted to tell you how lousy I felt about the affair – it must have been pretty rotten for you, at home with young kids. It was never serious for him, just one of those –'

'He told me,' Sarah interrupted.

Fanny got up and poured more champagne into the fluted glasses. 'What else did he tell you?'

Sarah thought for a moment. 'That you could recite Middle English poetry.'

She laughed, 'Could I? Christ, I don't remember.'

Sarah stood up and placed her glass on the desk. 'Thank you for the drink, but I must get back.'

Fanny nodded. 'Think about my offer. There's nothing for you outside. Conway is on the way out and Stiles already hates your guts.'

'Why?' Sarah asked.

'Because you're on Conway's side. It's nothing personal.'

Fanny smiled again. 'Anyway it's good to see you about the place, you don't seem to have changed at all.' She looked Sarah up and down again. 'Isn't it marvellous how those Jean Muir dresses just seem to go on for ever?'

When Sarah had left, the secretary waited for a few minutes and then tiptoed into the room to clear away. She found Fanny with her chair swivelled towards the window. The girl hesitated for a moment, and then said, 'Do you want anything else, Miss Hunter?'

'Just fuck off out of here,' she answered, in a voice as hard and cold as the ice bucket Jackie held in her hand.

CHAPTER
FOUR

GEORGE CONWAY was still away on Sarah's third day, and Stiles repeated the cold-shoulder treatment. The rest of the reporters were given jobs but there was nothing for her; instead of sympathising with her plight, Sarah found that the others seemed to resent the fact that she was doing nothing. The rest of the executives were equally distant. Whenever she approached the news desk conversation ceased and people glanced away as if she were an intruder. She tried not to mind, but she began to feel vulnerable and her loneliness caused her to strike up a conversation with Abbot, which subsequently proved to be a mistake.

It began simply enough. The two of them were the only reporters in the office when Sarah read a piece in that morning's paper.

'That girl can write,' she said to herself, and Abbot overheard her softly spoken words.

'Who?' he asked.

'Pauline Kaznovitch.'

'Oh, our little East European,' he replied. 'I would've thought

41

the time was ripe for her to go back to her own country and start another revolution . . . Kaznovitch,' he repeated. 'Remember "Lippy"?'

Sarah understood the reference. When she and Abbot had joined the paper there had been a policy on the *Gazette* that all staff bylines had to be British names, a rule that dated back to the Second World War. Like many archaic practices the habit had continued for years, until a distinguished commentator with the resonant name of Anton Lipsmitz, had been hired to write about the Soviet bloc. When his first piece appeared, a sub-editor had altered his name to Tony Smith. Lipsmitz's ensuing rage had been awesome to behold.

'She wouldn't have got a byline with that name in the old days,' Sarah said, and then she noticed that George Conway was back on the news desk.

Almost immediately, Alan Stiles called her over and told her to follow up a story in one of the other nationals. The briefing took some time because Stiles had only a sketchy grasp on the facts and kept having to refer to agency copy.

By the time she got back to her desk, Abbot was missing and Pauline Kaznovitch who had returned from her story, was waiting, hands on hips and clearly in a belligerent frame of mind. 'I understand you don't think I should have got a byline on my piece this morning?' she said in a voice of suppressed fury.

'I don't understand you,' Sarah said, bewildered by the girl's rage.

'Did you, or didn't you say my name wouldn't have appeared in the *Gazette* in the old days?'

Sarah shook her head. 'It wasn't like that,' she said. She looked around, but there was no sign of Abbot. Without waiting for any further explanation, Pauline stormed from the office.

Slightly flustered, and at the same time filled with anger at the mischief wrought by Abbot. Sarah sat down to tackle her first story. It was about a prominent Member of Parliament, whose cat had gone missing after a trip to the vet. By sheer luck, Sarah had brought an old contact book of Jack's into the office and it listed an ex-directory number for the man in question. His phone was answered by a housekeeper, who clearly wanted to talk.

It transpired that the old lady was about to be retired, and on less than generous terms, so she was prepared to be indiscreet about her employers. She told Sarah with a certain amount of grim pleasure that recently the MP's sleep had been ruined by the pet's nocturnal adventures and he had insisted that his wife must choose between the cat's manhood and her husband's continuing residence at their

London house. With some reluctance the wife finally agreed to have the cat neutered, but since the deed was done, both Member of Parliament and cat had been missing from home.

All was fine until Sarah came to write her story, and then the computer began to act in the most bizarre fashion, refusing to respond to any commands. After struggling for some time she felt a sensation close to panic. Once more she forced herself to read through her crib and carefully went through the motions with calm deliberation, but the terminal continued to flash warnings and Sarah had to restrain an impulse to burst into tears of frustration and smash her fists through the screen. Finally she remembered Claire Trevor's bleep number and called her.

'I'll be right there,' she answered when Sarah explained the problem. A few minutes later she arrived. 'It's not your fault,' she said as she rapidly entered instructions that restored sanity to the machine. 'I keep telling them this program is junk.' She sat back. 'There, you can start now.'

Finally Sarah filed the story; just as she logged off, Claire returned. 'OK?' she asked.

Sarah nodded gratefully. 'Thanks, you saved my life.'

Claire looked at her watch. 'I'm just about to have some lunch in the canteen. Would you like to join me?'

For a moment, Sarah was going to refuse. She found Claire Trevor's company slightly daunting. Her job as the systems editor gave her a status that was hard to define in the hierarchy of the office. Although she was not a journalist, her command of the electronic equipment meant that everyone to defer to her at times, which created a mild resentment, particularly among the men, who either talked to her as though she were a stern schoolteacher or overcompensated with clumsy, patronising banter.

Sarah really wanted to fit in with her new colleagues and thought that Claire as a companion would cause her to seem even more of an outsider. But she became ashamed of her reasons for refusing the invitation. 'I'd be delighted,' she said with a smile of gratitude.

A few minutes later they walked from the newsroom. Claire Trevor led her through a series of turns in the corridors that Sarah did not remember. Eventually they emerged in a brightly painted cafeteria, where tall windows lined one wall and filled the room with gloomy light from the dark, clouded sky. A row of white-coated women stood behind a stainless steel counter. When they had chosen their lunch they sat at small, formica-topped tables on metal seats that were anchored to the floor. The surroundings were pleasant enough: Sarah's vague memories of the old canteen were of a smoke-filled room, painted dark green, where the air was always impregnated with a mist evaporating from huge vats of boiling fat. This place was cleaner, and the tables were no longer filled with blue-clad men, sitting in varying states of stultified boredom, while they waited for a shift to pass so they could qualify for their casual payments.

'So, how is it going?' Claire asked.

'Oh, I mustn't grumble,' Sarah replied evenly.

'That bad, huh?'

Sarah looked up from her salad and Claire laughed. 'Listen, kid, I've been around Brits long enough to know when they say, "Mustn't grumble" what they really mean is: "Life is hell."' Sarah sighed. 'You're right: life is hell.'

'Tell me about it,' Claire said.

Normally, Sarah would have made a few evasive remarks and changed the subject; she had been taught at boarding school to believe that it was bad form to complain about personal difficulties. But now she suddenly wanted to talk, and somehow it was easy to confide in a stranger. She recounted the events of the past days and Claire laughed when she told her of Cat Abbot's duplicity. As her laughter continued, Sarah began to appreciate the pettiness of it all, and finally she began to laugh as well.

They continued to discuss the office for a time and then Claire asked about the children. Sarah told her about Emily and went on to describe the papers she had helped the boys prepare the night before. 'How do you manage while you're working?' Claire asked.

Sarah shrugged. 'The days aren't really a problem, but I'm starting to worry about working night shifts.'

'Why?'

'Emily is about the same age as the girls who have been murdered. Every time I read about them I think of her.'

Claire finished her food and pushed her plate away.

'Perhaps I could help,' she said. 'I'm free most nights.'

Sarah shook her head, almost in embarrassment. 'No, really, I couldn't impose.'

Claire leaned across the table. 'Look, I live alone in Swiss Cottage.' She paused and took a cigarette from her handbag, then leaned forward again. 'For God's sake, I need the company, why don't you invite me over. If we hit it off, great, if we don't you can think again.'

Sarah looked down at the table and after a brief hesitation made up her mind. 'Thank you,' she said. 'I'm sure the children will like you.'

'That's settled then, I'll come over tonight.'

'Well, if you're sure it's convenient. . . .'

Sarah looked down at the white surface of the table again, and at that moment a shaft of sunlight broke through the heavy clouds and streamed through a tall window; catching the glass, it refracted a small rainbow of light on to Sarah's hands.

Claire noticed the effect and smiled. 'That must be a lucky omen,' she said.

Suddenly Sarah felt a surge of confidence flow through her; it was as if the rainbow of light had charged her with a sudden resolve. Since the day she'd returned to the newspaper, she had only reacted to people's opinions, sought to please others, and accepted their reservations as justifiable criticisms. Now she was in the mood to attack. Curling her hand into a fist she rapped on the table top with whitened knuckles.

'I'd like to get back now,' she said. 'There's someone I must talk to.'

CHAPTER
FIVE

H ER spirits lifted, Sarah returned to the newsroom and found Cat Abbot seated at his desk. He glanced up furtively as she approached, then dropped his eyes when Sarah stood before him. She could see that he was doodling on a scrap of paper, filling the page with pin-men that dangled from gallows.

'Come outside to the landing,' she said in a low voice. 'I want a word with you.'

Abbot gestured towards his telephone. 'I can't, I'm expecting an important call.'

Sarah leaned closer to him and snatched the ballpoint pen from his hand, her eyes glittering with determination. 'Come outside or I'll ram this down your throat,' she said softly.

Abbot had angered enough people in his life to know when threats were likely to be fulfilled. Meekly he followed her from the room.

Sarah turned when they reached the empty area at the head of the staircase and Abbot stood with both hands dangling at his sides, his eyes still wearily flickering to the pen that Sarah held like a dagger.

'What's this all about?' he said plaintively.

Sarah was close enough to him to see a small patch of hair beneath his lower lip where he had neglected to shave.

'You told Pauline Kaznovitch that I said her piece didn't deserve a byline.'

Abbot raised his palms upwards. 'Christ is that what this is about?' he said in a wheedling voice. 'That was just a bit of fun to wind her up – a joke. Can't anybody take a joke any more?'

Sarah shook her head. 'I can't, Cat. I've completely lost my sense of humour these days. So let me tell you what I'm going to do.' She paused for a moment and jabbed him in the chest with the pen.

'Unless you explain clearly to Pauline the conversation that actually took place, I'll make sure everyone knows what you're really like – I don't mean my opinion, I'm talking about specific instances of your behaviour in the past.'

'Jesus, what's this?' he said, attempting one last bluff. 'Who the fuck do you think you are? Donna Corleone? Is this the offer I'm not supposed to refuse? Everybody knows me. What kind of secrets do you think you have?'

Sarah's smile made his heart sink.

'I could tell them about the "Miracle of Maidstone". That little boy wasn't blind at all, he just had conjunctivitis. I know you paid his mother to rub red pepper in his eyes. And what about the Runaway Nun series? You didn't put her in a country hotel, as you claimed on expenses. She was sleeping on a mattress in your garage because your wife wouldn't have her in the house.'

Abbot shook his head. 'No one is going to believe all that, and anyway it happened years ago. Who cares now?'

Sarah folded her arms. 'Some people don't forget, Cat. Remember the Maxton brothers? They were released from Parkhurst last month.'

'So?'

Sarah spoke slowly, with great deliberation. 'I know you visited their mother the night of her heart attack and showed her pictures of what her sons had done to Mick the Lip. Everybody still talks about how fond the Maxton Boys were of their old mum.'

Abbot licked his lips nervously. 'You shouldn't joke about that,' he said quickly.

She nodded. 'Fine, Cat. You tell the truth about me, and I promise I won't tell the truth about you.'

Sarah left him on the landing and returned to her desk. The rest of the day passed without incident.

When the time came for her to leave, both Conway and Stiles were missing from the desk. She logged off duty and, as arranged, met Claire Trevor in the vanway beneath the building. As they walked to where the cars were parked Sarah paused for a moment to glance through the long grimy windows of the old loading bays. Dim light illuminated a vast abandoned room where sheets of newspapers were spread on long tables.

'What went on in there?' Claire asked.

'It was the publishing room,' Sarah replied. 'When they printed the newspapers here the copies came up from the basement and were loaded into vans from these ramps.'

Claire nodded. 'They were the guys who had phoney names to beat the tax.'

'Some did,' Sarah replied. 'They weren't all bad.'

But Claire wasn't really interested. They stopped beside a small black car with smoked windows; it looked very smart and glamorous. 'Why don't you park here tomorrow?' Claire asked when they headed for Doughty Street to collect Sarah's car. 'It's first come, first served.'

They arrived at the house and Claire looked up at the ivy-clad front with admiration. 'This is going to be a pleasure,' she said, 'like visiting Harvard. My place is the size of a cigarette packet.'

The remark made Sarah feel slightly guilty. 'We bought it with money left to Jack by his parents,' she explained. 'Property was a lot cheaper then.'

Claire laughed as they entered the house. 'Don't apologise. We Americans approve of wealth, it says so in the constitution.'

Sarah found that the boys had already cooked something for themselves, but had forgotten to turn on the air extractor. The room was as smoky as a prehistoric cave and littered with debris. After opening the windows, Sarah found a bottle of white wine in the refrigerator and poured two glasses; it tasted good to her and for a moment the desire for a cigarette returned. While they were still in the kitchen, Emily came home. She was later than usual because she played the flute in the school orchestra and had stayed for evening practice.

After shaking hands with Claire Trevor she asked how Sarah's day had gone.

'I did a story about a cat,' she replied. 'Things haven't changed all that much.' She turned to close the windows. 'I'm making omelettes and salad, do you want some?'

'No, thank you,' Emily replied gravely. 'I had a large lunch. I may have some toast later.' She turned to Claire. 'It's a great pleasure to meet you, Miss Trevor. I'm glad mother has made a friend so quickly.'

They watched her go and when she was out of earshot Claire held up the palms of her hands.

'What an extraordinary child,' she said. 'It was like meeting someone from a Jane Austen novel.'

Sarah nodded, 'She was always like that – even as a baby she'd thank you when you handed her a toy she'd thrown from her pram. God knows where it comes from, the boys are complete hooligans.'

Claire sipped some of her wine and then turned to look at some photographs on a noticeboard next to the telephone. One had been taken the Christmas before last. It showed Sarah and Emily putting tinsel on the tree.

'It must be nice to have kids,' she said almost wistfully, 'Especially a daughter.'

'They're more of a worry than boys,' Sarah replied.

Claire glanced towards her. 'In what way?'

Sarah shrugged. 'I suppose because it's easier for boys to decide their own fate – that's what's expected of them, the way the system goes.'

'I thought all that stuff had ended. Isn't this the age of equal opportunity?'

Sarah shook her head. 'I didn't mean the sort of jobs available. Emily's always wanted to be a doctor, from the moment she could talk, and she's bright enough to make it, according to her teachers.' She looked towards the photographs. 'But suppose she falls in love with a boy who wants her to live on a farm; or follow him around the world as a soldier's wife. I worry if that would be enough.'

'So you want her to be a doctor?'

'Yes . . . well no,' she smiled. 'I mean I want her to be a doctor because I think it will make her happy – but her capacity for self-sacrifice worries me. I could see her giving it all up for somebody else.'

'Some selfish son of a bitch you mean.'

Sarah thought before answering, 'What I really mean is I just want her to be happy – and not discover when it's too late that life could have been better, more fulfilling.'

Claire held out her glass for Sarah to pour more wine. 'It sounds like a good thing I don't have any kids. It's tough enough coping with my own life.'

Sarah filled her own glass too. 'Don't you want children?' she asked without looking up.

'I can't see it, happening,' Claire replied quickly. 'For the past eighteen months I was involved with a married man. Being a mistress is a lonely business – you lose contact with other people.'

'Is it all over now?'

Claire nodded. 'Absolutely,' she said, and so finally that Sarah thought she'd better change the subject. 'Come into the living room,' she suggested.

They took the bottle of wine with them and Sarah looked around before they sat down. Already there were signs that she had ceased her tedious round of cleaning. Magazines were scattered about the sofa, there were loose record sleeves and two abandoned glasses of fruit juice on the coffee table in front of the fireplace. Strangely, she felt no compulsion to clear away the mess; she was quite content to sip her wine and listen to the distant thumping noises made by the boys.

'Who plays Trivial Pursuit?' Claire asked, noticing the box on a bookshelf.

Sarah had been looking into the garden. A shower of rain had streaked the french windows. 'Jack and the children.' She thought for a moment. 'I used to, occasionally,' she said after a time.

Claire Trevor could hear a trace of sadness in her voice. 'Well, you make the omelettes and I'll set up the board. We can play after supper.'

Sarah went to the kitchen and Claire followed a few minutes later. When Sarah served the food, Emily and the twins joined them at the table. Introductions were made, and Martin turned to Claire. 'Are you a journalist too?' he asked.

Claire shook her head. 'Nope, I teach people how to use computers.'

'Are you teaching mum?'

'She picked it up pretty quickly,' Claire answered. 'It takes some people a long time.'

'They teach us to use them at school,' said Martin. 'Actually I'm pretty good as well. We've got the Victor 500 series, do you know them?'

Claire smiled. 'I helped to develop it when I worked for the Rainbow Division in California. They're a bit out of date now.'

'Did you go to university?'

Claire nodded. 'MIT.'

'Where's that?'

'Massachusetts Institute of Technology – near Boston,' Emily said.

'Where they had the Tea Party?' Paul asked.

Claire laughed. 'That's right. They invented baked beans there as well.'

'I thought Heinz invented baked beans.'

'Don't be daft,' Martin interrupted. 'You might as well say they invented tomato soup.'

'Maybe they did,' said Paul airily. 'After all, tomatoes come from America, don't they?' he asked, appealing to Claire.

'That's right,' she confirmed. 'Tomatoes, bubble gum and banjos.'

'Emily can play the banjo,' Paul said. 'She can play anything.'

Claire looked at her. 'I bet you like maths as well.'

'How did you know?' Emily asked.

Claire shrugged. 'Just a guess – people who like music are often good at mathematics.'

Despite all the questions, Claire had almost finished her meal.

'Do you play Trivial Pursuit?' Paul asked her.

Claire laughed. 'I thought you'd never ask.'

A few minutes later they were all crouched over the game. The flow of conversation was as easy as if Claire were a member of the family.

At ten o'clock Sarah called it a day, and after groans from the boys, the children went upstairs. Claire and Sarah began to clear away the clutter.

'Did you enjoy the afternoon?' Claire asked as they stood in the hallway before her departure.

'Yes, I think so,' Sarah replied. 'But the atmosphere is so different now.' She paused. 'It's probably my age.'

Claire cocked her head to one side. 'How do you mean, different?'

'There seems to be something odd going on, it's as if there were a secret that only a few people know about.'

'What kind of secret?'

'I'm not sure. Perhaps it's just my imagination, but it's odd the way George and Alan Stiles keep disappearing from the desk. Maybe it's the computer terminals as well, everyone just seems to peer into them all day, they don't talk to each other any more.'

She opened the door, and Claire looked out into the rain-filled night. A hard wind shook the trees. 'More like winter,' she said

52

with a frown. 'I'll be glad to get to bed.' She turned to Sarah and they hesitated for a moment – then Claire leaned forward and kissed her on the cheek. 'The kids are great,' she said. 'I'll be glad to stay with them any time.' She walked swiftly down the path and waved without turning just before she crossed the road to where her car was parked.

Sarah stood at the open doorway after Claire had left and looked across to the house opposite. Undoubtedly the evening had been a success, and Claire appeared to have enjoyed it as much as the children. It seemed a pity that a woman who had so much to give should have been trapped in an affair without a future. Through the sound of the wind in the trees, she heard a dog barking at a darkened window: it sounded more frightened than angry.

CHAPTER
SIX

SARAH could not find her story when she examined the *Gazette* the following morning. Martin and Paul had brought the thick pile of newspapers to her bedroom. It was the first day they were delivered to the house, and all the nationals were soon spread across the bed. The boys began to study the tabloids. Emily brought her a cup of coffee and she watched her daughter after a moment's hesitation pick up the *Guardian*. Good old Emily, Sarah thought; as always, life was to be taken seriously.

When the boys had finished with the other tabloids she skipped through them and found two denials of an unhappy married life from the absentee Member of Parliament. She was disappointed but unconcerned that they hadn't used her story; it was common enough to be spiked. Only about half the material that came into the *Gazette* each day was printed and pressure of production could also keep good stories out of the paper, so she was in a relaxed enough mood when she arrived at the office.

George Conway was still away and Alan Stiles was in his chair. With his feet resting on a half-open drawer, not quite confident enough to place them on the desk top, he was talking in a conspiratorial manner with a young man called Sinclair, whom Gates had pointed out as one of the Chosen Ones. Stiles noticed her arrival and waved for her to come over, but continued the conversation with his companion while she stood next to them. Sinclair was now muttering details of what he had done to Thelma, the news-desk secretary, in the back of his car the previous evening, and it was clear that they wanted Sarah to hear every word.

She tried to remain out of earshot; she was not embarrassed by Sinclair's remarks, having become indifferent to this sort of conversation in her first months on a newspaper, nineteen years before. Her reluctance to listen was for the sake of the girl, who sat uneasily, a few desks away. It was clear she knew what they were talking about too.

Eventually, Sinclair's anecdote came to an end and Stiles glanced up at Sarah. 'That was a crappy piece of work you did on the cat story yesterday,' he said, and there was no humour in his voice now.

'Why was it crappy?' she asked, feeling a blush come to her face, which angered her more than Stiles's comment.

'Don't you read the other papers? Your stuff was balls – the MP issued a statement at midnight denying your story and saying he was perfectly happy with his wife, and so was the cat. We had to pull your copy after the first edition.'

'He lied,' Sarah said flatly. 'I have a full shorthand note of what the housekeeper said.'

'Well, we couldn't get her on the telephone last night to confirm your quotes, so the lawyer made us pull it. He was even talking of damages.'

'Why didn't you call me at home? I could have told you it was the housekeeper's last day. I have a telephone number for her.'

'How the hell would I know where you were?'

'By looking in the log. I wrote "Gone home", and my number.'

Stiles began to shift his ground. When he saw that her defences were solid his attitude altered from his previous cold nastiness. Now he smirked and said, 'There's no need to get catty,' in a camp voice.

'I just don't like to be accused of being unprofessional,' she replied, realising that her words sounded slightly pompous.

'Now she's got her claws out,' Stiles said to Sinclair, in the same tone.

Sarah walked away from the desk, and heard the sound of miaows from them both. She knew she was in the right, but she had not been completely vindicated by her answers and a vague feeling of not being trusted seemed to linger over the next few days. Whenever Sinclair saw her in the corridor he would give a slight miaow and make a scratching motion with his hands. George Conway was no comfort; he had taken some time off, so she felt completely at the mercy of Stiles, who continued to ignore her.

The frustration might have caused Sarah to quit, had it not been for the support given to her by Claire. Although there was nearly ten years' difference in age, Sarah never thought of Claire as belonging to another generation. In some ways she seemed even older than Sarah.

She mentioned it one day, when they were shopping and had stopped for a coffee in High Holborn.

'I never hung around with kids my own age,' Claire replied.

'What about your mother?'

Claire spoke matter-of-factly. 'She ran off when I was a kid. Dad was the one who brought me up. We travelled around a lot – I never made many friends in High School.'

Sarah looked through the window at the shoppers passing by. 'I never got to know my father very well. I was always away at boarding school.'

Claire lit a cigarette and tapped it quickly on a tin ashtray 'I didn't get to know the marines too well, girls don't make good leathernecks.' The words sounded bitter but Claire looked up with a smile. 'No mother, and tyrants for fathers – we could share the same shrink.'

'I've got a better idea,' Sarah replied. 'Let's save up and send Alan Stiles instead.'

They were still laughing when they paid the bill.

'Why don't you get a job somewhere else?' Claire asked as they walked back towards Gray's Inn Road.

Sarah shook her head. 'I'm going to stick it out.'

'Good girl.'

'Don't be too impressed,' Sarah replied. 'I couldn't have done it without you.'

On the Friday of her second week she was given a night shift. It coincided with a school concert in which Emily was to play and Sarah was disappointed that she would not be able to attend, but Emily comforted her while she prepared to leave for the office. 'Claire is coming, she can whistle it to you later.'

'I didn't know Claire could whistle.'

Emily nodded. 'She can play softball as well. We're going to a game on Sunday.'

'Are you?' Sarah asked. 'Where?'

'Regent's Park – then we're going to have hamburgers at the Hard Rock Cafe.'

'When was this arranged?' Sarah asked as she applied her eye make-up at the dressing table.

'This morning – don't you remember, I answered the telephone when she rang?'

'I think so,' Sarah answered. She got up and began to look in her wardrobe.

For a moment she felt a faint stirring of resentment that her children had taken so much to Claire's company and influence, but she dismissed it instantly, remembering how the friendship had eased the complications of her life.

'Wear the blue dress,' Emily as she left the bedroom. Sarah took her advice. A few minutes later, after calling goodbye, she left the house. The boys didn't want to go to the concert, but Claire was due to arrive at six o'clock and drive Emily to school, so Sarah's mind was at rest.

The traffic was heavy and by the time she got to King's Cross she was running ten minutes late. When she entered the newsroom it was almost deserted. At first she was puzzled, but then she remembered there was a farewell party for the sports editor in the boardroom. Brian Wallis had been a popular man and attendance was almost obligatory. The news desk was manned by a young assistant Sarah hardly knew. Production of the paper had been pushed ahead to allow for the festivities and the first edition was almost complete. A few sub-editors were still at their terminals but most were at the party. Sarah was urged to go up by the young man on the desk but she declined; she hadn't known Wallis and she really didn't feel like a drink. Instead she read the *Evening Standard* and then watched a television monitor above the news desk.

Time dragged past and she began to feel a slight sense of guilt that she was idling her time away here, rather than being at Emily's concert. Although she told herself it was illogical the thought continued to nag at her. She had just got her second cup of coffee when the young man on the news desk called her over. 'Hi,' he said in a friendly manner. 'We don't really know each other. I'm Arthur Swann.'

'Sarah Keane,' she replied.

'You live in Hampstead, don't you?'

'Yes.'

Swann looked down at the sheet of paper in his hand and frowned. I just got a call from a contact of mine. There's some kind of flap going on at Hampstead nick. He didn't know what it is but it's to do with some sort of problem in –' he looked at his handwriting. 'Kerris Avenue?'

Sarah nodded, 'That's right – it's close to me.'

He handed her the paper. 'Go and take a look, will you. It's probably nothing, but if you string it out for a bit you can go straight home.'

Sarah left the building and made the return journey to north London. She could almost feel frustration mingled with the exhaust from the cars that slowly moved forwards on the clogged roads. The traffic thinned out when she reached the pond at the top of the hill.

Kerris Avenue was a private, unmade road that led on to the Heath. Sarah parked her car and walked towards the entrance. A gusting wind blew through the horse-chestnut trees and there were no people about until she turned into the avenue. Halfway down she could see a yellow police tape across the width of the roadway. There were vehicles parked in a haphazard fashion and men standing in groups. The wind brought the sound of crackling radios. As she walked forward, a sheet of newspaper came tumbling towards her and blew about her legs. She reached down and was about to discard it when she saw it was the front page of that morning's *Gazette*. Then she noticed the blood: dark red, in a half-moon the size of a grapefruit. There was something else on the page, a curious black mark stamped over the newspaper's masthead. The image was roughly oval, about three inches long with a crude symbol cut in relief.

Sarah saw that some of the blood had marked her leg. The wind felt very cold. She folded the sheets and wiped the blood away with a handkerchief, then continued to walk towards the police tape. A constable wearing a bright yellow coat met her at the barrier. 'This road is closed to the public, madam,' he said in a toneless voice. 'I'm a reporter,' she said, and looked towards the cluster of cars and vans parked a few yards away. 'May I talk to the senior officer?'

While she spoke Sarah watched a thin man wearing a dark grey mackintosh with the collar turned against the wind. He was of average height and stood apart from the others. Although he did not look like a policeman, Sarah knew that he was in charge.

'The superintendent is busy at the moment,' the constable replied.

Sarah held out the folded sheet of newspaper. 'Will you give him this?' she said, 'I've just found it.'

The constable looked down, and without taking the paper walked swiftly to the thin man. There was a brief exchange between them and he looked towards Sarah. She could see his angry expression. Then he walked over to her, his shoulders hunched against the wind.

Sarah's curiosity was aroused. Most policemen come from fairly ordinary backgrounds and it shows in the manners they adopt and the clothes they choose. This man was different; she felt instinctively that he had known the rigours of a childhood spent in boarding schools. He was young for a superintendent, she thought when he stood before her. When he spoke she knew she was right.

'My name is Colin Greaves,' he said, without using the prefix of rank. He reached out and carefully took the pages from her.

'Where did you find this?'

'Back there,' Sarah replied. 'I'm Sarah Keane, a reporter with the *Gazette*. May I ask what is happening here?'

He studied her for a moment without speaking and Sarah suddenly thought that she had seldom seen such an interesting face. For a moment she remembered a painting she had once seen. It was of a saint, whose name she could not recall. The expression turned towards his tormentors had been the same: this man's face was long and thin, with hard blue eyes, and the flesh seemed to have been pared away so that the olive skin lay taut against the bone. His hair was light brown and flecked with grey; it was cut short and looked dry, like fresh hay. There was an air of sadness about him that she felt she could almost reach out and touch.

'Why are you here instead of Peter Kerr?' he asked, naming the *Gazette*'s crime reporter. The question was mild and the tone courteous.

'The news desk sent me, Peter Kerr was at a party.'

No sooner had the words been spoken than she heard hurried footsteps behind her and a voice say, 'Hello, Colin.' She knew it must be Kerr, although she hadn't actually met him. Still, he did seem familiar. Perhaps it was the type, she thought. He was quite young, but overweight, which made him look older, and dressed like a successful car dealer. Slightly out of breath, he looked less than pleased to see Sarah.

'This is my story,' he said. 'The news desk made a cock-up. Alan Stiles says you can take the rest of the shift off and go home.'

Sarah stood her ground. 'Another girl has been murdered, hasn't she?' and then a sudden, terrifying thought came to her. 'It isn't Emily Keane?'

Greaves could see her concern. He shook his head. 'No – it's somebody else's daughter.'

She looked at Kerr. 'Are you sure I can't help?'

'No,' he replied. 'Your instructions are to go home.' He looked at her closely and was about to say something else, but Superintendent Greaves interjected. 'Before you do, Mrs Keane, would you mind going to the police station with one of the officers. We need to take your fingerprints; for elimination you understand.'

Sarah nodded and looked towards the cluster of cars. Between a police van and an ambulance she could see a body being wheeled on a stretcher. The wind blew harder through the trees.

CHAPTER
SEVEN

WHEN she eventually got home Claire was full of praise for Emily's performance. Sarah listened and tried to seem interested, but her mind kept returning to the events she had witnessed.

Claire realised something was wrong, but did not ask any questions until Emily had followed the boys to bed.

'There's been another murder,' Sarah said in a low voice, when they stood in the living room.

'Where?' Claire asked.

'Kerris Road, just by the Heath.'

'Dear Lord.'

Sarah nodded and sat down on the arm of a chair. 'From now on I intend to know where Emily is every moment of the day.'

Claire sat down as well. 'I don't blame you,' she said with feeling.

Sleep did not come easily to Sarah that night. When it did, she dreamed of a street filled with the swirling pages of newspapers. Colin Greaves stood in the far distance, calling out to her, but the wind blew his words away.

63

In the morning she was angry and her mood had not altered by the time she reached the office. Alan Stiles was still running the news desk, and she had only been seated for a few minutes when a secretary asked her to go and see him. It seemed a curious formality; he could have called her over without having to raise his voice.

As she approached he employed his usual technique of beginning a conversation with somebody else, this time an assistant at an adjacent desk, so that she had to wait until he had finished the exchange of banalities. When he turned to her the friendly expression had gone. 'Sorry, Sarah,' he said abruptly. 'We've been told to cut back on casuals. This will be your last shift.' He turned away again. Sarah waited for a full minute, then tapped him on the shoulder. 'I didn't say you could call me "Sarah",' she said.

He looked up and a wary expression came to his pale eyes. 'I'm sorry. Mrs Keane – if you insist.'

She nodded. 'Now you can go and tell the editor that I'm happy to go today because I've got a story that I think any of the other nationals would be interested in taking. Tell him I know about the connection between the murders and the *Gazette* – and so will the rest of the country by tomorrow morning.'

It was partly bluff, but Stiles didn't have the stomach to call it. He stood up, and now his voice was less assertive. 'Just wait for a minute – I'll be back.' He gestured towards her desk, pulled his jacket on and headed towards the executive end of the newsroom.

Five minutes later she received a telephone call asking her to go and see the editor, Brian Meadows.

After a short wait in the outer office, she was instructed to enter. In the large room on a corner of the building double glazing muted the sound of traffic from Gray's Inn Road, and sunlight filtered through. The spartan room was furnished in bleached wood, with a pale fawn carpet and washed-out abstract prints on the walls. She remembered it as it used to be: scruffy leather and dark-red walls, lined with dusty books, photographs and cartoons. The editor was not behind his desk; he sat in a tweed-covered easy chair, facing a sofa that was occupied by Stiles and Charles Trottwood, the *Gazette*'s chief lawyer.

'Take a seat, Mrs Keane,' the editor said. 'Forgive us for not standing.' He gestured towards a matching chair and Sarah sat on the edge, as if she were about to take dictation. There was silence and each man in turn avoided her gaze. Brian Meadows was a stocky, middle-aged man, who wore styleless, chain-store clothes. His long greying hair hung below his collar and flopped over his brow. Trottwood was elegant in comparison, the Savile Row suit nipped and tucked to show his slender figure.

'Mr Stiles said you mentioned something about a connection between the murder of the girls and the *Gazette*,' the editor said finally.

Sarah did not reply.

'As an employee, I think it is your duty to tell us of any information you possess that involves the company,' Meadows continued.

'But I'm not an employee,' Sarah said pleasantly. She watched an exchange of glances between the men that reminded her of a violent rally of tennis.

'Mrs Keane is on a casual contract, Brian,' Alan Stiles said quickly. Sarah saw the lawyer catch the editor's attention and raise his eyebrows to the ceiling.

'No, I'm not,' she said. 'Mr Stiles has informed me that my services are no longer required by the *Gazette* after today.'

'I see,' Meadows said and he gazed towards the Gray's Inn Road and tapped with his finger on the arm of his chair. The lawyer fiddled with a fob that hung from his watch-chain and Stiles looked ahead, a dark-pink flush mottling his babylike complexion. Finally, Meadows put his fingertips together and touched his lips.

'I wonder if you would mind waiting in my outer office for a few minutes, Mrs Keane?'

'Certainly,' Sarah replied with her best smile. She knew she had won and she was prepared to be magnanimous.

Although the door closed behind her, she could hear the power of the editor's invective when he addressed Stiles. It surprised her that such a mild-looking man was capable of such startling passions. After a few minutes the door opened and a suitably chastised Stiles passed her. 'Will you go in again?' he said in a low voice and he walked towards the newsroom. This time when she entered the editor was seated at the desk and the lawyer leaned against the wall behind. Meadows told her to take a seat.

'Before we go any further, Mrs Keane, may I ask if you would like to join the staff of the *Gazette*?' he asked.

'That would depend on the position I was offered.'

'Quite so,' Meadows replied. 'Well, I am prepared to offer you the job of a staff reporter on a six months' contract, at a starting salary of . . .' he glanced down at the papers before him, 'Shall we say £35,000 a year? There will also be a company car.'

Sarah cleared her throat before she answered. It was a big

increase on the £95 a day she was paid as a casual. 'That would be satisfactory.'

'Now, will you tell us what you know?' Meadows asked.

Sarah smiled, 'I don't wish to appear impertinent, but until I receive my letter of employment I will still be a casual, and at the mercy of Mr Stiles.'

Meadows sighed and nodded to the lawyer. 'Charles, would you be so kind as to dictate the offer to my secretary?'

Trottwood went to do his bidding and Sarah sat in silence until Meadows suddenly said, 'Are you Jack Keane's wife?'

'Widow.'

'I'm sorry, yes, Good Lord. I hadn't made the connection until now. We knew each other a bit in the old days.'

Sarah smiled but didn't answer. She noticed how everybody now referred to 'the old days', not just as a description of the general past, but specifically to the times before the diaspora, when newspapers were still clustered around Fleet Street.

At last the lawyer returned and Meadows signed the letter, which he passed to her with a flourish. Then he leaned forward expectantly and clasped his hands together on the blotter before him. 'Now, Sarah, if I may, will you tell us what you know?'

'Of course,' she replied when she had placed the document in her handbag. 'The murdered girls have all been found with a copy of the *Gazette* and each paper was marked with a curious symbol.'

Meadows leaned even further forward. 'Go on.'

Sarah shrugged. 'That's all I know.'

'That's all?' Meadows repeated. 'We know that already.'

'I'm sure you do,' Sarah replied, 'but I wasn't sure until you confirmed it just now.'

Meadows and Trottwood looked at each other.

'If I can manage to convince you enough to give me a job,' Sarah continued, 'think of what I might achieve if you put me on the story.'

Meadows leaned back in his chair and expelled his breath with a sound like a train coming to rest at the buffers. He looked into his lap for a time and when he raised his eyes Sarah thought she could see a glint of admiration.

'This is an extremely unpleasant story, do you think you have the proper temperament to work on it?'

'Yes,' she said, hoping there was enough conviction in her voice.

Meadows paused again and then nodded. Reaching for the telephone, he did not take his eyes from her. 'Ask Peter Kerr to come here,' he said to his secretary. There was another silence as they waited for Kerr to enter the room.

He was surprised to see Sarah again, and even more surprised when Meadows told him she was going to work on the story.

When they left the editor's office, Kerr did not speak as he led her up a flight of stairs. The next floor was divided into metal-partitioned offices fitted with panels of reeded glass. But the one that Kerr stopped at was part of the corner structure of the building and the walls were solid. He tapped a code into a security lock. Before he pushed the door open, he turned to Sarah.

'You still don't remember me, do you?'

She looked at him, puzzled. Kerr was grinning and it was the first time she had noticed a missing tooth at the side of his mouth. Then she made the connection. 'Speedy?' she said, 'is it you?'

'The very same,' Kerr replied.

She reached out and touched his arm. 'So you became a reporter, just like you said you would.'

'Yeah,' he answered, still smiling.

Seventeen years before, Peter Kerr, then known to all as 'Speedy', had worked as a messenger boy in the post room. In those days he told everyone who would listen that he intended to become a journalist. Sarah was pleased that his dream had been realised.

Kerr continued to hesitate, then said, 'Listen, I was sorry to hear about Jack. He was a great bloke.'

'Yes,' Sarah said. There was an awkward pause and Kerr half held open the door to the office. 'Take hold of yourself,' he said softly, 'the pictures are a bit strong.'

She entered the room, which had desks for several people. One wall was covered by a green baize curtain. Kerr paused for a moment, then drew it back to reveal a series of large photographs. They seemed to Sarah, at first glance, to be more like abstract paintings. Swathes of colour, predominantly magenta and scarlet, dominated the images, but there were other tones: delicate shades of purples and glistening yellows. Then, as Sarah continued to study them, they focused into recognisable shapes, and she was overcome by a wave of shock that made her sway momentarily. Her throat constricted and her bowels trembled. The strength seemed to drain from her body so that her legs felt unable to support her weight.

'Why don't you sit down?' Kerr suggested softly. She shook her head but held on to the back of a chair.

'You know,' he went on in the same quiet voice, 'it makes me ashamed to be a man – that someone could do this to any kid.'

Sarah shook her head, then forced herself to look at the pictures again. 'What happened to them?' she asked. Kerr took a ballpoint pen from his pocket to use as a pointer. It was as if he didn't want to touch the pictures with his hands.

'They were each hit on the temple with a blunt instrument, something like a hammer or a monkey wrench. Then they were dragged a few feet to somewhere more secluded and this was done to them.'

'Were they all near their homes?' Sarah asked, trying hard to keep her voice level.

'The first, no. The second two, yes. In the case of the girl last night, she was literally yards from her home.'

'What happened then?'

Kerr pointed to the pictures once more. 'The victim was laid on her side next to an open copy of the *Gazette* and disembowelled, so that the contents of the body cavity spilt on to the newspaper.'

Sarah looked away from the photographs. 'What about the symbol stamped on the newspapers?'

'Scotland Yard forensic say that's prepared beforehand.'

'Do the police know what it signifies?'

Kerr nodded. 'They're pretty sure it's made with a ship's stone.'

'What's that?'

'Some sort of pre-Christian piece of mumbo-jumbo. The experts say it was used as a Nordic curse. If you wanted to bring bad luck on your enemy you hid the stone on board his ship.'

She forced herself to turn back to the photographs. 'What else happens?'

Kerr hesitated. He did not look at her as he said, 'The knife blade is repeatedly thrust into the vagina.'

Sarah sat down and looked at the table top while Peter Kerr covered the pictures once again.

'Is there anything else?' she asked.

Kerr went to a cupboard and poured two drinks. He did not ask if Sarah wanted the whisky, but she took it, and was glad of the burning liquid that stung her mouth. He sat opposite and sipped his own drink.

'London University say that the symbol represents the word "revenge". The expert was intrigued by the equipment. The ink is the stuff commercial printers use, you can get it anywhere, but he thinks the ship's stone could be a museum piece.'

Kerr stood up again and said, 'By the way, the telephones in here are linked automatically to a recording device, incoming and outgoing, so be careful with private calls. There's a direct hotline to the incident room the police have set up at Hampstead nick, but that's on the news desk.'

He held up his hands as Sarah was about to speak. 'I know it's bloody daft, but Stiles insisted. It reminds us that he's supposed to be in charge.'

'Why isn't George Conway?'

Kerr shrugged. 'He's been hitting the bottle pretty hard recently. I think Meadows has done it to give him a kick up the arse.'

'Who else is working on the story?'

Kerr drank some more. 'Kevin Sinclair, Don Bradley, Dave Thomas and Ian Bradshaw. All picked by Stiles and all useless. I keep them out of the way as much as I can.'

'I thought they were supposed to be the pick of the crop?'

Kerr shrugged again. 'If they're the best we've got, then God help the paper.'

He unlocked a filing cabinet, took out three tapes and slid the first into a cassette recorder that was on the desk. 'Listen to this,' he said. 'My phone was already rigged with a recorder. I got this call on the day of the first murder.'

The clear English voice of a man filled the room: 'Is your tape recorder running?' Then Kerr answered 'Yes.' The first voice continued, 'You may call me Castor. I wish to tell you that a girl will be killed tonight, and the *Gazette* will be useful in clearing up the mess.'

Kerr switched off. 'All three messages are the same.'

Sarah watched as he lit a cigarette. 'May I have one of those?' she asked.

He reached the packet to her and offered her a light. Two lungfuls of smoke were enough but she continued to let the cigarette burn in her hand.

'Is there any connection between the girls?'

'Nothing the police can come up with yet.'

'What about the paper. Why the *Gazette*?'

'God knows. The families don't even take the paper. There's nothing in the cuttings library to suggest any connection, we've tried every conceivable angle. Maybe Castor is just a dissatisfied reader.'

'What were the girls like – were there any special similarities?'

Kerr drew on his cigarette. Before he poured another whisky for himself he offered the bottle to Sarah, but she shook her head. He sat down heavily in the chair opposite.

'They were all middle-class, the parents are all comfortably off; in the case of the last girl, bloody rich. All aged sixteen. That's it.'

He shook his head and reached up to pull the curtain aside again.

'Look at them. Julia Morell, found on Harrow Hill. A really beautiful kid. Louise Cullen, Stanmore Common. Plain as a pikestaff. Susan Blair in Finchley, another good looker. Last night's victim: Helen Craig, an ordinary girl, overweight, not a pretty face. The only absolute thing in common is their age.'

'The age of consent,' Sarah said softly, almost to herself.

'Sorry?' Peter Kerr said, and moved closer to her.

'The age of consent,' she repeated.

Kerr drank some more whisky. 'I don't think that applies any more, does it?' he said in a distracted fashion. 'From all I hear, they're at it the moment they're old enough to go out of the house on their own.'

Sarah thought of Emily. Surely that couldn't apply to her. She would know when her daughter ceased to be a virgin. That air of innocence – the last link with childhood would be severed and Sarah would know the difference. Like the curtain pulled on the photographs, Sarah shut the thought from her mind. 'What sort of co-operation are we getting from the police?' she asked.

Kerr considered the question as he ground out another cigarette.

'Pretty good – about as much as we could ask for. None of the other papers know that he rings us, or that he uses the *Gazette* to collect the entrails. A lot of our own staff don't either. We have the direct line to Colin Greaves, he's the superintendent in charge, you met him the other night. At the normal press briefs we go along with the others, but we can call him at home and we go there sometimes if he wants to tell us anything special. It's all a bit cloak and dagger, but I suppose it's the only way.'

'What's Greaves like?' Sarah asked. 'He didn't seem like the usual policeman.'

Kerr nodded. 'I know what you mean. . . .' He was about to say more when they heard the musical notes of the code lock and the door opened to reveal Alan Stiles, whose mood had changed since Sarah last saw him. Clearly he had recovered from the harsh words of the editor. Now he swaggered into the room, sat down and picked up Sarah's empty glass, which he slowly raised to his nostrils without taking his eyes from her.

'Whisky,' she said in the sort of voice one would use with a stupid child. Stiles put down the glass and began to fiddle with the cord of the curtain that concealed the photographs. 'Meadows tells me you're on my team,' he said after a time.

'That's right,' Peter Kerr answered. He had gone to one of the filing cabinets and was flicking through a sheaf of papers.

Stiles chose to ignore the remark. Instead he gestured with his thumb towards the wall of pictures. 'Can you cope with this sort of thing?' he said.

'As much as anyone can,' Sarah answered.

Stiles swung round and folded his arms. 'Right,' he said, 'Now here's what I want you to do. Kerr is chief crime reporter, he's got the rest of the team working with him, but they're out on the road most of the time. I'll co-ordinate from the news desk, but up until now, we haven't had anyone to cover here full time. Now you can be the link between all of us. This room will be the nerve centre of our activities. At the moment it's empty most of the time. With you here we can get some kind of order to the operation.'

Sarah laid both her hands flat on the surface of the table.

'You want me to be a secretary.'

Stiles shrugged. 'If you see yourself in that kind of role. . . .'

He let the sentence hang between them, then he got up and stood by the door. 'I've always found that women tend to gravitate to women's work.' He spoke with a smile that Sarah wanted to knock off his face.

There was silence for a time when Stiles had gone. Then Peter Kerr put on his raincoat, stood awkwardly beside her and said, 'I've got lunch with a contact.' He made it sound like an apology.

'What number will you be on?' Sarah asked. He told her and as he was about to go, she asked, 'How do I get access to VISOR?' Kerr wrote down the sequence of characters and then left.

It seemed very lonely in the bleak little office, so she turned to her terminal and called up the VISOR file. For all its secrecy, it did not contain much information. She copied some telephone numbers and addresses into her notebook and then called Claire Trevor. 'How goes your day?' she asked.

'I'm working in the advertising department,' Claire replied. 'It's a hell of a job getting all of this stuff on to a computer – like translating the Dead Sea Scrolls.'

'Do you fancy some lunch?'

'Sure, but let's get out of here.'

'There's a smart Italian restaurant near Holborn. I'll take you there.'

'That sounds like a celebration,' Claire said.

Sarah laughed. 'I'm celebrating one part of the day and drowning my sorrows about another.'

71

'I'll meet you in the entrance hall at one o'clock.'

Sarah hung up and turned her attention to the screen. It was almost time to go when Emily called her.

'Do you mind if I go out tonight?' she asked.

'Where?' Sarah asked. There was something curious in her daughter's voice, a note she hadn't heard before.

'To a concert.'

'With whom?'

Emily hesitated. 'Ric Daggert, one of the boys at school.'

Sarah didn't like the sound of Daggert; it conjured up images of bodies packed together in sweating rooms, writhing to discordant rock music. Ric Daggert was the sort of name that would go with black leather and a hollow-cheeked, sneering face. 'Where is this concert?' she asked.

'The Wigmore Hall.'

'Is he coming to the house to pick you up?'

'Oh, for God's sake, mummy! I'm meeting him at the station.'

'I want to see him,' Sarah said firmly. 'No introduction – no concert.'

Emily conceded after a final wrangle, and when she hung up, Sarah saw it was time to meet Claire.

She was waiting in the entrance hall as arranged, studying a plaque on the wall that commemorated the opening of the building.

'The first edition of *The Gazette* to be prepared and printed on these premises was on 21 July 1951,' she read, as Sarah walked over to join her. She looked up. 'Did they really use to print a million and a half copies from this building every night?'

'That's right,' Sarah answered.

'How many presses were there?'

'Haven't you ever seen them?'

Claire shook her head.

'Come and look now,' Sarah said, 'it'll only take us a few minutes.'

She walked over to a door next to the lifts, but one of the commissionaires called out, 'That's locked now. The only access is from the yard.'

'Thank you,' she replied, and she led Claire along the vanway until they stopped at another door. This one was unlocked. Once inside and descending the metal staircase, Sarah caught a familiar mixture of scents: ink, newsprint and oiled machinery. Claire looked down at the metal treads of the stairs and noticed the highlights on the bubbled surface where the steel had been polished by use in the past. The only sound was the hum of the air-conditioning plant and the clatter of their footsteps. After going deeper than Claire expected, they walked along a short corridor and emerged in a vast, gloomy room that was completely empty.

'The newsprint was stored in here,' Sarah explained as they walked on, and Claire noticed that her voice was hushed by the cathedral-like space. They crossed the concrete concourse and passed through a wide opening into another equally cavernous space that housed lines of massive machinery.

'This is the old press hall.'

Claire looked up in wonder at the lines of presses that stood before them, and Sarah thought how impressive they still looked. The matt-black and polished steel gave them the appearance of monstrous weapons from an ancient war that were still capable of sprouting barrels from their innards and firing great shells against the bare concrete walls. From somewhere, they could hear the sound of metal clinking and a tuneful whistling.

They walked forward again, and Claire noted that at various intervals there were gaps where men had once reached into the bowels of the machines to replate the presses and feed through the massive reels of paper. The whistling started again, and from one of the gaps a small man in baggy, ink-stained overalls emerged.

'Hello girls,' he said cheerfully. 'Sightseeing? We don't get many visitors down here.'

'I'm just showing my friend,' Sarah replied. 'She's never seen the old presses.'

The man nodded. 'Better take a good look, you won't get a chance to see them much longer.'

'Do they still work?' Claire asked.

The man rubbed his face with a rag before he answered. 'Oh yes.' He pointed to a button on the machine next to him. 'Press that and off she'd go.'

'Why do you still keep them in working order?' Claire asked.

The man smiled. 'Because they're worth money.' He nodded. 'This lot's going to be dismantled soon and shipped off to India.' He looked around again. 'Everything's going. I remember when Old Burntwood started this press for the first time: "I stand here at the heart of the *Gazette*", he said.'

He pointed to where Sarah stood. 'That was the spot.'

'The heart of the paper,' Claire repeated, 'that's kind of poetic.'

The little man laughed and shook his head. 'There's bugger all poetry left in the newspaper business now, love.'

They lingered for a bit longer after Sarah thanked him. He

73

returned to his work, and they walked the length of the press hall before returning to the surface.

'It was like being down a coal mine,' Claire said when they stood in the fresh air.

'You should have seen it when the presses were running,' Sarah replied, as they turned into Gray's Inn Road. 'The sensation was overpowering.'

In the restaurant they ordered white wine. Sarah opened one of the cellophane-wrapped packets of breadsticks and broke a piece off. 'Emily wants to go on a date tonight,' she said.

Claire nodded. 'With Ric Daggert?'

'How did you know?'

Claire smiled. 'I saw him hanging around when I took her to the school concert. She introduced me.'

'What is he like?' Sarah asked, and there was no concealing the concern in her voice. Claire took a breadstick and snapped it between her teeth. 'Oh, you know what they're like these days – long greasy hair, a scar on his cheek, one earring and tattoos all the way up his arms.'

'Tattoos?' Sarah repeated.

Claire laughed. 'You should hear yourself. Just relax, the kid doesn't even shave yet, and he plays the cello.'

Sarah drank some of the wine. 'I can't help it,' she said. 'This is the first time she's been out with a boy. It's all happened so fast.'

'She's nearly sixteen. That's pretty old for a first date.' Claire paused. 'How old were you?'

'My first date?'

'You know what I mean.'

Sarah drank some more wine before she answered. 'That was the sixties, wasn't it expected then?' Claire smiled at the question and Sarah decided to change the subject. She talked about the events of the morning but did not mention the link to the *Gazette*. It was Claire who raised the subject of the symbol that had been stamped on the sheet of newspaper.

'How did you know?' Sarah asked, astonished that Claire possessed that piece of information.

'It's in VISOR,' she replied with a hint of satisfaction.

'I thought access was strictly limited?'

'Remember I installed the system,' Claire answered. 'Like the cook said, only I know the entire contents of the stew.'

Sarah said 'The trouble is, Stiles isn't going to let me really work on the story. He's got me nailed to the desk, and there isn't a damned thing I can do about it.' She took another sip of wine and let the cold summery taste linger for a moment in her mouth. 'Still,' she added in a more determined voice, 'my nights are my own to do what I will with.' She broke off another piece of breadstick but did not bother to eat it. A heavy lorry rumbled past the window and she noticed it had begun to rain. 'I wondered – if it's not too much trouble – would you mind spending a bit more time with the children, just until this story is finished?'

Claire took the piece of bread that Sarah had discarded and added some butter.

'Only if you promise me to go easy on Ric Daggert,' she said finally. 'Remember the love of Romeo and Juliet, and Emily is a lot older than Juliet.'

'Juliet was dead before she was Emily's age,' Sarah said, and then regretted the words, remembering a saying of Sister Veronica: 'The Devil is always open to suggestions.' It's just a silly superstition, she told herself quickly.

The food arrived and Sarah began to eat with an enthusiasm Claire could not equal.

'You make me feel like a navvy!' Sarah said when she had finished her pasta. Claire's food seemed untouched; despite all the prodding she had done with her fork, very little had actually been eaten. She shrugged and raised the palms of her hands. 'I should never order lasagne. No matter how much you eat, it just seems to go on expanding, like some science fiction threat to the planet.'

After a few more minutes she gestured for a waiter to remove the plate. Sarah asked for zabaglione. When he returned with the order he nodded across the room. 'The gentleman in the corner asks if you will have a drink with him, ladies.'

They followed the direction of his glance and saw George Conway leaning forward to wave. He was sitting on his own and had been hidden from their view by a corner of the bar and some potted plants.

'Say yes, and ask him if he would care to join us,' Sarah replied.

Conway came to their table. They refused his offer of brandy, settling instead for glasses of the house wine.

'Where were you this morning?' Sarah asked. George sat with hunched shoulders, his powerful hands wrapped around a large tumbler of Scotch. When he drank from the brimming glass, Sarah could see how strong the drink was from the darkness of the liquid.

'Visiting my lawyer,' he answered with slow deliberation, then smiled at Sarah and she could see that his eyes were not quite in focus. 'My wife and I have decided to go our separate ways.'

'I thought you divorced years ago.'

George fumbled in his pockets and produced a packet of ciga-rettes. He lit one with an old-fashioned lighter and the scent of petrol and tobacco smoke mingled about them.

'That was my first wife, the once-beloved Jean,' he said in the same slow voice. 'This is number three.' He waved with his glass to emphasise his words and some of the whisky spilt on to the table-cloth. Realising just how drunk he was, Claire now sat stiffly in her chair. 'I think we'd better be getting back to the office,' she said quietly, and Sarah could hear her disapproval.

'You go on,' Sarah said gently, 'I'll stay for a bit.'

'Are you sure?' Claire said. She hesitated, wanting to rise from the table but reluctant to leave Sarah alone with a companion who might prove difficult.

'I'll be fine,' Sarah said. 'See you later.'

'Give me a ring,' Claire replied, continuing to watch George, whose head had slumped on to his chest. The sound of her chair scraping on the tiled floor caused him to jerk up his head. 'She'll be all right with me,' he said clearly. 'You run along.'

Claire continued to hover until Sarah smiled her reassurance.

When they were alone Sarah said, 'Are you upset by all this? . . . the divorce, I mean?'

George laughed, a loud, rumbling sound that caused heads to turn nearby. 'Only by the cost.' He inhaled deeply on the remains of the cigarette before he continued, 'Mind you, it's not all that much, I suppose. The other two took all my worldly wealth; this one's only getting part of my overdraft.'

He stubbed out the cigarette, finished his whisky and waved to the waiter. 'Same again?'

Sarah shook her head. While the drink was coming George took the remaining breadstick and fumbled with his thick fingers to extract it from the wrapper.

'Everything's complicated these days,' he grumbled, 'and every-thing is over-packaged. When I was a kid you bought things straight from the barrel.' He gave up the struggle with the cellophane. 'These must have been supplied by the manufacturer of Miss Trevor's knickers. Good to look at but impossible to get into.'

'Have you tried?' Sarah asked.

He shook his head. 'I'm fifty-one years old. We wouldn't have a lot in common, but some of the younger-generation have given it a go.' He turned down a thumb. 'Access restricted. Sinclair says it's because she's always got the cursor on.'

Sarah didn't think the remark funny. 'My God, you men never change, do you?' she said in a sudden angry voice. 'Just because a woman won't roll over the moment she's asked, you have to find an excuse for your own inadequacies.'

George held up his hands. 'Peace, peace! I was only reporting what they say. You know I love women. Look how many I'm supporting!'

Sarah leaned back and relaxed again. She even smiled at his contrition. 'I'm sorry, it's just that I like Claire. She's been kind to me and the children. Besides, I think it's a pleasant change these days if she chooses not to sleep around.'

George was about to say something but thought better of it. Instead he pointed at her. 'So how are you enjoying the job?'

Sarah pushed her glass aside. 'Hasn't Stiles told you, I've been taken on the staff?'

His head jerked up again and there was a surprised look on his face. 'No, I haven't been in the office yet. How did this come about?'

Sarah described the events leading to her appointment and he sat in silence for a time.

'You don't mind, do you?' she asked.

George shook his head. 'No, I'm delighted for you, just a little surprised. It's always pleasant to see Stiles thwarted in his grubby little machinations. This will put some sugar in his petrol tank.'

She leaned forward and rested her elbows on the table. 'Why does he want to get me? What have I ever done to him? We didn't even know each other until a few days ago.'

George leaned back in his chair, which creaked under his weight. 'It's because of Jack,' he said eventually.

'Jack?' Sarah repeated. 'How can he have anything to do with it?'

George rubbed his nose, moving the flattened cartilage from side to side. 'Jack stitched him up on a story, years ago, when Stiles was still a reporter.'

'What was the story?'

George shrugged. 'Some crooked businessman we exposed. Stiles was freelancing at the time, for the opposition. Jack knew Stiles was trying to buy one of his contacts, so he passed on phoney information, it sent Stiles off on a wild-goose chase to the East Midlands. While he was away, Jack nailed the man they were both after. Stiles never forgave him.' He looked out into the roadway where the rain had begun to slow the traffic. 'Funny really. Jack left the paper to go to television a few weeks later and recommended Stiles for his job, and he got it, but he never forgave Jack.'

'So you think he's taking it out on me. I didn't think anyone still remembered Jack on the *Gazette*.'

George nodded. 'One or two, you'd be surprised. He was the best reporter we ever had. Lucky old Jack.' He looked out at the street for a time, then turned back to her. 'I was always crazy about you, did you know that?'

Sarah laughed. 'Come on, George, it's me you're talking to – not one of your wives!'

He shook his head slowly. 'I thought you knew. I remember the night Jack first took you out, I walked down to Blackfriars Bridge during my break. Christ, I think I was going to throw myself in the river. I stood there, looking down, and then I told myself, it's just another of Jack's flash romances: we used to call him that, you know: Jumping Jack Flash, like the song.'

Sarah was unable to think of anything to say.

George continued, 'Then I thought, it'll be over in a few days, I'll get her on the rebound.' He held up a large hand and made a catching motion.

Sarah looked into his face. 'Are you sure you're not imagining how you felt, George?' she said gently.

He shook his head and then reached into his pocket and produced his wallet. After a moment's fumbling, he drew out the snapshot of her and pushed it across the table. 'I never forgot how you were.'

She looked down at the photograph and could feel her eyes fill with tears. With a great effort she regained her composure. 'That was taken a long time ago, George, eighteen years. I'm not the same person any more.'

'You look the same.'

'No, that was Sarah Linton, a twenty-year-old girl. I'm a woman with half-grown children. If I met her now I wouldn't even know what to talk about.' Sarah glanced at his miserable expression and tapped her watch. 'Time to go,' she said gently. She called for the bill while she waited for him to finish his drink.

'I'll get this,' he insisted, pulling a wad of ten-pound notes from his pocket. Sarah protested but he waved aside her objections. 'Let me, please, to make up for my remarks about Claire Trevor.' He managed to smile. 'Besides, it'll be something my wives won't be able to get their hands on.'

The rain was over and the short walk back to the office seemed to sober George, but Sarah knew all about the illusion some heavy drinkers managed to convey. It was as if he had switched to another part of his brain that was unaffected by the alcohol. Her father had once said it was similar to the watertight compartments on a ship; one part of the hold flooded but the engine room still operating.

George wasn't really fit to work though, and it caused her some concern. Luckily he solved the problem by announcing that he was going to take the rest of the day off; hailing a passing taxi, he gave the address of a street in Soho. Sarah watched him go and turned to enter the imposing building, but a small delivery van was driving out between the two stone pillars that flanked the driveway before the entrance. She stepped aside and stood in an alcove in the high dividing wall that separated the offices of the *Gazette* from the premises next door. The moment she entered the spot, Sarah was engulfed by a memory. Jack had kissed her there one wet, dark night. It seemed like a hundred years ago.

CHAPTER
EIGHT

WHILE she waited for the lift, Sarah remembered George's confession. She admitted to herself that she had always known of his true feelings for her, and also knew that they could never be reciprocated, so she had pushed the knowledge deep into the recesses of her mind, where thoughts that could hurt others, and herself, lay hidden from conjecture.

Now the prospect of returning to the claustrophobic little office with its gruesome pictures was deeply unappealing. Nonetheless, she made her way there and found Kevin Sinclair typing his expenses. He looked up at her for a moment, as though she were meat on a butcher's slab, but did not speak. Recalling his remark about Claire, and the conversation about the secretary, she wanted to escape from the room more than ever. An excuse was needed.

Like all good reporters, Sarah possessed a certain reserve of guile. She knew that if she asked Stiles for permission to leave the office, perversely he would insist that she stayed. The only solution was to arrange that he send her somewhere under the illusion that it was his own idea.

She called up VISOR on her terminal and read through the reports for some time, then, after looking at the terrible photographs again, she rang Stiles.

'Can we talk about the story on the telephone?' she asked.

'Yes,' he answered, without any noticeable enthusiasm.

Sarah took a deep breath: 'According to VISOR, all the girls were dragged just a few feet from where they were originally attacked to where they were murdered, is that correct?'

'Yes.'

'And according to forensic experts the girls were hit from behind by a right-handed person of average height.'

'What are you getting at?' Stiles asked impatiently.

Sarah paused. 'Well, it occurred to me that it should be possible to work out exactly where the girls were when they were attacked, so I could write a description of the last thing they saw when they were alive.'

'They were just ordinary surroundings,' Stiles said, and then he got the point. 'I've got a better idea,' he said. 'Take a photographer and shoot it. There's no need for you to write anything, the pictures will tell it all.'

'Yes, I hadn't thought of that,' she said, managing to sound disappointed.

'Hang on,' Stiles said abruptly, and she could hear him making arrangements with the picture desk. Eventually he came back on the line. 'Be downstairs in the entrance hall in five minutes. Harry Porter will meet you there.'

'Harry Porter,' Sarah repeated. 'I thought he had retired long ago.' But Stiles did not hear. He had already hung up.

After the call Sarah turned to Sinclair. 'I've got to go out for Stiles,' she said. 'Do you want my telephone switched through to the news desk?'

He waved a hand dismissively, without bothering to speak or lift his head from the sheet before him. Sarah studied his hunched form and made a silent resolution that her own sons would never treat other human beings, men or women, with such discourtesy. She guessed that Sinclair was in his early twenties, judging from his unlined skin and fashionably baggy clothes. All of the insolence of youth and none of the uncertainties.

Impulsively, she wrote the telephone number of her local Chinese restaurant on a piece of paper, then sat down opposite him and said, 'Kevin, I know what's worrying you and I want to help. Why don't you ring this number? He's a very good doctor.'

He looked up puzzled, and took the scrap of paper. 'Worried about what?' he asked suspiciously. 'What doctor?'

'He specialises in your sort of problem.'

'What problem?'

Sarah smiled sympathetically and shook her head. 'It's all right, I'm practically old enough to be your mother, there's no need to be shy. A lot of boys have the same trouble with sex when they start.'

'What trouble?'

Sarah continued to gaze at him steadily. 'You must know what's written about you on the wall of the ladies' loo?'

She now had his full attention, and a flush of sudden panic had begun to suffuse his cheeks.

She nodded again: 'That's why the girls refer to you as Swifty.' She got up before he could answer and left the room.

On her way out she stopped to call into the advertising department, where she knew Claire was working. She found her seated before a computer terminal next to a miserable-looking girl, who was listening to her patient instructions with an expression of blank incomprehension. Claire looked up and Sarah said, 'I have to go out, I'll call you later.'

She was about to leave the room when she paused. Something had brought back memories; it was the smell, she realised finally. Newsprint. There were stacks of old papers piled at one end of the room and the musty scent permeated the air and reminded her of other times. So did Harry Porter when she saw him in the entrance hall, photographic bags heaped at his feet, puffing on a small cigar.

'I thought you'd retired?' she said as she approached him.

'Nah – I was on me holidays in Broadstairs, bloody awful it was, rained every day.' He took hold of both her hands and she hugged him, like an old dog. Despite the mildness of the day, he wore an overcoat that would have protected him from a Siberian winter.

'I heard you was doing casual shifts,' he said gloomily. 'You must be bloody mad coming back to this business.' Then he held her at arm's length. 'Well, let's have a look at you.' He nodded his approval. 'Bloody hell, girl, you still look twenty.'

Sarah leaned forward and kissed him. 'You haven't changed either, Harry, still the same old charmer.' The words were true. His red face, as raw and round as a roll of beef, was surmounted by a small brown trilby of the sort favoured by the sharper members of the racing fraternity. Bright blue eyes, magnified by the thick lenses of his horn-rimmed spectacles, continued to study her. 'You'll do,' he said finally. 'Now what's this load of old rubbish Stiles wants?'

Sarah explained while they walked to the vanway. 'Your car or mine?' she asked, as they skirted a large puddle of rainwater.

'It'll have to be yours, I don't drive any more,' Harry said. 'It ruins your drinking.'

While Sarah headed towards Harrow, the location of the first murder, he began to recite a litany of those who had been fired from the *Gazette* in the years since her departure. Each name was accompanied by an expression of regret. Sarah smiled as the list continued. It was as if Harry were discussing members of a closely knit family, when she knew that he had detested most of the people mentioned. Eventually, when he spoke warmly of Nat Goldman, a long-time picture editor of the paper, she was forced to protest.

'But Harry, you loathed Nat Goldman. I remember you once told him you were going to eat a ham sandwich while you were standing on his grave.'

'That's not the point,' Harry replied, as he puffed on another cigar. 'Nat and I hated each other for forty-five years – we started as darkroom boys together on the same day. I may have fought with the little prick, but I still miss him. They hire people these days with personalities like pigeon shit.' His eyes glistened. 'That's why I treasure Stiles. He's the last of the old-fashioned bastards, untrustworthy, devious, disloyal. He'd stab you in the back just to check if his knife was still sharp.'

Sarah laughed again. 'Oh, Harry, you are wonderful. I was beginning to think everything had changed utterly, thank God you're just the same.'

The tour through the locations in the north London suburbs did not take long, despite squalls of rain that fell intermittently from the ragged clouds. Finally they stood in the same spot where she had spoken with Colin Greaves the night before. So much had happened since then, it seemed like a week ago. The memory of his melancholy face came to her as she waited in the quiet road. The surroundings looked different now; the last of the clouds had blown away and the wet surface of the road was dappled by sunlight that streamed through the foliage of the trees. The only sounds were a blackbird singing and the occasional hissing click of Harry's camera.

'All done,' he announced at last. 'I could do with a beer now.'

'How about at my place?' Sarah offered.

'Can I get a taxi from there?'

'Easily,' she answered. 'You know the house.'

Harry thought for a moment. 'Are you still living in the same place where you had that New Year's party?'

'The very same, it still bears the scars.'

They got back into the car and when they turned into Sarah's street a few minutes later, Harry said, 'Sorry about Jack.' She was busy parking the car, so he could not see her eyes. 'I know that, Harry,' she replied quickly.

Emily opened the front door before she could take out her keys. At first Sarah thought she had forgotten to put on a skirt; all she wore was a pair of black tights that showed every contour, and a long white blouse that did little to disguise the rest of her body. She was also wearing more eye make-up than usual and her loose hair fell almost to her waist. It made her look much older than she had that morning. Sarah felt a sudden anger rising.

'How many times have I told you to always get dressed properly before you answer the door,' she said crisply.

Emily raised her eyes to the ceiling of the hallway as Sarah swept past. 'Oh, mum, everyone's wearing this sort of thing now,' she said in a martyred voice.

'I think she looks great,' Harry said as he followed them. 'That stuff's all the rage, according to my granddaughter.' He turned to Emily. 'I don't suppose you remember me, do you, love?'

Emily studied him. 'I've seen pictures of you in dad's room,' she said eventually.

'Are you still going to be a doctor?' Harry asked.

'Yes,' Emily said with surprise. 'How did you know?'

Harry followed Sarah into the kitchen and pointed to a large pinewood bench. 'When you were five years old you sat on my lap over there and told me.'

'Did I?' Emily replied, 'And you still remember?'

Harry tapped his nose, which was the pitted texture of coke. 'Anyone with a trunk like mine forgets nothing.'

Sarah handed him the promised beer and he drank half of it with the first swallow. Then he turned to Emily again and winked. 'So where are you off to all dolled up like that, young lady?'

'To a concert at the Wigmore Hall.'

'Are you now?' Harry said. 'I once photographed Pablo Casals there.'

Sarah could see that Emily was impressed. 'You actually knew Casals,' she asked.

Harry nodded and drank some more of his beer. 'He even played me a tune afterwards.'

'Pablo Casals is Ric's god,' she said.

Sarah noticed the reverence in her voice and could not decide if it were for Pablo Casals or Ric Daggert.

'When are we going to meet this young man?' she asked.

Emily looked at her watch. She had been glancing at it continually since they had entered the house.

'Any time now,' she answered casually.

They heard the front door opening again, and the boys came into the house. It seemed they were generating an energy field that caused winds to swirl about them. Then Sarah saw they were accompanied by a tall youth she did not know.

'We found him in the garden,' Martin said and he nudged Emily. Sarah could see two high spots of colour on her daughter's cheeks and she had lowered her eyes to study the tiled floor of the kitchen.

Sarah studied the youth and was filled with foreboding. He was strikingly handsome, tall and dark, his well-built frame clad in a fashionably ill-fitting suit. All of her worst fears were fulfilled. She doesn't stand a chance, she thought with a sinking feeling. And I shall have to nurse her broken heart.

But then she heard Emily speak, 'You're late!' she said in an unexpectedly firm voice. Ric Daggert looked doleful, and when he spoke Sarah felt a wave of relief break over her. The high, hesitant voice that now stammered an apology was still that of a boy, and one who was in considerable awe of her daughter. The wolf had not yet found his teeth.

When introductions had been made, Sarah issued a warning about being late. As they were about to depart he paused and stood before her. 'She'll be safe with me, Mrs Keane,' he said. 'I promise I'll look after her.'

His words touched Sarah to the heart. 'I know you will, Ric, thank you,' she replied.

Martin and Paul made for their part of the house. Harry accepted another beer and leaned against the sink. 'They look just like Jack,' he said.

Sarah agreed. 'But Emily takes after my mother,' she said.

Harry put his empty glass down on the draining board and looked around the room. 'We had some good times in this house.' He lit another little cigar and studied the glowing tip for a moment. 'Funny how you see a lot of friends for a few years, and then things change and you lose touch.' He slapped the steel sink behind him. 'Well, I'd better be on my way.'

'I'll phone for a taxi,' Sarah said. 'Help yourself to another beer.'

She went to the living room to make the call. As she replaced the receiver, it rang again.

'Gotcha!' Fanny Hunter said. 'I've been trying to find you all afternoon.'

'What's the matter?' Sarah asked.

'Nothing's the matter,' Fanny said. 'I want to invite you to a knees-up I'm having tonight. Sorry about the short notice, it's a last-minute do.'

Sarah hesitated.

'Come on,' Fanny urged, 'put your glad rags on, it'll do you good.' Sarah realised a refusal would sound churlish. 'What time, Fanny?' she asked.

She made a note of the address, then rang Claire at the office. They chatted for a few minutes and at the end of the conversation Sarah said, 'May I beg a favour. I'd like to go out for a few hours later. It's just Paul and Martin at home, Emily's on her date. Would you mind?'

'Feel free,' Claire replied. 'I've got to write a report tonight so I won't be very good company.'

'I'm cooking lamb chops for the boys' supper, will that suit you?'

Claire laughed, 'Are you kidding, after all that lasagne? I couldn't eat a thing.'

Sarah told Harry of the invitation when she returned to the kitchen and he was impressed. 'She doesn't usually have riff-raff like us at her parties,' he said.

Sarah glanced at her hands. 'Look at these,' she said. 'People will think I'm just there to do the washing up afterwards.'

'I shouldn't worry,' Harry said drily. 'If Fanny's flashing it about no one will be looking at your hands.'

CHAPTER
NINE

UNSURE how smart the occasion would be, Sarah finally settled for a dark grey silk dress and a string of pearls left to her by her mother.

'How do I look?' she asked Claire when she arrived at 7.30.

'Like a million dollars,' she answered. 'Fanny's tits won't stand a chance in the light of your cool sophistication.'

'The cab's here,' Martin called out, and with a final glance in the mirror in the hallway, she set off.

The journey to Kensington was unsettling. The minicab smelt like an ashtray, and the surly driver cornered the reeking car ferociously, causing her to sway violently in the back seat. But it wasn't just the unpleasant quality of the ride; Sarah was also aware that this was the first time she had attended any sort of social function alone since before she had been married. The thought so daunted her that at one point she almost told the driver to turn around and take her home to Hampstead. The cab deposited her before an imposing, white-painted house in The Boltons. By the time she'd walked up the steps to the pillared portico, a manservant in striped trousers and black jacket had opened the door and with a few words of greeting, indicated that she was to go up to a reception room on the first floor.

Although she was fifteen minutes late Sarah was still one of the first arrivals. There was no sign of Fanny, just a group of young people in fashionably casual clothes, who made noisy conversation round a grand piano that stood in the wide bay windows overlooking the rear garden.

Sarah took a glass of champagne from a tray offered by a white-coated servant and, leaving the reception room, looked for somewhere to hide. She was lucky with the first door she tried. It led into a smallish sitting room comfortably furnished with Edwardian furniture, the walls covered with paintings. Sarah noticed a book, open and placed face down on a small table next to the most comfortable chair, and a tumbler half full of whisky.

Glad of the solitude, she began to study the paintings; all seemed to be by the same artist, very English and mostly of domestic scenes: children playing in gardens, portraits of confident men and women, landscapes of a rocky coastline she did not recognise and still lifes that she thought must have been painted in this house. The pleasant record of an upper middle-class life that had taken place long before she was born.

Sarah was so absorbed by the pictures that she looked up in some surprise when a tall, white-haired man, wearing a dinner jacket and fumbling with an unfastened cufflink, entered the room.

'Forgive me,' he apologised, 'I didn't mean to startle you.'

It was clear by his manner that the man lived in the house, and Sarah knew instinctively that this was his room.

'It's I who should apologise,' she replied. 'I'm afraid I'm an intruder.'

'Not at all,' he said. 'I suppose you were driven to take refuge in here by my granddaughter's friends. Very wise, they know they're forbidden to enter this room.'

Sarah saw that he was still struggling with the cufflink. 'May I help you with that?' she asked.

'I should be eternally grateful,' he answered, and held out his hand. While she inserted the gold link through the starched cuff he studied her. 'I'm sorry I wasn't there to greet you,' he said, 'but Fanny left it rather late before reminding me I had to dress for the occasion. My name is Osbert Hannay.'

'Sarah Keane,' she replied, remembering vaguely that Fanny had married someone called Hannay. 'You must be. . . .' She left the assumption unspoken. It was clear that this man was much older than Fanny, and the fact that he had his own quarters in the house suggested that he could be her father-in-law.

'I'm Fanny's husband,' he said. 'Are you an old friend of Fanny's?'

'We've known each other for a long time.'

'But this is the first time you've been to one of these parties?'

'We haven't seen each other for a number of years.'

Hannay stroked his freshly shaven chin. 'They tend to be a trifle confusing for the newcomer. My friends and relations are older and not very fashionable, you may find them a bit stuffy. You've already seen my granddaughter's crowd – being young, they seem to me as foreign as Hottentots. Fanny's friends tend to be very smart; famous faces, that sort of thing.'

He picked up the glass of whisky and gestured towards the pictures: 'Do you like my paintings? I saw you looking at them when I came into the room.'

'You did them?'

He laughed, 'Oh, no. They're by my mother, Beatrice Hannay. She was quite well known – once upon a time.'

'They're lovely,' Sarah replied. 'This must have been a very happy house.'

'It was,' he said after a moment, and then the sound of loud voices came from the other room. 'I think some more adults may have arrived by now, shall we join them?'

When she re-entered the reception room, Osbert Hannay's prediction proved correct. It was now filled with people, but they had divided into three quite distinct groups. The young were still gathered about the piano. Near the door was a cluster of famous faces, most of whom Sarah recognised from television and politics. In between was a wedge of more elderly people, who seemed to be shepherded by a youngish woman. She was stamped with the same long, thin features Sarah had noticed in the family portraits in the other room.

'Honestly, daddy,' the woman whispered, just loud enough for Sarah to hear, 'you might have been here to meet your own friends.'

'Sorry, darling,' he replied. 'May I introduce you to Sarah Keane. She's just been admiring your grandmother's pictures.'

'Leonora Hamilton,' the woman said. She shook hands in a firm manner and immediately began presenting the elderly people in her charge. As she spoke, the names seemed to echo in Sarah's memory like the words of a half-forgotten hymn.

'And this is Mary and Frederick Fortescue,' she continued, and Sarah looked more closely at the couple before her.

'Do you come from Dorset?' she asked with sudden interest.

'Yes,' the man answered. 'Why do you ask?'

Sarah smiled. 'My mother's maiden name was Anne Fortescue.'

He studied her briefly and said, 'Did she marry a doctor called Linton?'

Sarah nodded.

'Bless my soul,' he exclaimed, 'Anne was my second cousin.'

Now Sarah understood the familiarity of the names, having had them recited to her by her mother when she was very young. They were all descended from recusants, members of the old Catholic families who had refused to convert to the Church of England during the Reformation.

'It's odd that we haven't met before,' Leonora said. 'Where has daddy been keeping you?'

'I don't actually know your father,' Sarah said. 'We only met this evening.'

'Really,' Leonora said. 'Who did you come with?'

'Fanny invited me.'

'Fanny?' she repeated. 'But Fanny doesn't know any of our friends.'

Just then there was a whooping sound and two of the elderly couples parted to allow Fanny through to Leonora. 'What are you doing down here?' she asked as she took Sarah's arm and tugged her towards the other end of the room. 'Come away from all those bead-rattlers and meet some interesting people,' she went on, in a penetrating whisper. Fanny seemed to part the crowd like waves before the prow of a ship until they stood in front of a cabinet minister and the host of a television game show. They smiled uneasily at Fanny's introduction and reluctantly made some space so that Sarah could listen to their conversation about the tax advantages of tree farming.

Sarah accepted another glass of champagne from a circulating waiter and glanced about her. Standing a few feet away was Brian Meadows. She was surprised to see that he was talking to the police superintendent Colin Greaves, a guest who seemed out of place among the glittering media personalities that pressed about them. She could not see any other people from the *Gazette*. Greaves caught her eye and gave a half smile. Sarah was about to sidestep the cabinet minister and join him when a voice behind her said, 'Sarah?'

She turned, and for a moment had difficulty in recognising Patrick Stone, husband of Philippa, the woman of a thousand varied sexual encounters. His shambling figure had been remodelled completely, gone were the baggy corduroys, hairy tweed jacket and ragged beard. In their place, a slimmer Patrick wore designer jeans and an expensive-looking silk jacket with wide lapels. She studied his hair, puzzled, then realised it had been streaked with highlights.

'Hello,' she said quickly. 'Is Philippa here?'

He shook his head. 'Didn't you hear? We're divorced.'

'No, I'm sorry, Patrick.'

He shrugged. 'That's the scene now, we're both doing our own thing. I guess we just needed more space.'

Sarah noted that, like his choice of clothes, Patrick seemed to have settled on the early 1970s for his new vocabulary. In the past his speech had been filled with academic jargon.

'Are you still working in television?' she asked.

'Same old grind,' he replied. He looked at her more closely. 'You look wonderful. What are you up to?'

'I'm reporting on the *Gazette*, my old job.'

'It obviously suits you,' he said slowly. 'Strange how things change, isn't it?' He gestured to his clothes and smiled ruefully. 'Look at me, I feel like Gary Glitter in this ridiculous outfit.'

Sarah was warmed by his self-awareness. 'Who chose them?'

He indicated a slim, blonde girl who was laughing at an actor Sarah thought she recognised.

'Karen,' he said, taking a quick swallow from his glass.

'Who is she?'

Patrick laughed. 'The only known predator who lives on lettuce leaves.'

He turned and looked at Sarah. 'Do you know, I haven't tasted meat in eight months. It's ludicrous, a man of my age should be obsessed by sex, not fillet steak and pork chops.'

Sarah looked towards the still laughing girl. 'I'm sure there must be compensations.'

Patrick took another glass of champagne from a passing tray.

'Well someone else can enjoy them from now on. The fair Karen and I have decided to call it a day after tonight.' He paused before asking, 'I don't suppose you'd join me for a mixed grill one evening?'

Before she could answer, Fanny took her by the elbow again. 'Come and talk to Colin Greaves, he just told me he knows you.' Fanny pulled her into the crowd and looked about her with a slight frown of frustration. 'He seems to have gone,' she said with a hint of disapproval. 'Oh, well let me introduce you to my accountant.'

Sarah found herself pressed upon Lionel Holt, a fussy little man, one of those individuals who could separate a chosen victim from the other company in a room and transfix them with an endless monologue of self-centred platitudes. After a few minutes she looked around, seeking other company, but he continued to press on, oblivious of her boredom. Finally, realising there could be no escape, she said it was time for her to leave. Despite her protest he insisted on driving her. As they left, Fanny nodded towards Patrick, who was standing with Karen, and winked. Then Sarah realised she had been set up. She thought about Fanny's motives all the way home with Lionel Holt's voice droning in the background.

The next day, Sarah stayed in the operations room and spent her time there classifying the VISOR file, which had been assembled in a haphazard fashion. Claire called her at one point to say she had promised the children she would come over for the evening. Late in the afternoon, when she had finished entering a list of all the contact numbers relevant to the story, Sarah made a sudden decision and reached for the telephone.

A police sergeant answered. After a brief pause Colin Greaves came on the line. Sarah reminded him of their meeting. 'I remember,' he said. 'I was going to talk to you at Fanny Hunter's party, but you seemed rather involved, then I had to leave.'

'The *Gazette* has put me on the story now,' she answered. 'I wondered if I could speak to you this evening. I don't mind when.'

He hesitated and said, 'I'll be home at ten o'clock.' Then he gave her his address. Sarah studied it, puzzled for a time. It did not seem the usual sort of area policemen lived in.

Later that evening, coming from the direction of Kilburn, Sarah noted how the streets rose through the social scale as she approached Notting Hill. Bleak, soot-stained Victorian houses, divided into bedsitters and small flats, gradually gave way to elegant villas, their tree-filled gardens protected by high walls. Eventually she stopped the car at the address given to her by Greaves. It was in the smartest part of Ladbroke Grove. She studied the little Georgian house for some time, wondering if there could have been some mistake. The small garden surrounded by iron railings looked well kept, but lacked the signs of a loving hand, and there were no lights showing at the windows. The building had the effect of being maintained rather than lived in.

She rang the brass doorbell and waited. After a time she heard footsteps and Colin Greaves opened the door. He was wearing an old cricket sweater over an open-necked shirt. Sarah thought it somehow seemed frivolous; a monk's habit would have been more suited to his grave countenance. Without speaking, he gestured for her to enter and she followed him across the hallway. The house smelt musty and when they passed an open doorway she saw a room shrouded with dust sheets.

'I live upstairs,' Greaves said, sensing her puzzlement. 'I only use part of the house.'

He led her to the top floor and into a pair of connecting rooms at the back of the building. It was not women's territory. The darkly painted room was furnished with a large leather sofa, and tables piled with books. A single armchair stood next to a reading lamp and in one corner a small military desk was heaped with papers. In the alcoves on either side of the fireplace were bookshelves and, on top of cupboards, a small television set and a large record player. Although the weather was mild, a fire burned in the grate. There was little space in the room, but everything was carefully placed. He was clearly not a man who lived in disorder.

By the light from the reading lamp she could see a single bed in the connecting room. It was made with the sort of precision that would earn the approval of a hospital matron.

He took her coat and indicated for her to sit on the sofa.

'Did you enjoy the party last night?' she asked.

Greaves shook his head. 'It wasn't really the sort of occasion I care for, I only went because Meadows said he wanted to talk to me. He seems rather in awe of Fanny Hunter.'

'She's very important to the paper,' Sarah answered.

He considered her words then said, 'I was just about to make myself some coffee, will you join me?'

'Yes, fine,' Sarah replied and he opened another door. She heard the sound of cupboard clicking and there was the sudden buzz of an electric grinder. The aroma of freshly ground coffee drifted to her and after a few minutes he reappeared carrying a tray, which he placed on a table next to his chair. Sarah noticed he took both cream and sugar; somehow she had imagined he would forgo such earthly pleasures. Although there was a definite care about every-thing he did there was nothing fussy or old-maidish about his manner; it seemed more like the actions of a good mechanic, neat and competent without any wasted effort. She tasted the coffee. It was delicious.

'Sorry about the mug,' he said. 'I should have asked, but it seems silly to make it properly and then serve it in thimbles.'

'This is lovely,' she replied. Then she looked at his sweater again. 'Where did you play cricket?'

'New College,' he answered, 'long ago.' He smiled as he spoke, but Sarah thought he still looked sad.

'I hope you don't mind me coming at this hour.'

Greaves drank some more coffee and then shook his head. 'No, I stay up late and there's no one else to disturb.' He spoke factually, without any trace of self-pity, but still sounded melancholy.

Sarah sat forward. 'The reason I came was because I'm new to the story and I wanted to see if there were any points I hadn't picked up on.'

He rested a hand on the table next to him and drummed his long fingers on a book before he answered. 'There's little to know,' he said, 'I can't understand why the *Gazette* has so many people on the story. We still don't have any positive leads, just fragments. We're groping in the dark hoping for a mistake or something that will match on the computers. So far we appear to be searching for a psychotic who's named himself after one of the heavenly twins. The voice experts tell us that he's fairly young, and he has a middle-class accent; one that came naturally, there's no sign of elocution lessons. And he probably lives somewhere in the Greater London area.' He drank the last of his coffee. 'Meanwhile, the press and the politicians castigate us for lack of action.'

'That's all, there's nothing else?'

'Some people think they saw a blue van parked in the vicinity of the first two murders. We have part of a number plate. That's all.'

'And no logical connection with the *Gazette*?'

He nodded but did not answer.

'But the blue van, it could be something.'

Greaves smiled. 'We can only hope.'

She waited to see if he would add anything else, but he was content with the silence between them. Sarah was intrigued. Past experience told her that most policemen who are articulate want to speak about themselves when they are with a reporter, unless they have something they wish to conceal, but Greaves did not fall into either category. He was content to make brief statements that did nothing to enhance his standing in Sarah's eyes.

'Do you think he'll kill again?' she asked eventually.

'He'll try, but it won't be so easy from now on.'

'Why, has he changed?'

Greaves poured himself some more coffee before he answered. 'No, but you must remember most murder victims, outside the domestic variety, are poor. Killers who do it for thrills or compulsion usually choose drifters, prostitutes, the outsiders of our society. Castor is killing children from middle-class homes, who have parents.' He halted for a moment. 'I know, I've talked to them. What's interesting is how vulnerable they've been in those quiet streets. You can almost imagine them saying to themselves, "Nothing terrible could happen here, not where I live. Murders take place in slums, meaner surroundings than mine." Now they know different.'

He looked up at Sarah. 'Do you have children?'

'Two boys, and a daughter almost the same age as the victims.'

'Do you know where she is tonight?'

'Yes.'

He held up a hand. 'You see. No parent will let their daughter out on the street alone now, no matter what time of day it is. It will be harder for him to kill,' he paused again, 'and harder for us to catch him.'

A clock on the mantelpiece softly chimed the half-hour and Sarah glanced at her watch. Greaves noticed. 'Doesn't your husband mind you working so late?'

Sarah looked down at the cup she still held in her hand. 'My husband was killed more than a year ago.'

He studied her with the same sad expression. 'I'm sorry, Mrs Keane, you have my sympathy.' The words were plain, but she did not doubt his sincerity.

She looked up and tried to smile. 'For a long time I wouldn't face up to the truth. I just pretended it hadn't happened, he was away a lot, always abroad. I would tell myself he was on another job and one day soon he'd come back to us.'

Greaves seemed about to say something but instead reached out to a cupboard beside the fireplace and took out a bottle and two glasses.

The brandy was very old; she could feel the smoky fumes when she inhaled. Then she remembered the journey home and put down the glass. 'I really shouldn't, I have to drive home to Hampstead.'

Greaves smiled again and she suddenly thought how kind his face was now, even though the sadness seemed to linger around his eyes.

'Do you need your car in the morning?' he asked.

'Yes, I have to drive my children to school.'

'Don't worry about it, I'll call you a taxi.'

'How will I get my car?'

He poured more brandy. 'I'm going to Hampstead before seven o'clock, that's where the operations room is set up. I'll drop the car off and put your keys through the letterbox.'

She hesitated but realised that she didn't want to drive home. The brandy and the warmth of the room were comforting after the long day and she was beginning to feel sleepy. She handed him the keys and sipped some more from her glass.

'Tell me about your husband,' he said, and to her surprise she found that she could talk of Jack to him without difficulty. Thoughts and feelings she had told nobody else, not even Claire, were suddenly easy to speak of, and she talked on until the clock on the mantelpiece chimed midnight.

'I really must go,' she said.

'I'll ring for a taxi, it won't take long,' he replied. He went to the extension in the bedroom to make the call. After summoning the cab he rang another number, but she could not hear much of the conversation he conducted in a quiet voice.

Sarah stood up and looked around the room. Noticing a silver-framed photograph on the little desk piled with papers she picked it up, and by the light of the reading lamp saw that it was of an attractive young woman with short blonde hair, who had her arms around a boy and a girl. The boy was the image of the woman, the same flaxen hair and snub nose. The girl looked like Greaves. Sarah put the picture down quickly, feeling that she had made an intrusion into his privacy, and then he came back into the room.

As he had promised, the taxi came quickly; he walked with her to the end of the path and shivered in the cool night air. 'I hope you come again,' he said.

Sarah shook his hand. 'Next time we'll talk about you.'

Greaves stood with his hands thrust into his pockets. 'There's not much to know.'

She smiled. 'You mean you're only a humble policeman?'

He shook his head. 'No, sadly, I can't count humility among my virtues,' he said, then reached out and touched her arm. 'Good night, Sarah, sleep well.'

She looked back as the taxi drew away but he was gone. Once more the house was shrouded in darkness.

CHAPTER
TEN

WHEN she got home she found Claire with her feet resting on the sofa, surrounded by scattered papers.

'I'm sorry I'm so late,' she said, knowing that the hour would not bother Claire.

'No problem,' Claire replied. 'I might as well be burning your electricity as my own.'

'What time did they get to bed?'

'Just before eleven o'clock, exactly as you stipulated, Colonel.' She gathered the spread of papers into a neat pile and put them into her briefcase. 'How was your saintlike policeman? What's he really like?'

Sarah didn't answer at once. Thinking back, she realised that she had learned nothing. She had told him of her deepest feelings and he had been sympathetic, but it had been a one-sided conversation. 'I don't know anything about him at all,' she said finally.

Claire smiled. 'Don't you? – I know lots.'

Sarah looked at her with interest. 'How?'

'Stiles,' he replied. 'He's got another file, apart from VISOR. He thinks nobody knows about it – but there are no secrets from Wonder Woman.'

'Why do you think he does it?' Sarah asked, puzzled by Stiles's actions.

Claire shrugged. 'Information is power. Secret information is very powerful. I suppose it's just one of the ways Stiles is trying to screw George Conway. He bought the stuff on Greaves from a freelance, I'll give you the access code tomorrow.'

Sarah was tired after Claire had gone, but knew she would not sleep easily. She looked into the boys' room and saw them sprawled awkwardly across their beds, duvets on the floor, unable to conform even in sleep. Emily stirred and looked up when she opened her door.

'Sorry, darling,' Sarah said softly, 'I didn't mean to disturb you. How was the concert? I forgot to ask last night.'

'Lovely,' she replied sleepily. 'I wish you could have heard it.'

'So do I.'

'I want to get up early in the morning, will you wake me?'

'What time?'

'Six-thirty.'

'That is early.'

'Ric's taking me to see a fox on the Heath. He says the cubs come out before anyone is about. Oh, and there was a call from a Patrick Stone, he left a number and said can you call him in the morning, he doesn't mind how early as he's got a location shoot.'

'Thank you, darling,' Sarah replied, then kissed her and went to her own room. She set the alarm clock for six, knowing she would be awake before it rang.

Sarah stood at the kitchen window early in the morning, and while she waited for the coffee to brew she found Patrick Stone's message and dialled the number.

'Hi,' he said and she could hear the enthusiasm in his voice. 'Thanks for ringing back. Now, how about this meal – you wouldn't refuse a starving man, would you?'

Sarah felt odd. Although they had known each other in the past, this was hardly an outing with an old friend; there were new implications in the relationship he offered.

She took a deep breath and said, 'Yes I'll come.'

'Great,' Patrick replied 'How about tonight?'

That was sooner than she expected, but she realised it was possible.

'I'll pick you up at nine o'clock,' Patrick said and he hung up before she could add anything further. Nine o'clock sounded rather late she thought, it would be nearly ten before they began to eat. Then she smiled. A late night wouldn't do her any harm.

She looked into the garden. A soft light fell on the treetops and beads of dew glittered on the uncut lawn. The morning sky was made a paler blue by high thin clouds but she thought it was going to be a fine day. For a moment, while the perculator bubbled beside her, she felt a contentment that had been absent from her life for a long time. She poured the coffee and was about to take a cup to Emily when she heard the letterbox rattle beside her in the hallway. Colin Greaves was halfway down the path when she opened the door. He turned and she held up the mug in her hand, 'It's not as good as yours, but it's freshly made.'

He retraced his steps and followed her into the kitchen. Before Sarah could pour another cup, Emily joined them.

'This is Superintendent Greaves,' Sarah said, 'and this is my daughter, Emily.'

Greaves stood up and shook hands.

'Are you in charge of the murder investigation?' Emily asked.

'Yes, I am.'

'I hope you catch him soon.'

Greaves nodded and changed the subject. 'Why are you up so early?'

Emily told him about the foxes. Hearing a gentle tap on the door knocker she said, 'That will be Ric. I told him not to ring the bell.'

When Emily left Greaves put down his coffee. 'They're nice at that age. I hope she sees the foxes.'

Sarah thought of the photograph she had seen on his desk a few hours earlier, but didn't say anything. He stood at the window and looked into the garden.

'Shall I give you a lift to the station?' she asked.

He shook his head. 'No, I'd like to walk.' He turned and looked at her for a time and then said, 'Would you care to go out for a meal one evening?'

Before she answered Sarah took the cups and placed them in the sink. After all, there was no long-term commitment to Patrick Stone 'Yes, I would,' she answered at last. Greaves said, 'I've got out of the habit of speaking to people like this, I hope you'll bear with me.'

Sarah looked down, made suddenly shy by his own difficulty with the request.

'Well, goodbye then,' he said. 'I'll ring you to arrange things.'

His invitation had made things curiously formal. They shook hands at the front door and she wished that she were wearing something other than her old housecoat.

It was early when Sarah got to the office. She rang Claire at home for the code to the Greaves file and was about to enter it on her terminal when it occurred to her that another of the reporters might come into the room. The thought concerned her. There was so little space it would be easy for anyone to read her screen without much effort. Remembering that the editorial floor would still be deserted she made her way downstairs and found George Conway already at the news desk.

He looked awful. She could tell he had not been home all night; the crumpled shirt was the same one he had worn the previous day and his eyes were raw at the rims. He had shaved but the blade had nicked his chin and he was attempting to staunch the flow of blood with a piece of newsprint torn from one of the morning papers. But he seemed cheerful enough.

'You sound better than you look,' she said when he called her over.

'That's because of clean living,' he answered with a smile. 'I am the bird that has caught the early worm.'

'Is that supposed to be me?' she asked.

George shook his head. 'You are the stitch in time that saves nine.'

Sarah sighed, 'I'm sorry, it's too early to play word games.'

He handed her a sheet of copy paper which was spotted with his blood. There was an address scrawled on it.

'A mother of one of the victims wants to speak to us. She just rang.'

'Why did she call?'

George rubbed his eyes with the back of his hand. 'Because of my extraordinary charm, of course,' he said. He looked up. 'I wrote to them all. This one liked my letter.'

Sarah looked down at the sheet of paper. 'Shall I ring to confirm the appointment?'

'No, it would give her an opportunity to change her mind. Take Harry Porter with you, he's in the canteen,' he said with another smile.

'What else is making you so cheerful?' Sarah asked.

102

George slapped the desk with one of his slabby hands. 'My first wife is going to South Africa with a man she met at a divorced and separated dance. I don't have to pay her maintenance any more.'

'Is that what you were celebrating last night?'

'No. I was drowning my sorrows last night, I didn't get the news until this morning. Tonight I celebrate.'

'What will you do?'

He thought for a moment. 'I might give my second wife a ring.'

Sarah turned away shaking her head, and George watched her as she walked through the newsroom.

She found Harry Porter sitting at a window seat in the canteen eating a dainty little bacon sandwich.

'Look at this bloody thing,' he complained by way of greeting, and he waved half of it in the direction of the white-coated woman who had prepared the offending article. 'They call this a sandwich!' he said with disgust. 'Who the hell do they think they're cooking for, Princess Di?' Harry looked out at the grimy buildings opposite. 'In the old days you could get a bacon sandwich in here and you wouldn't want to eat again for a week.'

Sarah smiled. 'That's because you had to go to Bart's Hospital afterwards and get your stomach pumped out. The food used to be disgusting, Harry, and you got printer's ink all over your clothes whenever you sat down.'

'That's another thing,' he said, undaunted by her challenge. 'I miss the comps, and the warehouse boys. All you've got now are office staff. If I swear in here, all I see is swivelling heads looking at me as if I'd farted in the bath . . . sod 'em!' he said in louder voice and the white-coated woman looked up from behind the counter in disapproval. This clearly caused him some pleasure. 'What job are we doing?' he went on more cheerfully.

'We're going back to the last house you photographed yesterday,' Sarah answered. 'The mother of the girl wants to talk to us.'

Harry pushed aside the remains of his food. 'Oh, Christ,' he said in a much softer voice, 'I'm getting too old for this sort of story.'

His grip had tightened around the mug before him and Sarah noticed that his hands were like her father's: long, slim and very clean, as if they had been bleached by frequent washing.

'Did I ever tell you about the job I did with Dixie Walker?' he asked after a time. Sarah shook her head.

Harry looked up at her. 'Of course not. It must have been before you were even born. This bastard had been killing little boys and hiding their bodies under coke dumps. They found one of the kids

in Willesden and Dixie got the family's address from a local copper.'
He paused and drank some more tea. 'We went around to the flats
where the parents lived. The mother let us in, she thought we were
from the Council. We didn't know the police hadn't been yet. It
was Dixie who told her the boy was dead.' Harry shook his head.
'I can still remember her face . . . Jesus, I thought she was going to
die of grief.'

Sarah reached out and touched one of his hands. 'Would you
prefer it if somebody else did the job?' she asked softly.

Harry searched his pockets for a cigar. 'No,' he said flatly. 'I'll
do the work, as always.' But she saw that he had left the rest of his
food untouched.

Helen Craig looked vaguely familiar to Sarah, when the Spanish au
pair showed them into the living room of the Hampstead house.
The surroundings were very bright, despite the sadness that seemed
to enfold her.

Everything in the room was pale: carpets, upholstery, walls. The
furniture was white, and a crystal chandelier reflected darts of light
about them. There was a full-length portrait of Helen Craig above
the pink and white marble fireplace. When Sarah studied the painting, she realised that the woman who sat stiffly before them on
the delicate sofa had been famous many years before. From her
appearance in a series of advertisements for washing powder, Helen
Craig had for a brief time been as recognisable to the public as a
member of the Royal Family.

When she stood up to shake hands Sarah said, 'Wasn't your
maiden name Gaynor?'

The woman smiled, but the sadness did not leave her. 'You have
a good memory, Mrs Keane.'

As he sat down again Sarah noticed that she maintained the careful posture taught to her in her youth; only her hands, restlessly
intertwining, showed the tension in her still body.

'Do you really think this interview will do any good?' she asked
in a voice that was suddenly unsure. 'In his letter Mr Conway said
it might help some other parent.'

Sarah glanced at Harry but he had his eyes down, making adjust-
ments to his camera. She looked about the pale room that was
flooded with light from the tall french windows and the words
seemed to linger between them, like cold breath on a winter's day.

'It might,' Sarah said eventually. 'Perhaps some parent who believes such a thing couldn't happen will be more careful.' Her eyes went to the photographs arranged on the piano. She could see the murdered child's pictures quite clearly. The unexceptional and beloved daughter of a beautiful mother. She turned to Helen Craig again. 'Maybe somebody saw something and forgot – the article may jog a memory.'

She looked away and saw that Harry now had his camera ready.

'Will it bother you if Mr Porter takes photographs while we talk?' she asked.

Helen Craig shook her head, 'I was used to it once, I don't mind.'

The interview began, and after a time the woman began to tell the whole terrible story of how the death of her child had affected her life. While their voices murmured softly in the light-filled room, Harry Porter worked to catch the gestures and expressions that came as she spoke of her daughter.

It wasn't until the end of the interview that she began to falter. For most of the time her voice had been firm and controlled, even when she told of the discovery of the body. The breakdown came when she said what it was like to stand in a bedroom filled with toys and memories of her daughter's childhood, knowing it would now remain empty for ever. Then Helen Craig's shoulders bowed and, covering her face with her hands, she began to rock backwards and forwards. Sarah moved from the chair opposite and sat beside her on the sofa. She reached out and Helen Craig leaned into her arms, her body contracting with helpless sobs.

Harry Porter put his camera aside. This scene, he decided, would remain private. Silently he got up and left the room, while Sarah administered what comfort she could. Slowly, she began to tell of the pain in her own life, and how time had numbed the grief. She told Helen Craig how her mother had died when she was a girl, and the long, lonely days that followed. Then she began to talk about Jack.

Gradually the sound of Sarah's voice seemed to comfort the woman and she recovered some of her composure. Sarah judged she could be left alone once again.

Harry had smoked a cigar in the garden by the time she joined him. They drove back to the office in silence, still carrying the atmosphere of the house with them.

Sarah stopped at the news desk to tell George that she would file the story in good time for the first edition.

'Make it your best,' he replied. 'I got a roasting at morning conference for sending you on the job.'

'Why?'

He smiled sourly. 'The assistant editor in charge of features demanded to know why we hadn't assigned his star writer to the task. He said there was no one to touch Fanny Hunter when it came to hearts and flowers.'

'It wasn't hearts and flowers, George, believe me; you can judge for yourself when you read the copy.' He nodded to the reporters' desks, where Sarah saw Pauline Kaznovitch taking things from her drawers and placing them in a cardboard box. 'She's got the hump with you as well,' he said in a low voice.

'Why?' Sarah asked again.

George looked up to the ceiling. 'Because she thinks you got in early and pinched the job she would have done. God protect me from women!'

Sarah walked over to Pauline and said, 'I didn't ask for the assignment.'

The girl continued to pack her belongings and answered without looking up, 'It doesn't matter, I'm taking up an offer from Fanny Hunter to work in her department. I suppose I just don't have what men want on this paper.'

Sarah watched her for a moment and then said, 'If I were you I'd stay with George.' But Pauline ignored her. Sarah shrugged and made her way to her own office.

The piece took longer than expected; she made several starts, but each time the words she wrote seemed cheap and loaded with false sentiment. Finally, almost in desperation, she stopped trying so hard and just wrote plainly, and as swiftly as she could.

George rang as she typed the last sentence. 'How you doing?' he asked, 'Harry's pictures are excellent.'

'Coming now, sorry it's been so long,' she replied, glancing at her watch. 'I'm just putting it over to you.'

She made the various command instructions to the computer and electronic transference to the news desk took place.

Now the job was done she felt drained. The little room was still claustrophobic, even though the other reporters were out of the office. Her notebook was open on her desk and she noticed the code she had jotted down earlier. Deciding to risk someone coming into the room, she sat for a while, reading about Colin Greaves until her phone rang again. It was Claire. 'Hi,' she said crisply, 'do you need any babysitting tonight?'

Sarah could feel the knot of muscle in her neck caused by the tension of typing her copy. It was an irritating pain.

'Yes,' she replied. 'I'll tell you why later.'

'Have you read the stuff on Colin Greaves yet?'

'I've just finished it.'

Claire paused. 'Divorced – I guess you can understand why he looks so sad now.'

'Yes,' Sarah replied. It was a day for sadness. Suddenly she looked forward to the meal with Patrick, something that would take her away from her melancholy mood.

'Well, I'm off,' Claire said. 'See you later.'

Sarah sat for a little time longer and then realised that she was hungry. She rang the news desk and got one of the assistants. 'I'm just going to the canteen if there are any questions on my copy,' she explained.

'OK,' the voice replied without any interest.

She found Harry in the same seat he had occupied earlier in the day. 'Is that the same bacon sandwich?' she asked when she sat down with him again.

'Tastes like it,' he replied.

She ate some of her salad before she spoke again. 'George says your pictures are very good.'

Harry nodded. 'I could tell that when I was taking them.'

'I found the piece hard to write.'

'I can imagine.'

Sarah had almost finished when a call came through from the young news-desk assistant she had spoken to earlier.

'Features are handling your stuff. Edward Carter says will you both go to his office when you've finished.'

Sarah told Harry and, pushing their plates aside, they both made for the exit.

The secretary in the outer room told them to go ahead and they entered the office of Edward Carter the assistant editor in charge of features.

George Conway was there with Carter, a tense, energetic young man to whom Sarah had never spoken before now. He smiled when he looked up from behind the desk, where he had been studying a layout of page one. 'Come and look at this,' he said, and they stood beside him.

The layout was carefully drawn. They could see quite clearly that a large picture and a quote from Sarah's copy ran on the front page with a reference to the main story inside.

'The editor just wanted the pair of you to know that you've cost the *Gazette* £18,000,' Carter said. 'That's the amount of revenue we would have earned from the two advertisements we've taken out of the paper to accommodate your pictures and copy.' He sat back in his chair and swivelled round to face them more squarely. 'Well done, both of you. It really is remarkable stuff, I'm proud to put it in the paper.'

They muttered their thanks in an embarrassed fashion and George Conway ushered them from the office. 'Come on, I'll buy you both a drink,' he said gleefully. 'Carter even admitted that Fanny couldn't have done better.'

Sarah looked at her watch and thought it was way past closing time, but remembered that pubs now stayed open in the afternoons. Conway took them across Gray's Inn Road and into the Red Lion. There was a scattering of people in the bar, mostly of the sort Sarah would have expected to find drinking their way through the afternoon. One or two furtive faces glanced towards them over lonely glasses, but the main group, which dominated the far end of the bar, consisted of a noisy, red-faced collection of men who seemed to be laughing in a desperate manner, as if to convince themselves they were having a good time. Sarah asked for a glass of wine that she really didn't want, but it would have seemed ungenerous to refuse George, who was clearly pleased to be vindicated in his decision to use her on the story.

Her own mood was mixed: the memory of Helen Craig's grief was still fresh in her mind and it was difficult to celebrate something that was the result of so much anguish, but at the same time she was pleased that her work had earned so much praise. Harry guessed at her feelings. 'Cheer up,' he said gruffly. 'You're not responsible for the state of that poor bloody woman.'

Sarah wondered if he were right. Had she actually done any good, or had she merely rekindled Helen Craig's pain for the sake of a good story? She raised her glass with the others, but did not enjoy the taste of the wine.

She bought the next round, then made her excuses. 'Do you mind if I go early, George? I'm going out this evening.'

He shook his head. Sarah dutifully drank up and said goodbye. As she crossed the road to collect her car, she suddenly wished that Jack could have read the piece. He would have known if her misgivings were well founded.

CHAPTER
ELEVEN

C HECKING the time, she made a diversion in her route and, as expected, found Emily and the boys walking home from school. Usually they went their separate ways, but in the last few weeks she had insisted that they make the journey together.

'What's all this?' Martin said as they got into the car. 'Have you got the sack?'

'On the contrary,' Sarah replied. 'My work was so excellent I was given the rest of the day off.'

When they reached home she made a pot of tea and sat down in the living room. She noticed how frowsy the house was beginning to look. 'Come on,' she said, putting aside her weariness, 'let's get this place habitable again.'

Despite their protests, the boys helped and after an hour or so the rooms were restored to some kind of reasonable order.

Sarah left it for some time until she told them about her dinner engagement. Although she tried to be nonchalant about the whole business she actually felt quite nervous when pressed for details by the children. They followed her about and crowded in the doorway while she ran her bath.

'He's an old friend of the family,' she reassured Emily, who seemed more concerned than the boys. 'He and his ex-wife used to come here for dinner often when you were small.'

'Where's his wife now, mum?' Martin asked, grinning. 'Did he give her the elbow for you?'

'Certainly not – they separated a long time ago.'

'Did he fancy you in the old days?' Paul said, nudging his brother.

'Look,' Sarah said in a lecturing voice. 'This is not a romance, I'm merely having dinner with an old friend.'

'How old is he?' Emily asked.

Sarah paused with a bottle of bath salts in her hand.

'About forty-five I suppose, I really don't know.'

The doorbell rang and she ushered them from the bathroom. 'That will be Claire. Go and keep her company.'

Even though she deliberately chose a sedate dress, the boys wolf-whistled when she came downstairs at 8.30. Emily had taken to her bedroom from where the sound of Bach emanated in gloomy grandeur. The boys stayed in the kitchen while Sarah and Claire watched television.

The clock hand crept towards nine o'clock, but there was no sign of Patrick Stone. By 9.30 Sarah was rather on edge, her feelings mixed between concern that something unpleasant might have happened to him and annoyance if his behaviour turned out to be simply bad manners.

Then there was a long ring on the doorbell and he entered, full of apologies and carrying a bottle of champagne.

'Work,' he said with a shrug. 'Bloody producers – they only feel necessary when they're making life totally impossible for us mortals.' Patrick shook hands with Claire. 'Shall we have some of this?' he said, holding up the bottle.

'Do we have time?' Sarah asked.

'Oh yes,' he replied easily. He looked towards the door where Emily and the twins now stood, gazing at him as if he were an interesting species of pond life.

'You remember the children,' Sarah said quickly and as she spoke she wished Patrick had worn one of his old tweed jackets rather than the silk she'd last seen at Fanny's party.

'Hi,' he said with less assurance. 'Do you want some champagne too?' The boys pressed forward, but Sarah held up a hand. 'You can have a little with orange juice,' she said. 'Go and get the glasses.'

It was well after ten when Patrick led her out to his little Japanese sports car.

'Will the table be all right?' Sarah asked.

'Oh, sure,' he replied and gunned the engine before driving off with tyres squealing.

The restaurant turned out to be a club near Seven Dials, where the waitresses wore fixed smiles and very few clothes. Deafening rock music thundered from the disco area and coloured lights slashed through the gloom.

Sarah felt depressed the moment she entered. After a few minutes seated at a table they were shown to, a squat man with a ravaged face and spiky dyed blonde hair came to shake Patrick's hand.

'This is Dave, the owner,' Patrick shouted above the music.

Sarah shook hands and a waitress handed her a massive padded menu. The only choice seemed to be varieties of junk food. She ordered a hamburger and sat watching Patrick and the owner holding a conversation that they could only manage by speaking directly into each other's ears, as one would to the profoundly deaf. Eventually Dave departed and Sarah ate her hamburger, which was rather good. Occasionally Patrick would point into the room, which was gradually becoming more crowded, and name some individual, usually a football star.

Midnight finally came with the steady pace of a glacier and Sarah said it was time to go home.

Patrick looked surprised. 'Don't you want to have a bop?' he shouted, nodding towards the packed little dance floor.

Sarah smiled and shook her head.

'I'll just be a few minutes,' he said and wormed his way into the writhing mob.

The music changed to a quieter selection and Sarah felt as if a band of pressure had been released from her forehead. She looked up and saw Karen, the girl Patrick had escorted to Fanny's party, standing before her.

'Do you mind if I sit down?' she asked.

'Please do.'

Karen chose the chair next to her and said, 'I'm glad Patrick's back with you. He needs someone his own age.'

'Back with me?' Sarah repeated. 'I don't understand.'

'Aren't you an old girlfriend of his?'

Sarah shook her head. 'We know each other – that's all.'

Karen sighed. 'Jesus, he told me you were an old flame. I suppose it's another one of his bloody fantasies.'

111

Sarah folded her hands together. 'He told me he'd been living with you for the past eight months.'

The young girl laughed. 'No way – he's been pestering me for a year. It's getting embarrassing. Everyone calls him the last swinger.'

'Thank you for telling me,' Sarah said in a firm voice. 'I think I'll leave now.' She collected her handbag and was almost at the door when Patrick caught her up.

'I'm sorry,' Sarah said, 'I must get home.'

They walked to the car in silence and then he began a monologue about how he had been constantly pursued by young women since his wife had left him. Sarah listened quietly, just wanting to get home now.

It wasn't until he had stopped his car outside her house that Patrick ceased talking about himself. She was trying to think of an excuse not to invite him in, when he solved the problem by making a sudden lunge for her.

'Patrick, please –' she protested, feeling slightly ridiculous as his hand fumbled for her breast.

'Don't pretend to be shy, baby,' he grunted. 'Fanny told me how things were for you, just relax.'

Evading his grasping hands she wriggled from the car. He got out and followed her to the gate, which she shut firmly behind her. 'Go away!' she hissed.

'OK, just cool it,' he answered as she hurried along the pathway, and then he called out as he was getting back into his car, 'I don't need this, you know, I was only doing a favour for an old friend.'

The children were asleep but Claire was still up, watching a late-night film.

'So – how was it?' she asked

Sarah beckoned her into the kitchen and threw up her hands. 'Complete disaster,' she said. Halfway through relating the events of the evening, Claire began to laugh, and Sarah joined in.

Two days passed and Sarah was deeply bored with the ritual of her routine in the operations room, when Colin Greaves rang 'I thought you might feel like that meal we talked about. This evening?' he said.

'If you'd rather not . . .' he added when she did not reply at once, and she could hear the sudden reservation in his voice.

'No,' she said, 'I mean yes, I was going to eat at home tonight. Why don't you come?'

This time he paused. 'What are you having?'

'Just a Chinese takeaway from the local restaurant.'

'I'll come if you let me order it,' he said finally.

Sarah laughed. 'How do you know what we like?'

'Trust me,' he replied. 'I'll be there at eight.'

'Another boyfriend,' Paul said when she told them of the dinner guest.

'He's not a boyfriend,' Sarah said firmly. 'Just someone I know through work.'

'Is he like that Stone man?' Emily asked. She was standing on the coffee table, examining herself from different angles in the large mirror over the fireplace.

'Nothing like Patrick Stone,' Sarah replied emphatically and they noted the tone.

Emily was now thrusting her chest out, so that her breasts were taut against the blouse of her school uniform. 'Do you think I'll get any bigger?' she asked.

'Why do you want to be bigger?' Sarah asked. 'Models have to starve themselves to have your figure.'

'What shape do you want to be?' Martin asked.

'Cello shaped,' Paul said quickly. 'So Ric Daggert will love her all the more.'

'Shut up, you,' Emily answered. 'If you ever get a girlfriend she'll have to be like a rugby ball. It's the only thing you know how to hold.'

'Patrick Stone has a head like a rugby ball,' Martin said. 'What's this new man like?'

'Very nice,' Sarah answered. 'Actually, he's a policeman.'

'I didn't think you knew any policemen,' Paul said.

'Look on me as a mystery woman,' she replied. 'Someone with an interesting past.'

'You don't really have a past,' Martin said. 'You went to school, got a job on the *Gazette*, married dad and lived here for the rest of your life.'

I suppose I did, Sarah thought. Thirty-eight years, told in a single sentence. Not a story to hold the attention for long. She went into the breakfast room. While she set the table with the bowls and chopsticks that Jack had brought back from one of his trips to Hong Kong, she continued to think about Martin's remark. He hadn't intended it to be hurtful, but the truth of it rankled. The boys, sensing her change of mood, had followed her.

'Candles!' Paul said when she took down the holders from the dresser. 'Is this going to be a posh meal?'

'As posh as a takeaway can be,' Sarah said, recovering her humour. 'That means you've got to wash and look presentable.'

By the time she got into the bathroom herself it was 7.30. She was still wearing her dressing gown when the doorbell rang.

'You get it, Emily,' she called. 'I won't be long.'

When she stood before her wardrobe, trying to find something to wear, a sudden thought came to her: I'm dressing for a man again. It was a curious feeling and it affected her choice: a blue dress Emily had said would be suitable for Speech Day when she'd first bought it.

The boys and Emily were sitting on the edge of the sofa listening to Colin Greaves when she came down. She could hear through the open door that he was telling them about Hong Kong.

'Mr Greaves can speak Chinese,' Martin said as Greaves stood up.

'I know,' Sarah replied and she accepted the bunch of flowers he had brought with him. They were all white: carnations, Michaelmas daisies and roses. A memory stirred and she remembered that white was the Chinese colour for death.

'A bit anaemic, I'm afraid, but they were all that was left on the flower stall,' he said quickly.

'They're lovely,' she replied. 'I'll put them in water.' She looked around. 'Is the food already in the kitchen?'

'It's being delivered,' Greaves said, glancing at his watch. 'It should be here in a few minutes or so.'

'Would you like a drink?'

He nodded. 'There's some Chinese beer in the fridge, I brought it with me.'

'Chinese beer? I thought they only drank that dreadful stuff that comes in little pottery bottles?'

'Mao Tai,' he said. 'They do, but they also brew good beer.'

'In that case I shall have one,' Sarah answered and she turned to Martin. 'Be a dear and bring us two beers, darling. Use the glasses that are on the top shelf of the first cupboard.'

'Do they really use hatchets?' Paul said, trying to bring the conversation back to the gang wars of Hong Kong.

114

'Oh yes,' Greaves replied and was about to elaborate when the doorbell rang.

Sarah answered it and was confronted by a scowling Chinese gentleman; he was carrying a large wickerwork basket, and spoke to her in his own language. She could not understand a word but the tone sounded faintly hostile. Feeling slightly helpless, she was joined by Greaves, who addressed the man in the same rapid tones. He now smiled, and his features were transformed. Pushing Sarah aside, he followed Greaves through the hallway and placed his load on the dresser beside the table in the breakfast room. There was another incomprehensible conversation in the hallway and then the man departed.

There were no cardboard and tinfoil boxes inside the hamper. Instead it contained sealed crockery pots, vacuum flasks and a nest of round wooden baskets.

'Some of this should be eaten very hot,' Greaves explained. 'Do you have a microwave?'

Sarah showed him where and he directed how the meal should be served. The boys were dubious at first.

'This looks like spaghetti,' Paul said as he lifted a few strands of noodles from his plate.

'That's right,' Greaves replied. 'The Chinese invented spaghetti.'

'Did they?' Martin said and he nudged Paul. 'He thought it was Heinz.'

'Marco Polo bought it back from his journey in Cathay,' Emily said.

'How do you know that?' the boys asked together.

'Trivial Pursuit,' she answered. 'It was one of the questions when Claire and I were playing the other night.'

'Who's Claire?' Greaves asked.

'She babysits for us when mum goes out on dates,' Martin said innocently and earned a killing glance from Sarah.

'This beer is good,' she said, changing the subject. 'It's sweeter than lager.'

Greaves produced a final dish. 'I like this,' he said. 'But it's only for the brave.'

'What is it?' Emily asked.

'Sea slugs.'

The boys could not resist the challenge, but Sarah and Emily declined.

'How are they?' Sarah asked as the boys chewed thoughtfully.

'No worse than escargot,' Paul replied.

'What language were you speaking with the man who delivered the meal?' Emily asked.

'Chinese, of course,' Martin interjected.

Greaves shook his head. 'Cantonese.'

'How many other languages do you speak?' Emily asked.

'Three,' he answered, 'Mandarin, Portuguese and French.'

Sarah noted that he had not included English. There was no hint of a boast in his voice. It was as though he were presenting evidence.

'How did you come to learn Portuguese?' Paul asked. Greaves drank some more of his beer before he answered. Although he had loosened his tie, he still wore his jacket and Sarah realised that the evening had become quite warm. He smiled suddenly and two lines deepened at each side of his mouth.

'I spent part of my childhood in Hong Kong; my father was a civil servant there. Macao is not far away and they speak Portuguese there. After university I joined the police. They sent me back to Hong Kong on secondment. I was taught French at boarding school in England, that's why it isn't so good as my other languages.'

The bell rang again and Emily said it would be Ric. She thanked Greaves for the meal, made her excuses and disappeared upstairs with Ric. The boys remembered a television programme they wanted to watch and left Sarah and Greaves at the table. He poured some more beer. After a time, Sarah loaded the dishwasher with all the used crockery from the hamper, then turned to Greaves, 'Shall we go outside?' she suggested. 'There's seats in the garden and it may be cooler.'

He followed her through the darkened living room, past the boys who were illuminated by the soft glow of the television screen, and into the garden. Sarah paused by the french windows to turn on a lamp that hung over a wooden bench from one of the apple trees. She brought cushions from the conservatory, and when they were seated Greaves lit a cigarette. The tobacco smelt delicious to Sarah. It was quite dark now, except for the pool of light from the lamp, and all of the surrounding gardens were silent. Greaves leaned forward and rested his forearms on his knees. He looked up at the house. The sound of Mozart came from Emily's lighted window.

'Why do you live in that house on your own?' Sarah asked eventually. He did not answer immediately, watching a fluttering moth that had been drawn by the brightness of the lamp. 'An aunt left it to me,' he said. 'I used to stay there in the school holidays; I suppose it's the place I think of as home.' He was silent for a time and then he said, 'We may have found the blue van.'

116

'When will you know?'

Greaves waved smoke away from his face before he answered. 'Tomorrow morning for sure. Maybe tonight.' Then he turned to look at her. 'How did you know I spoke Cantonese?' he asked.

Sarah looked into his eyes to try and read his mood, but his expression told her nothing.

'I saw a file on you today,' she answered.

'What did it tell you?'

'Not much. Your education, the stuff you told the boys. It said you transferred from the Hong Kong police and that you were a high-flyer.' She paused. 'It also said you were divorced.'

'Did it tell you why?'

Sarah shook her head. He was about to speak again when the french windows opened and Emily called out, 'Mr Greaves, there's a telephone call for you.'

He followed her into the house, and after a short time returned to Sarah. 'Work,' he said with a shrug.

'Must you go?'

'Yes, they've sent a car for me.' He paused. 'They've picked up the van driver. Do you want to do the story?'

Sarah thought for a moment, then shook her head. 'Give it to Peter Kerr, he's the chief crime reporter.'

Greaves nodded. They stood in the hall to say goodbye.

'Thank you. It was good to be with a family.'

'Come again. Next time I'll cook.'

'Are you a good cook?' he asked, without smiling.

'Exceptional!' she replied, and she didn't smile either.

'Then I'll come.' He walked away, holding his hand up as a salute of farewell, but he didn't look round.

After she had heard the car drive away she went to the kitchen and began to wash the delicate Chinese bowls by hand. There was still one of the beers left in the refrigerator. She poured it into a clean glass and was about to drink it when the doorbell rang. It was the Chinese man who had delivered the food. He followed her into the kitchen and saw the beer standing next to the packed hamper.

'Chinese beer?' he asked.

'Yes,' Sarah replied, 'would you like it?'

The man picked up the glass and drank the contents very quickly. He lifted the hamper from the table. 'Are you a friend of Colin's?' he asked, and there was no trace of an accent in his voice.

'Yes,' she answered, 'I suppose I am.'

'He's a very good man,' he said, and then he left the house.

CHAPTER
TWELVE

THE following morning Martin woke Sarah with a cup of coffee. 'The police have arrested someone for the murders,' he said. Sarah glanced at the alarm clock. It was almost 7.30. 'It's on the television news and the front page of the *Gazette*,' he added, passing the papers to her.

The quotation from her interview with Helen Craig and Harry's picture were still there on the front page, but above them, separated by a thick rule, was a bold headline that read:

MURDER HUNT – 2 a.m. MAN HELD BY POLICE

Martin looked over Sarah's shoulder: 'Why don't they say who he is?' he asked.

'It's not allowed,' she answered, not looking up from the paper. 'It's against the law.'

'Why?'

'It could prejudice a fair trial.'

'Why do they have to make it fair for a murderer?'

Sarah put the newspaper aside and drank some of her coffee. It

119

tasted awful and she remembered for a moment Colin Greaves's skills.

'It's not to make it fair for murderers, it's to make it fair for the rest of us,' she answered eventually. 'There are laws for everyone, even the police.'

Emily entered the room as she spoke and went to the window to look into the quiet street. 'Ric says the police are as bad as criminals anyway,' she said.

Sarah decided it was too early for that kind of debate. 'Some are, some aren't,' she said briskly. 'Nothing is all black and white. There's good and bad everything: doctors, journalists, policemen. Even cellists.'

Emily turned and smiled. 'He's not a cellist yet.'

'Well, let's hope he's a good one when he is,' Sarah said as she made for the bathroom.

She got to the office early but George Conway and Stiles were already on the desk.

'Peter Kerr is upstairs,' George said, 'he stayed here last night. Let's go up and see him.'

The little room felt as if it had been well used. Stale tobacco smoke still lingered in the metallic, air-conditioned atmosphere and there were plates holding the crusted remains of sandwiches next to an empty whisky bottle. Plastic cups littered Sarah's desk. One of them was half filled with tea with the remains of cigarettes floating like bloated brown maggots. Peter Kerr looked up when they entered. He was blowing into an electric shaver he had just used.

'It looks as if it was a good party,' George said drily. 'I wish somebody had invited me.'

Stiles heard the inflection in his voice.

'I'm sorry, George,' he said quickly, 'but it was all moving so fast we just got on with it. I said to Brian Meadows you would be sorry you missed it.'

'The editor was here, was he?' George asked mildly.

'Oh yes, he gave us a drink at the end of the night. He was very happy.'

'Well, he's not so happy now,' Peter Kerr said. 'He's just been on to me. Colin Greaves rang him.'

'Why?' Stiles asked warily.

George and Kerr exchanged knowing glances. 'I told you before I filed the story that Greaves had reservations,' Peter Kerr said.

Stiles folded his arms defensively. 'But my contact was sure they'd got the right man.'

Kerr nodded. 'The other blokes on the case thought they had him, but I kept telling you Greaves had doubts all along.'

Conway sat down. 'Tell me what you know: everything.'

Kerr lit a cigarette. 'I got a call from Colin Greaves at midnight. They brought the man in at one o'clock but they hadn't charged him; by that time we'd gone to press with the last edition.'

'But my copper was sure,' Stiles said plaintively. 'The man is an out of work actor called Edward Marshall. He did a bit of carpentry on the side. He's even interested in astrology, and his birth sign is Gemini. The heavenly twins, Castor and Pollux. It all fits.'

George turned to Peter Kerr. 'Any previous form?'

Kerr shook his head. 'Nothing. He lived with a girlfriend until recently, then he went home to his parents' house in Camden Town. His old man was a carpenter until he retired, he had a bloody great shed in the back garden, full of tools. Forensic even checked some of them.'

Stiles was looking at the ceiling as if seeking inspiration. 'He was definitely seen in two of the areas.'

Kerr stubbed out the cigarette. 'That checks, he owned up to working on jobs nearby.'

'There!' Stiles said. 'It can't just be a coincidence.' But the others ignored him.

'That's all?' George asked.

'That's all.'

Conway drummed his fingers on the edge of the littered table. 'No wonder Greaves is dubious,' he said finally, 'it's all pretty thin.'

'We didn't say he was the actual one,' Stiles said, 'just that they were holding someone. We didn't even name him.'

Peter Kerr looked at him scornfully. 'You were the one who wanted to say he was charged.'

The telephone rang and Conway answered it. All he said after listening for a few moments was, 'OK', then he hung up.

'That was Sinclair,' he said to the room. 'Edward Marshall has just been released from police custody. They're perfectly satisfied with his alibi.'

There was a silence and then Sarah said, 'Oh, God,' very softly.

'What's the matter?' Stiles asked. 'They can't blame us for anything.'

'People will read our story and think that he's been caught,' George said wearily. 'They might start relaxing again.'

'Nonsense!' Stiles blustered, 'the radio and TV will say that he's not the one.' He got up. 'I think I'll give Reg Stenton a ring. He was the night editor. It was his decision to go with the story. I'd better warn him that the old man is angry.'

Conway looked at Peter Kerr when Stiles had left the room. Kerr held up his hands. 'Stiles urged Stenton to run the piece, he even wanted to name Marshall. They were arguing with the night lawyer for a long time, then the editor came back to the office. He'd been to some advertising piss-up. He sided with the lawyer.'

George nodded. 'It still makes the paper look lousy,' he said. 'I'd better get back to the desk. We'll be taking calls from readers all day on this one.'

Sarah did not enjoy the rest of the morning, although several people called with congratulations about her interview. Eventually she met Claire in the corridor.

'Was it a good dinner with Superintendent Greaves last night?' she asked and Sarah thought she could detect a note of disapproval in her voice.

'How did you know?' Sarah asked.

'Martin rang me about the softball match,' she said.

'I'm sorry,' Sarah replied, 'it was just a spur of the moment thing, I wish you could have been there.'

Claire laughed at Sarah's evident discomfort. 'It's all right,' she said, 'I'm just an old spinster, jealous of my friends.'

Sarah reached out and took her arm. 'You know how much you mean to us now,' she said. 'The children love you.'

Claire put her own hand on Sarah's. 'I'm glad,' she said. 'They're great kids.'

'Are you doing anything lunchtime?' Sarah asked.

Claire held out a plastic laminated card. 'The world of computers calls. I'm off to a two-day exhibition at Olympia.'

'Why don't you come over later?' Sarah asked, 'we can have a natter – two old spinsters together.'

Claire thought. 'I'll do my best. There's film shows until eight, but I'll try and sneak off.'

Sarah did not feel like eating lunch, but she wanted to escape from the office for a time. She walked as far as St Paul's Cathedral, enjoying the warm day, despite the heavy roar of traffic about her.

When she returned she could hear the telephone ringing as she walked towards the little office. The monotonous sound continued while she tapped in the code to open the door. When she lifted the receiver the tape recorder clicked on automatically.

The voice was unmistakable; high-pitched, cultivated, feminine almost. It was Castor.

'Tell Superintendent Greaves that another girl will die tonight,' he said. There was no emotion in the sentence, he could have been reading the weather report.

'Why are you doing this?' Sarah asked. She tried to remain calm but there was anger in her voice.

There was a pause. 'I presume you are Sarah Keane? I read your article this morning. A little mawkish for my taste, but admirably suited for the great family of *Gazette* readers.'

'Why are you killing these children?' Sarah insisted.

'I told you. Revenge.' His tone was normal; he could have been talking about the weather.

'But these girls have done nothing – how can they have harmed you?'

'I keep telling you,' he said in a chiding voice, 'I'm looking for revenge, not retribution.' Then the line went dead.

Sarah replaced the receiver and began to tremble uncontrollably. She felt as though she had been actually touched by the voice, and her body taken with a sudden fever. It took a great effort to make the necessary calls.

Less than an hour later, Conway, Kerr and Stiles waited with her when Colin Greaves entered the little office. He was accompanied by a detective-sergeant he introduced as Nicholas Holland, and a small, thick set man whose dark eyebrows met above the bridge of his fleshy nose. The man's head was so large it did not seem to be in proportion with the rest of his body.

'This is Doctor Carlyle,' Greaves said, 'a psychiatrist who has been assigned to the case.' He nodded to Conway, who held his hand above the switch on the tape recorder. They listened three times to the brief exchange of sentences.

'What the hell does he mean?' Conway said eventually.

'Do you have the complete *Oxford English Dictionary*?' Doctor Carlyle asked. His voice was deep and soothing.

Conway called the library and spoke to one of the assistants.

'There's about four feet of it,' he said.

'Ask for the volume containing R,' Carlyle said. Conway made the request and replaced the receiver. 'It's on its way.'

While they waited, they played the tape again and again until the news-desk secretary arrived with the book.

Carlyle studied it for a few minutes and then shrugged. 'I cannot be sure what he means,' he said petulantly.

'Make a guess,' Greaves said in a hard voice.

Doctor Carlyle shrugged his tweed-clad shoulders again.

'Retribution means recompense for evil. One definition of revenge is to satisfy oneself.'

'I don't follow,' Stiles said.

Doctor Carlyle turned to him. 'Perhaps there is nothing personal in the attacks on these girls. Maybe he is doing it to revenge himself on somebody else, or society as a whole.' He leaned against the desk and folded his arms. 'You must realise, his deeper motives come from the labyrinth of his lifetime's experiences. His understanding of the words "revenge" and "retribution" may be subjective, and therefore bear nuances I have no way of interpreting without extensive consultation with him.'

While he spoke, Brian Meadows had entered the room. He shook his head at Carlyle's little speech. 'So what you're saying is you can't be sure what he means, unless you have a long chat with him?'

Carlyle looked momentarily ruffled. 'You could put it that way,' he said stiffly.

Greaves took the detective-sergeant by the arm and said, 'Get on to the radio and television people. Say, Castor has told the police that he will kill another girl tonight.' Brian Meadows looked worried by the instruction. 'Do we really want all the lunatics in Britain to know he's telephoning the *Gazette*? Our switchboard will be jammed with impostors?'

'We won't mention the *Gazette*,' Greaves answered, 'but I want as many people as possible to learn of his intentions. It may save someone.'

'You don't sound very convinced,' Sarah said.

Greaves nodded towards the tape recorder. 'Listen to that again,' he said, 'and then tell me if you've ever heard anyone so confident of anything. There must be 50,000 sixteen-year-old girls in London. That's a lot more than we can look after.'

The rest of the day and the early evening passed slowly. Sarah picked Emily and the boys up from school and at eight o'clock Claire arrived, explaining that she had managed to slip away from the exhibition. Ric called and stayed in another part of the house with Emily, listening to records until it was time for him to leave. After supper, Claire suggested that she teach Sarah and the boys how to play poker. Gradually they became absorbed in the game and no mention of the murders took place until Sarah finally sent the boys upstairs.

'I saw the news on a monitor screen at Olympia. The whole place practically came to a standstill,' Claire said softly, when they had settled down in the living room. The children were out of earshot, but they still discussed the case in quiet tones.

'At least Ric is always around Emily,' Sarah said. 'Any other time and I might have grown weary of his constant presence.'

'Or his voice,' Claire answered. 'I know love makes one blind but I didn't realise it deafened as well!'

'Thank God,' Sarah said. 'I'd be really worried if he sounded as good as he looks.'

Claire got up from the sofa and reached for the empty coffee cups.

'Don't bother,' Sarah said, 'I'll clear up.'

'Aren't you tired?'

Sarah shook her head.

'Would you like me to stay the night?'

'No, you run along. I've got some ironing I want to do.'

'That's a lonely job,' Claire said. 'Oh well, back to Olympia tomorrow.'

Sarah watched her drive away. Everything was quiet now. She sighed when she returned to the living room. The housework she had recently done without thought now seemed an endless and irritating task. There was dust everywhere. She remembered being told that dust was, for the most part, dead skin particles. She wondered if it were true or just one of those pieces of nonsense people repeated without ever checking. She decided to find a few more examples and put the idea forward as a feature for the paper: Myths of our time, she thought, like the idea that sex is more important for men than for women.

Prompted by sudden guilt she decided to clean the living room, concentrating on the mundane work until the room glowed with polish. Then, after loading the washing machine in the kitchen, she ironed for the next few hours.

Although she was now physically tired, her mind was still alert. She ran a bath and lay for a long time in the deep water, looking down at her slim body. When she had dried herself she was more relaxed but still not ready for bed. There was a bottle of brandy in the kitchen cabinet, she remembered. After pouring herself a measure she returned to the living room. Standing in the darkness, the silence seemed absolute. The brandy reminded her of the visit to Colin Greaves's house.

She wanted to go to bed now, but something stopped her – a

125

feeling that the night was not yet over, that there were events yet to come.

She heard a sound; something indefinable that came from the front of the house. She told herself it was a roaming cat or the wind in the trees, but the night was quite still. Then another slight noise came from somewhere in the garden. She trembled as she had done earlier in the day, but now there were children in the house and other, primitive instincts prevailed.

Common sense forgotten, Sarah did not think of the telephone. Instead she reached out in the darkness and took a poker from the fireplace. Holding the heavy iron rod seemed to transform her fear into anger and her body suddenly felt stronger. The noise came again; now she could identify soft footsteps that moved from the windows to the pathway. Adrenalin surged through her and an anger now approaching rage. Sarah moved quickly from the living room and threw open the front door, stepping back to wield the poker with full force in the wide hallway.

Colin Greaves stood beneath the porch light. He held up his arms in surrender and she slowly lowered the poker and stepped aside to let him enter.

'I couldn't sleep,' he said, 'and I wondered how you were.'

She held her fingers to her lips and led him into the living room. Without asking, she brought him a brandy and he stood at the cold fireplace with both hands wrapped around the glass.

'I feel a little foolish now. I hope you forgive me for hanging around.'

Sarah shook her head. 'It's rather flattering. Is there any news?'

He shook his head. 'Nothing.'

Without thinking, both of them put down their glasses and Greaves wound his arms about her. His body felt different to Jack's, slimmer; his embrace was so fierce the breath was squeezed from her body.

Then they heard someone calling from the top of the stairs: 'Is everything all right?' It was Martin, his voice full of sleep. Sarah went to the hallway to answer. 'It's fine, darling, go back to bed.'

When she returned, Greaves had picked up his drink and was sitting in an armchair next to the fireplace. He looked exhausted. The deep upholstery seemed to engulf his slim frame. Sarah sat down in the chair opposite.

'How long have you been divorced?' she asked.

Greaves glanced up and thought for a moment. 'Seven years.'

'Are your children with her?'

When he replied there was no emotion in his voice. 'My children are dead. Didn't the file tell you that?'

Sarah shook her head. 'No, I'm sorry. It only said you had done brilliant work in Hong Kong. The only personal thing mentioned was the fact that you were divorced.'

He looked up again and rested his head against the back of the chair: 'They drowned,' he said softly. 'It was a boating accident. My wife blamed me. I was at work when it happened. She couldn't save them.'

He looked down into the brandy glass. 'Perhaps she was right.'

'Do you miss her very much?'

He held his chin for a moment and then let the hand fall back to rest on the arm of the chair: 'I miss them all – sometimes I dream that we're all together again.'

'I have those dreams,' Sarah said and they were silent for a time.

'I came here hoping to make love to you,' he said eventually.

'I know.'

'Don't you mind? Perhaps you should report me to the police.'

She left her chair and came to kneel before him, holding his hands in her own.

'I was attracted to you from the first moment I saw you,' she said. 'I've felt guilty about it ever since.'

'Because of disloyalty?'

She nodded.

'Yes,' he said, 'I've been the same.' He reached out and held her face with both his hands. The kiss was gentle; she could feel that he needed a shave and he tasted of brandy. She didn't think of anything else.

'Do you want to?' he asked, softly.

Sarah nodded and then looked up at the ceiling.

He followed her gaze. 'A bad time?'

'And place,' she replied.

'If we could find the right time and place?'

'I think I'd like that very much.'

He smiled, and this time it reached his eyes. It's a good face, she told herself, harshly treated by life, but still kind.

'I'd better go before my resolve fades,' he said, and he reached down to help her to her feet. When they stood together their bodies touched again and Sarah almost changed her mind, but the thought of the children above them brought her back once more.

Greaves put his hands in his pockets, as if to keep them from temptation. 'My sister has a cottage near Oxford. Perhaps we could go there for a few days, if you could get away?'

'Yes, I'd like that,' she answered. She heard the sound of a door opening above.

'I'd better go,' he said.

He left as silently as he could and when Sarah reached the top of the stairs she found Emily standing on the landing.

'I couldn't sleep, but I didn't like to come down,' she said.

'Why?' Sarah asked.

'You were with Mr Greaves.'

'We were only talking.'

'Were you? I didn't hear much talk.'

'We spoke softly,' Sarah replied, but Emily had already turned to go into her bedroom. Sarah watched as the door slowly closed.

CHAPTER
THIRTEEN

T HE following afternoon, Sarah sat in the operation room reading agency copy on her terminal. Peter Kerr was humming tunelessly while he browsed through a selection of travel brochures. Kevin Sinclair was murmuring into the telephone at the far end of the room. Kerr's telephone rang and he reached out without taking his eyes from the photographs of sunny beaches.

'Jesus Christ!' he said in a voice that caught the attention of both Sarah and Sinclair, then he glanced towards them and covered the mouthpiece. 'They've found another body – Barnes, this time.'

He listened for a few minutes longer and then replaced the receiver. 'Is it definitely Castor?' Sarah asked.

Kerr nodded. 'Exactly the same ritual, only this time he's killed the parents as well, so he could get to the girl. The police discovered it this morning. There was some cock-up in communications – that's why they haven't told us until now.'

He stood up. 'I'm going down to the news desk. I want both of you on this, so make your arrangements.'

Sarah looked at her watch. Nearly five o'clock; it was going to be a long night. Claire had gone to Olympia for the second day of the seminar; she wondered if she would still be there, but she answered Sarah's call.

'I know,' Claire said, 'you're going to be late. Sure I'll sit with the kids. I've bought a new set of Trivial Pursuit questions; those boys have memorised all the old ones.'

'How did you know what I was going to ask?' Sarah asked.

'I was close to the news desk a few minutes ago.'

'I don't know how late I'm going to be.'

'That's OK. I think I'll cook hamburgers, do you want me to save you one?' Sarah sensed she was being as normal as possible for her sake.

'Thank you,' Sarah said and she hung up. Another girl, Sarah said to herself, and it was Emily's birthday the following week. Her thoughts were interrupted by the return of Peter Kerr.

'Harry Porter is meeting us in the entrance hall,' he said. 'You drive him, Kevin. I'll take Sarah. We may need to split up, so we'll take two cars.'

The cross-town traffic was so heavy that Peter Kerr cursed all the way to Kingsway.

'What's the address?' Sarah asked. He handed her a sheet of paper and she looked it up in a street guide Kerr kept in the glove compartment.

'Let me out here,' she said, when they were close to Holborn underground station. 'I may get there quicker if I go by tube. It's not a long walk from Hammersmith.'

'It's worth a try,' Kerr replied and he pulled to the side of the road.

Sarah had forgotten how crowded the underground was in rush hour. Part of the solid wall of humanity, she stood crushed against blank-faced fellow travellers, until, forty minutes later, she scrambled gratefully from the swaying carriage and tried to hurry from the station. But the crowds that trudged along a network of crowded pedestrian tunnels beneath Hammersmith Broadway frustrated her. Eventually she emerged into a bleak landscape that was divided into odd-shaped sections of municipal grass by roads, heavy with slowly moving traffic. After a few minutes' walk the crowds thinned when she began to cross the wide metal span of Hammersmith suspension bridge. Beneath her, the choppy waters of the Thames sparkled with light from the evening sun. Sarah lengthened her stride, aware that the other people about her were on their way home, while she was about to visit the scene of a murder.

130

All the world seemed peaceful. Castelnau, the road she now hurried along, was lined with quiet houses, each looking safe and secure. Eventually she reached the street Kerr had named, and turning from the major road entered another world. There was the same cluster of police vehicles with their squawking radios and the familiar tapes stretched across the width of the street.

Sarah had been right about the traffic; there was no sign of Kerr or the others. In fact she was the first reporter on the scene. As before, she was stopped at the barrier, but this time she was spotted by Colin Greaves, who was making a telephone call from the front seat of a police car. He waved to the policeman who was barring her entry and beckoned her to sit beside him. They were parked before an imposing, double-fronted house. The rose-pink walls were covered with wistaria and steps led up to a doorway flanked with pillars. The door was open. At any other time the elegant house would have looked inviting, but now there was an ominous feeling to the brightly painted hallway that was half revealed.

'Are they still inside?' Sarah asked.

Greaves shook his head.

'Is it possible for me to go in?'

He looked sideways at her. 'It's still pretty gruesome.'

'I can manage,' she answered.

He led her up the flight of steps to the open door. 'Careful here,' he instructed, and she could now see the blood that had soaked across a carpet and on to the polished wooden floor of the hall.

'The father opened the door,' he said. 'We think it happened at about midnight. Castor entered the house and ran him through the throat with a long-bladed knife.'

'Like the one the other murders were committed with?'

'No, this was more like a butcher's knife, quite wide near the hilt, judging from the wound. It severed the jugular and cut the vocal cords.' He gestured for her to follow him into the house. 'Walk between these chalk marks,' he told her, then he pointed down. 'There was a lot of blood from the father's wounds. Castor stepped in it as he moved down the passageway to here.' He pointed again. 'The wife was coming from the garden room. This time the blade was driven through her body with such force the point entered the doorpost.' In a matter-of-fact way he showed her the small scar on the paintwork. 'The wife clutched at the blade with her right hand. It almost severed two of her fingers when he withdrew it.'

Sarah looked down at the crudely drawn outline of a body on the wooden floor. The blood had congealed into a dark thickness.

Greaves stood for a moment looking down. 'He must have moved with an extraordinary speed and agility,' he said, almost to himself, 'like a dancer. Strange, considering how he was dressed.'

'You know how he was dressed?' Sarah said.

Greaves looked up. 'We think so. Two neighbours saw a motorcyclist leave the house. They say he was from one of these delivery companies. We've got a fair description.'

'What about the girl?'

Greaves turned and walked to the staircase. Halfway up, he stopped. 'She must have heard something and come here to look. You can see from the marks of the mother's blood on his hand where he touched the wall as he ran after her. She tried to hide in the bedroom. That's where he caught her. He didn't kill her immediately. She was only stunned, like the others. He dragged her out on to the landing and finished it there.'

Sarah stopped and breathed deeply.

'Are you all right?' he asked.

Sarah nodded. 'Just give me a minute,' she said. She looked briefly into the girl's bedroom before following him down. At the foot of the staircase she began to pray. I hope there's a God, she said to herself. An Old Testament God who punishes evil.

'Do you want to see anything else?' he asked.

Sarah shook her head. She had seen enough.

Detective-Sergeant Holland came in from the street and spoke quietly to Greaves. 'There's a lot of reporters out there now, and television crews.'

Greaves spoke to Sarah. 'I'll go out and talk to them. Give me a few minutes and then we'll see if we can slip you out without attracting their attention.'

'If you'll wait in the kitchen,' Sergeant Holland said, 'I'll make you a cup of tea.'

Sarah followed him to the rear of the house and sat down in surroundings that felt familiar. She looked around at the stripped-pine furniture, bunches of dried flowers and tiled floor. There was a large calendar pinned to a noticeboard with dates ringed and notes scribbled in the margins with a fibre-tipped pen. Around it were snapshots of the family. Some showed a girl in riding clothes.

'What were their names?' Sarah asked.

Holland continued to search for cups while he answered. 'Lindsay,' he said in a preoccupied fashion. 'Robert and Marion. The daughter was called June.'

Sarah reached out and touched one of the photographs. 'She liked to ride.'

'Yes,' he answered, 'there are cups and ribbons in her bedroom.'

Sarah looked at the calendar again. There was a ring around the date for the following Saturday and the word 'Gymkhana' written and underlined. She began to make notes until the Sergeant handed her a cup of tea. He was a hard-looking young man, with short hair and blunt features, but his hand trembled slightly when he handed her the cup.

'What do you think of all this?' she asked.

He turned away to look at the noticeboard, aware that she could tell how affected he was by the events in the house.

'I'd string the bastard up,' he said. 'I don't care if he is a nutter. He should pay for what he's done to all these people.'

Revenge, Sarah thought. She remembered her own prayer: the same motive as the killer. To forgive seemed an impossible act of charity.

She drank the tea gratefully and Greaves returned a few minutes later.

'Kerr and Sinclair are with the crowd outside,' he said. 'There's an alley at the end of the garden. If you go that way you can come round from the next street and the others won't know you've been here.' He looked at his watch. 'Do you know the London Apprentice?'

It was a pub on the river, quite close, near Brentford. Sarah had been there a few times. She nodded.

'I'll meet you there in an hour or so.'

Sarah made the circuitous journey he had suggested, and when she re-entered the street saw that the road was now choked with reporters' cars and neighbours stood in their gardens looking out on the scene. She found Peter Kerr and Harry Porter standing together. Sinclair was at the police line, talking to a group of reporters from the other papers.

'Christ, the tube was slow, wasn't it?' Kerr said when he saw her.

'I got here ages ago,' Sarah muttered. 'I've been inside the house. Greaves wants to meet us in an hour at the London Apprentice.'

'You'd better file,' Kerr said. 'Use the telephone in my car, it's parked there.' He handed her the keys. She got on to the news desk and found Stiles in charge. He put her on to the copy-takers and she dictated for more than half an hour, until she was longing to get into the fresh air again. As with most reporters, Kerr kept the interior of his car like a rubbish tip. Old cigarette packets, sweet wrappers, discarded toys and crumpled newspapers formed layers of trash at her feet. The street outside looked neat in comparison.

'Let's go,' Kerr said to her. 'Harry's staying with Sinclair. I'll send my stuff on the way. You drive.'

The traffic was lighter now and it did not take long to get to Brentford. Sarah turned alongside the high wall that skirted the grounds of Syon House and eventually stopped the car in the narrow road that ran alongside the river bank.

The evening was fine; sunlight still fell on the island opposite the public house, slanting through the high branches of the trees. Colin Greaves had not arrived. While Peter Kerr bought them drinks, Sarah stood on a little balcony and watched a racing eight pulling through the narrow channel. The other people about her were mostly young. They looked relaxed, enjoying the pleasant spring weather. She suddenly felt a long way from the house in Barnes.

'One glass of white wine,' Peter Kerr said, as he handed her the drink, and they stood talking in low voices until Greaves arrived. Sarah watched him walk slowly along the roadway towards them.

'He's making sure none of the others are about,' Kerr said, referring to the reporters who had congregated at Barnes.

When Peter Kerr had bought him a pint of bitter, Greaves repeated most of the information Sarah had already learned at the house.

'So you're sure it's this cowboy on the motorbike?' Kerr asked.

'Not yet, but I give it a good chance.'

'How long do you think it will take to find him?' Kerr asked in slightly louder tones.

Greaves looked towards a group of laughing people near to them before he answered in a softer voice. 'When we've traced the company – maybe tomorrow. They should have records of all their assignments and the bikes keep in touch by radio.' He paused and drank some beer. 'The problem is, there's a hell of a lot of people doing this work. It's still a matter of grinding through the routine and there haven't been any lucky breaks on this job so far.'

They stood in silence for a few minutes, then Kerr said, 'Nature calls,' and went inside the public house.

Greaves looked down into his glass with a half-smile. 'I hardly ever drink English beer,' he said, 'but somehow it seems obligatory when you're beside the river.'

'You sound like a foreigner,' Sarah replied.

He nodded. 'I feel that way quite often. Remember, I was born in the Orient.'

'Why did you ask us to come here?' she asked.

Greaves looked at her again. 'I didn't expect Peter, I wanted to see you.'

'Why?'

His gaze was steady and unsmiling. 'Just to be near you for a time, I suppose.'

She blushed at the compliment and lowered her eyes from his. 'Thank you,' she said. Greaves thought he could see how she had looked when she was a girl.

'Is your car here?' he asked.

'No, but I must go back to the office with Peter.'

He looked over the river. 'How about this weekend? I think I can get away. We could go to my sister's cottage on Saturday.'

Saturday, she thought, and she remembered the murdered girl at Barnes, June Lindsay, was to go to a gymkhana on Saturday. She shook her head. 'It's Emily's birthday, I must be at home.'

Greaves looked away and slowly drank his beer. Sarah could see Peter Kerr returning. He had bought more drinks and was moving through the crowd with care so that he would not spill the three glasses.

'We could go on Sunday,' she said quickly.

Greaves nodded and smiled as Peter Kerr arrived.

'It was my round,' Sarah protested.

Kerr laughed. 'I was passing the bar and I just couldn't stop myself. No sales resistance, it's the story of my life.'

CHAPTER
FOURTEEN

T HERE were no questions on her copy when they returned
to the office. Sarah and Peter Kerr were standing by the
coffee machine when the chief sub passed with a page proof
in his hand.

'Nice stuff, Pete,' he said, 'I like the bit about her missing the
gymkhana.'

'I didn't write that,' Kerr said. 'Show me.'

The chief sub held out the proof. The only byline on the page
was Peter Kerr's, although most of the copy was by Sarah.

'Where's her name?' Kerr demanded 'She wrote most of this.'

The chief sub shrugged and took back the page. 'Sorry, Stiles said
it was all your story.' He began to walk away as he spoke. 'It's too
late for any changes now.'

Sarah did not feel angry. In truth, she did not want any praise for
the work she had done: it would have seemed like profiting at the
expense of the murdered family. But Kerr was outraged. 'Where's
Stiles now?' he called out after the retreating figure.

'Gone to the pub,' he replied, as he pushed open the swing-doors at the end of the newsroom.

'Do you want to come and sort him out?' Kerr asked.

Sarah shook her head, 'I'm too tired, Peter. I think I'll just go home.'

'Well I will,' Kerr said resolutely. 'I love being nasty to the little prick.'

She walked down to the vanway with Kerr, who continued to point out Stiles's evident defects. Sarah was only half listening, but she was thinking of the same subject.

How are people's characters formed? she wondered. At what age did Stiles decide how he was going to behave in life? Surely no one would want to be such a failure as a human being? She thought of her own children. The boys were so much like Jack: their lives already seemed to be set on a course that she could do little to alter, and didn't want to. But what of Emily? She loved her absolutely, but sometimes she seemed like a stranger. Their tastes were often the same, but Sarah always thought Emily was just running in parallel rather than being influenced by her. Until Ric had come on the scene, the person with whom she had shown the most affinity had always been Sarah's father. She knew they often spoke on the telephone; Long conversations of the sort she had never held with him. Her train of thought was interrupted by Peter Kerr saying good night.

She picked up her own car and drove slowly. She was very tired and the breeze from the open window felt soothing on her hot forehead. The boys were already in bed when she got home. Ric Daggert had gone, but Emily sat with Claire on the sofa, surrounded by photograph albums, cuttings books, and some old copies of the *Gazette* that had been preserved, for some forgotten reason, in black plastic bags.

Claire was yawning as Sarah came in. 'I'm bushed,' she said. 'I'm taking up your offer to stay the night. Your hamburger's in the microwave, bun under the grill, salad in the refrigerator. Goodnight.'

She looked down at the scattered books and papers when she stood up and then turned to Emily. 'Give your mother a hand clearing up, young lady. This old girl is hitting the sack, as my daddy, the marine, used to say.'

She kissed Emily on the forehead and left the room.

Sarah sat down in Claire's vacant seat, too tired to begin.

'Shall I get you a drink?' Emily asked. Sarah reached out and hugged her. 'Do you know, a cup of cocoa would be perfect.'

Emily stopped at the door. 'I'm sorry about last night.'

Sarah smiled back. 'That's all right.'

Emily paused again, 'It was Claire who told me to apologise.'

Sarah nodded.

'She's nice, isn't she?'

'Yes, darling, a good friend.'

As Emily closed the door the telephone began to ring. Sarah reached for the extension on the table next to her. She expected it to be the news desk with a question about her copy, but it was Osbert Hannay.

'Forgive me for calling so late,' he said, and she could hear the concern in his voice. 'But I wondered if Fanny is still with you?'

His question puzzled Sarah. 'I haven't seen her today,' she answered.

'Oh!' he replied after a pause. 'Well I apologise for bothering you.'

'Who told you, Fanny was here, Osbert?'

He paused again, clearly finding the conversation difficult. 'She didn't come home last night. I spoke to her on the telephone this morning and she gave me the impression she'd spent the night at your house. I assumed she was still with you.'

Sarah did not wish to tell tales but she refused to provide an alibi for Fanny Hunter. 'I'm sorry, but she's never been to this house.'

'This is rather worrying,' he said flatly. 'When she has stayed away on previous occasions it's always been another man.'

'Previous occasions?'

'Oh, yes.' Hannay said. 'Fanny rarely spares me any details of her affairs.' He hesitated again then continued, 'I think I should tell you, Sarah, my wife is not a very . . . reliable person. I have no right to try and influence your relationship, but I wouldn't place too much confidence in her friendship.'

'Why do you stay with her, Osbert?' Sarah said gently.

'Habit, I suppose,' he replied. 'Actually, she stays with me. I can't think why – we've more or less led separate lives for some years.'

Sarah could not think of anything to say, other than 'I'm very sorry.'

'Thank you,' Hannay replied, 'and once again, I apologise for calling so late. May I beg one last favour?'

'Yes,' Sarah said after a moment of hesitation.

'Please don't mention this to Fanny.'

'If that's what you want.'

Hannay said goodbye and Sarah thought about the conversation for a few minutes. Then she lay back and felt the tension in her shoulders. Next to her was an old photograph album. She turned to the early pages and glanced at the little black-and-white snapshots her father had taken during her childhood. Beaches, pets, groups posed around motor cars on summer days. She wondered if people still took photographs of their motor cars. 'It's one of the family' her father used to say of their old Riley.

Some of the newspapers had spilt out of their plastic bag. She reached down and pulled them out, puzzled about why entire copies had been kept. Then she saw they were editions which contained a series of Jack's reports from the Far East, pieces that had won him an award. She picked up the first paper. The *Gazette* had still been a broadsheet in those days. It surprised her a little to see how respectable and staid it had looked. She read through Jack's piece and thought how well-written it was, and that time of her life returned with a rush of memories. She had been pregnant with Emily and had not long left the paper. Other names came up from the pages, some half forgotten, others fresher in her mind. She found a large picture taken by Harry Porter of the Prince of Wales smiling at a crowd of women outside a factory in the Midlands. He looked young and carefree. Like all of us then, Sarah thought.

Emily came in, carrying a tray that held Sarah's hamburger and a cup of cocoa. She laid the paper aside and realised that she was famished when she began to eat. The food tasted delicious.

'Claire says only Americans know how to make hamburgers properly,' Emily said as she watched Sarah eating. Sarah looked up and noticed Emily toss back her long hair. The movement made her look older and Sarah had one of those jumping little shocks that came occasionally. Because Emily had always been so slender it had been easier to see her as a child, but these days the woman was showing more and more.

'Do you mind if I go away the Sunday after your birthday?' Sarah asked.

'Why should I?' Emily replied, without looking up from the photographs she was now studying. 'Besides, Claire is taking us all to a game of softball – you don't have to come.'

'As long as you don't mind,' Sarah said, and she suddenly noticed her hands. They were starting to lose their raw roughness.

She finished her meal and took up the old copy of the *Gazette* again, flipping through the pages. The City page stopped her, and she held it closer to the reading lamp.

A picture across seven columns had caught her attention. It was of an elegant man leaning against a desk, arms folded nonchalantly and head tilted towards the camera. His smile was quizzical and filled with self-confidence. Surrounding him were the trappings of a splendid office: beautifully carved rosewood furniture, showcases filled with fragile porcelain, painted vases, delicate scroll paintings of birds, warriors and mountains. On the huge desk were models of ships, ivory boxes, small brass cannons, nautical instruments and a curious, stone object with some sort of characters carved into it. The symbol seemed somehow familiar, but her tired brain would not make the connection. Then she realised. Standing up, she held the paper to the mirror above the fireplace and saw that it was the runic sign for revenge.

Sarah continued to study the picture for some time and read the headline accompanying the article: BALTIC-MARINE 'SAFE AS ROCK OF GIBRALTAR' CLAIMS SIR GAVIN TEMPLE. The piece was by the city editor and told of the growing doubts in financial circles about the stability of the Baltic-Marine Insurance Company – doubts that were strongly refuted by Sir Gavin. Wearily, she picked up a large leather and canvas satchel she had taken to carrying with her and took out her notebook. She wrote down Sir Gavin's name and then, with one last effort, she and Emily cleared away the scattered books and papers before they went to bed. Just before falling asleep a strange image came to her. She saw herself looking into a mirror; but the reflection was of Emily.

CHAPTER
FIFTEEN

SARAH was pressing a blouse when Martin entered the breakfast room with the post.

'A big thick one for you from the *Gazette*,' he said, placing the envelope next to her on the ironing board. She opened the letter, and seeing that it was her formal contract of employment, set it aside and continued with her task.

'What is it?' Martin asked.

'Office stuff.'

'May I look?'

She nodded and he sat down at the table to study the document. 'So you're on a month's trial,' he said after a few minutes.

'No,' she replied, 'three months' notice.'

'It says a month's trial here.'

'Show me!'

Martin held up the letter and indicated the paragraph. The Agreement will be subject to one month's trial period, it read.

'I suppose that's standard,' she said lightly.

Martin shrugged. 'The form's printed, so everyone must get the same thing.'

'Yes,' she replied, but a whisper of doubt still lingered in her mind.

The operations room was empty but there was a scrawled note from George Conway asking her to call him. She knew there was a problem the moment he spoke.

'Did you see the programme?' he asked.

'What programme?'

'The Fifth Estate, it was on last night.'

'No,' Sarah said. 'Why?'

George paused. 'They gave us a bit of a kicking.'

'What for?'

'Your interview with the dead girl's mother. It seems Mr Craig knows Sir Robert and he's been on to him this morning about the paper upsetting his wife. Sir Robert doesn't like complaints, especially from friends in the City.'

'We didn't do anything unethical, George. She volunteered for the interview, didn't she?'

He sighed. 'You don't understand our chairman, he's a bloody box-wallah, not a newspaperman. I once heard him say that investigative journalism was just muck-raking and bad for the country.'

'But we're supposed to be muck-rakers; at least, that's what I was always taught.'

'Not in Sir Robert's book.'

'Well, which book has he been reading?'

'The one entitled: How to Get a Peerage. Anyway it's happened. I've got a tape of the programme in my office. Come down and we'll watch it together.'

Depressed by the conversation, Sarah made her way to the cubby-hole off the main newsroom that Conway shared with the picture editor. George was waiting. When she entered he started the tape.

The Fifth Estate was a late-night chat show conducted by a woman called Tilly Roche, who had made her mark by castigating the methods of journalists who operated at the lower end of the trade. After the opening credits, the camera closed in on a blow-up of Sarah's interview while an unseen actress read extracts in a breathless, prissy voice.

Then the camera cut to Tilly Roche, looking suitably concerned.

Speaking to camera, she questioned the motives of the *Gazette* in running such an interview. Was it necessary to expose the private grief of an individual who had suffered such an appalling experience? Did such an article add to the public's understanding of the case, or was it just a sordid form of voyeurism, calculated to increase the circulation of the newspaper? Then she introduced her guests, who were to comment on the article, and the camera pulled back to reveal Doctor Carlyle and Fanny Hunter.

'Doctor Carlyle,' Tilly Roche continued, 'as a consultant psychiatrist, in your opinion would such an article prevent the killer from going for another victim?'

Carlyle shook his head slowly. 'You must understand that the perpetrator of these dreadful acts does not react in the same way as a normal person. For him such a public display of grief would be counted as a triumph.'

Tilly Roche interjected. 'So what you're saying is: the murderer might actually be encouraged to kill again if he read the article?'

'Jesus,' George said softly.

Carlyle thought for a moment, realising the legal implication of his words. 'All I am saying is, we cannot know the reasons that motivate these acts until this man has been subjected to lengthy analysis. By studying his patterns of behaviour we may be able to predict what course his future actions may take, but his motives will remain buried in his subconscious until they can be unlocked by –'

Tilly Roche did not wait for him to finish. Instead she turned to Fanny.

'Well, this is something of a hotseat for you. As I'm sure the viewers will know, Fanny Hunter is the leading columnist on the *Gazette* and therefore in the difficult position of commenting on the shortcomings of her own paper. I for one applaud her courage on coming on to the programme tonight.

'So what do you think, Fanny, was the *Gazette* right to print the story?'

Fanny's pause was perfectly timed, just long enough to convey proper consideration, then she looked up. 'Luckily, I work for a marvellous man called Sir Robert Hall, chairman of the Gazette; we talk about the paper all the time, in fact I'm having lunch with him tomorrow to discuss just this sort of thing. So it really doesn't take courage for me to speak out. He's always backed me when I've disagreed with my own paper in the past. That's why I admire him so much, but in one way I am in a difficult position on this, because the girl who wrote the article is a personal friend of mine. I'm sure it was only inexperience that caused her to put her name to the story, but I know that's no excuse. Until journalists learn that they can't ride rough-shod over the feelings of the public we're going to have these unnecessary blots on the profession. I just think it's a shame that standards aren't the same as when I first came to Fleet Street.'

'But surely, it is the editor of the paper who makes the decision whether to print an article or not?' Tilly Roche said. Fanny shook her head. 'It just doesn't work like that. The editor of a modern newspaper has a thousand things to do; like the Prime Minister, he has to rely on subordinates to carry out his policies. Sometimes, in the rush of the day, misjudgements are made. Brian Meadows is a brilliant editor of the *Gazette*. I'm sure he feels as let down on this one as I do.'

Conway stopped the tape. 'The rest is waffle about a piece in the *Spectator*,' he said, then he turned to Sarah. 'Fanny was brilliant, she kissed Sir Robert's arse, excused Meadows from blame, kicked Carter and me in the guts and put the skids under you.'

Sarah was too angry to speak at first. Then she said, 'Will you run the final credits for me?'

George wound on the tape, and there, among the many names, she found Patrick Stone, Executive Producer.

Sarah glanced at her watch as she left George's office and half blundered into Harry Porter. 'Did you see the TV last night?' he asked.

She nodded. 'George played me a tape.'

'Come over here,' he said, and led her to a quiet corner of the newsroom. After a few minutes conversation, he patted her arm and Sarah looked at her watch again. She made her way to the library and asked for cuttings on the Oaklands air disaster.

'Good Lord, that's going back a bit. Anything else you want from the last century?' the assistant said.

Sarah was about to say no, when she recollected the name she had made a note of the previous night. 'And everything you've got on Sir Gavin Temple,' she added, and he went off to make a search.

Twenty minutes later, her arms full of photocopies, Sarah left the library and called a telephone number Harry Porter had given her. Then she made her way to Fanny's office.

Jackie stood up and barred the doorway to the inner sanctum at the sight of Sarah's fearsome expression.

'She's not in there, honest*leeeee*,' Jackie said, giving one of her animal cries.

'Where is she?'

'In her private loo, making up for lunch.'

'Where is it'

'Along the corridor on the right, but you can't go in there!' Jackie called after her.

Ignoring the PRIVATE sign, Sarah pushed open the door and entered a room considerably larger than Conway's office. Apart from the usual equipment, it was furnished with rugs, a large sofa and a dressing table where Fanny sat, attending to her face. She looked up at Sarah in the reflection of the mirror and there was no friendship in the glance.

'Yes?' she asked and returned to the task of applying eyeliner.

'You're having lunch with the chairman,' Sarah answered quietly.

'That's right.'

'Will you discuss last night's programme?'

'I imagine the subject will crop up.'

'They say he listens to you.'

'He appreciates my contribution. I have a certain influence. Why?'

Sarah leaned forward. 'I want you to use that influence to repair the damage you've done.'

Fanny turned round in the chair. 'Sorry, sweetie,' she said, 'I can't let personal feelings interfere with the good of the paper. If he asks me what I think, I'll tell him the truth, like I always do.' She turned back to the mirror and said, 'Now will you please piss off, I'm rather busy.'

'Like you were the night of the Oaklands air crash?' Sarah said softly.

Fanny suddenly became preoccupied with a box of tissues. 'I don't know what you mean,' she said, but her voice lacked conviction.

Sarah took one of the sheets she had brought from the library and held up a cutting with the headline: TRAGIC MOTHER TELLS HOW HER FAMILY DIED. 'Remember when you wrote this?' Sarah said. 'How will Sir Robert be able to tell the difference from my piece?'

'I was ordered to write that,' Fanny replied. 'Besides, it happened before he took over the paper.'

Sarah nodded. 'Would he feel so forgiving if he knew the whole story? I seem to remember he made a speech recently on the standards of the press, and you did set yourself up as the Mother Teresa of Fleet Street on television last night. Think what the gossip columnists would do with the truth.'

147

'You're bluffing,' Fanny said in a harsh voice. 'You don't know anything – you weren't even on the paper then.'

Sarah agreed. 'You're right. I was at home with my children, but Jack was on the story, he told me what happened.'

Fanny shrugged dismissively: 'But he's hardly in a position to corroborate what you say, is he? Unless of course, you're contemplating one of those clairvoyant interviews from beyond the grave, which the *Sun* do so well.'

Sarah noticed that under pressure Fanny's voice became erratic. She had spoken the last sentence in the cultivated tones of a Cambridge graduate.

'That won't be necessary. Think back, Fanny,' Sarah prompted. There were eight of you from the paper covering the story. The office had booked you all into a motel near the airport and the walls were thin enough to push a pencil through them. Everyone went out on the job except you and Cat Abbot. You were still angry that Jack had broken it off with you, so you tried to make him jealous with the sound effects of your orgasms as he was in the next room. You didn't leave that double bed all night.' She held up the cutting once again. 'This interview with Mrs Watling was pure invention.'

'You can't prove that,' Fanny said quickly.

Sarah took a deep breath. 'Yes, I can,' she said. 'I've just spoken to her on the telephone. Her sister gave me the number. She's remarried now, her name is Daphne Cooper. She remembers it well, and the letter she wrote to you complaining – the one you never answered.'

Fanny stood up. 'This is blackmail.'

'That's right,' Sarah answered calmly, and she walked from the room.

'What's that you've got?' George asked as she passed the news desk.

'Cuttings on Sir Gavin Temple,' she said, holding up the bundle.

'Temple?' Conway repeated, as if the name had stirred a memory. He shook his head; the thought had eluded him. 'I know what I keep meaning to tell you,' he said, 'Get your expenses done.'

Sarah returned to the fourth floor and laid the photocopies beside her telephone. Sinclair was muttering in the corner with Don Bradley, a young man she had hardly seen in the office. For the next few hours she laboriously filled in expense sheets. It was a dreary task that somehow reminded her of housework. When the forms were

148

finally completed, she took them downstairs to the news-desk secretary. Stiles was standing next to George.

'Sarah,' he said with an ingratiating smile, 'you must know how sorry I am about your byline. Believe me, it was a cock-up. I hold myself to blame, but I do think the subs were equally guilty.'

Sarah looked to the rows of empty chairs where the sub-editors would be sitting later in the day. She doubted if Stiles would have made the same claim if any had been present. She shrugged and was about to hand in her expenses when Stiles reached out for them. 'Here, I'll sign those now, you don't want to be waiting for the money, do you?'

Sarah was beginning to understand his devious qualities. She realised that his sudden change of attitude towards her was the result of the trouble Fanny had caused. He took the sheets, with barely a glance, initialled each one and then handed them to the secretary.

'Anything else we can do for you?' he said, continuing his display of new-found friendliness.

There was, but Sarah wanted the request to go through George, who was taking a call.

'I'll just stand here until I think of something,' she replied. With another smile, Stiles returned his attention to the desk.

When George hung up she said, 'I'm down on the rota to work this Sunday. May I swap with Sinclair? He's already told me he's happy to change.'

George considered the request and then nodded. It had not been an automatic agreement: news editors could be insistent about reporters sticking to their allocated duties. Sarah was about to leave when George beckoned for her to lean closer.

'My spy has been talking about your behaviour. What went on in Fanny's boudoir?' he asked in a whisper.

'I'll tell you when it's easier to speak,' she replied in the same quiet tones, and glanced at Stiles, who was now straining to hear their conversation.

'Great,' George said in a much louder voice. Then he looked up at the wall clock, which stood at 11.45. 'Let's go and have one to celebrate.'

Sarah followed him with a wry smile and a few minutes later they sat at the bar of the Red Lion.

'White wine,' he said, placing Sarah's drink before her. 'I can remember the days when you couldn't buy wine in a pub.' He drank some of his own whisky, then continued, 'Tell me about your talk with Fanny.'

When she had described the encounter, George smiled. 'I don't know what part she'd dread getting out most,' he said happily, 'the fact that she made up a story, or the fact that she slept with Cat Abbot.'

Sarah thought back. 'Oh, Cat wasn't such a laughing stock in those days, a lot of women fancied him. Fanny wouldn't care about that getting out. If you want to damage her, you've got to hit at her reputation.'

He glanced at her again. 'You've toughened up in your old age.'

Sarah sipped some of her wine before she answered. 'I've got children to feed now, George. Call it a mother's instinct for survival.'

He nodded and then frowned in irritation at a sudden burst of electronic burps and bleeps from the video game that was placed a few feet from him. 'Is there to be no sanctuary left on earth from those blasted idiot boxes?' The youth who was playing the machine looked up from the screen and Sarah could see anger on his slack-mouthed face.

'Something wrong, John?' he asked belligerently.

In his sitting position, George looked like a portly, middle-aged man. But when he stood up the power in his frame showed through the fat.

'Go away, you vile little person,' he said in a low, menacing voice, 'or I shall squash you like a garden slug.'

The youth did not contemplate his looming presence for long. He gave the machine one last jab and then walked hurriedly from the pub, leaving the bar to George, Sarah and the barmaid, who now said, 'Don't let the guv'nor hear you speaking to the punters like that, George. You'd be surprised how much money that thing brings in every week.'

'Really?' he replied. 'How much, would you say?'

'I don't know exactly,' the barmaid said, 'but the guv'nor says it took him and his missus to Florida for their holidays last year.'

George glared at the machine in disgust. 'Florida,' he repeated. 'That's just the sort of destination you'd expect from a contraption like that.'

Sarah nudged him. 'Don't be such a curmudgeon, you sound like Harry Porter. Next thing you'll be asking them to put sawdust on the floor again.' Noticing the greasy impregnations in the carpet, she said, 'On the other hand, that might not be a bad idea.'

Conway looked around the empty bar and leaned closer. 'What does Greaves say about the chance of an arrest today?'

Sarah shifted her wine glass along the mahogany counter and looked at him. 'He really doesn't have any idea.'

'Doesn't he have a guess? Christ, you can't stop most coppers from telling you their hunches!'

'He isn't like that. He doesn't seem to care what people think of him. He says they've just got to work through the list. It's a question of luck if they hit the right one early.'

George now sat with his back to the bar and gazed at the machine, which continued to flash lights and emit occasional bleeps to attract the attention of other players.

'We should do a piece on those lumps of rubbish,' he said with a thoughtful nod. 'It's the sort of thing my first wife would enjoy, she bought anything with a plug on it. God, how do I find such women?'

Sarah rummaged in her bag for her purse. George was now entering a reflective mood and she did not want to risk a repeat of the conversation they had held in the Italian restaurant. She decided to leave. 'I'm going to buy you a drink and then I've got to go,' she said firmly.

'Got a better offer, eh?' he said with a slight edge in his voice.

Sarah shook her head. 'Actually, I'm going shopping. Did you know that you can buy lamb chops in Smithfield meat market at almost half the price you'd pay for them in Hampstead?'

Before he could answer, she tapped him on the chest with a forefinger. 'And the fruit sold in Leather Lane is a real bargain.'

'I'll take your word for it,' he replied. 'Personally, I never eat fruit. If you drink enough beer it does the same job and you don't litter up the world with peel and apple cores.'

Sarah ordered him another Scotch but before she paid, Harry Porter came into the bar. She bought him a pint of beer and soon he and George began a conversation about the days when pubs had been the proper refuge of drinking men and not the playgrounds of overpaid youths.

'There was no money for bloody machines then,' Harry agreed. 'I used to give my mother a quid every week, and I only earned thirty bob.'

George agreed heartily with Harry's inaccurate recollections.

Sarah walked from the pub down Gray's Inn Road. It was just after twelve o'clock. Leather Lane market would now be filling with people from the nearby offices, but she didn't mind. She enjoyed the bustle.

151

Just over an hour later she returned to the office loaded with shopping. Sinclair and his companion had left and she sighed with relief. Their secret, sniggering conversations were irritating, and sometimes made her long for more adult companionship.

Her telephone rang and when she answered, Colin Greaves said, 'This is a personal call.'

She turned off the recorder and said, 'Go ahead.'

'I just wondered if you could get away for an hour or so?' She looked at the clock. It wasn't quite 1.30. 'I think so,' she answered. 'Where shall we meet?'

'That depends. Do you want to eat?'

'I'm not bothered.'

'In that case I'll meet you by the seals' pool at the zoo in about half an hour.'

She took a cab to Regent's Park and arrived at the rendezvous before him. It was a cold, overcast day and there were few other spectators watching the browsing seals; just a middle-aged couple, who still stood beside her when Greaves touched her arm to announce his presence. Before they spoke, the woman suddenly said, 'Poor buggers, it's not very natural for them, is it?'

The man with her contemplated her words for a moment. 'Perhaps they should put the polar bears in with them,' he answered finally, then walked away. The woman hesitated, and then followed him.

'Is there anything you want to look at?' Greaves asked.

'No, but I would like a cup of tea,' Sarah replied.

They walked to the cafeteria, and sat in the middle of a sea of empty tables. Sarah glanced out at the dismal day while he brought the cups to her.

'I like the zoo, but I'm not really sure that I should,' she said when he was seated. 'Sometimes it seems cruel to keep animals locked up.'

'I would have answered that once,' he replied.

'You went to university, didn't you?' she said, remembering his file.

He nodded.

'Why did you become a policeman?'

He smiled. 'Because of Reg Bolton.'

'Was he one of your teachers?'

152

'No. He was a detective-inspector from Leeds.'

'How did you meet him?'

'It's a longish story,' he said lightly, and once again she sensed his reluctance to talk about himself.

'I don't mind,' she answered.

He looked at her as if to make sure she was not just being polite, and then began. 'I'd almost settled on an academic career,' he said, 'then one day, in my final year, I was driving north to see a friend and my car broke down. Reg gave me a lift, although he had his wife and two kids in the car. He asked me what I did and I told him.' He paused. 'I used to talk more in those days.'

Sarah nodded encouragement and he continued. 'I'd been reading the doctrine of the superman . . .' he broke off again. 'Are you familiar with it?'

'No.'

'It's to do with the idea of man evolving into a higher species, one that goes beyond the concept of good and evil. Anyway, Reg listened and I prattled on until we stopped at a motorway cafe for a break. It was crowded but we got a table near a group of drunks who had been to a football match. They were making a bloody nuisance of themselves and everyone just pretended they weren't there. Then a couple of them started to get nasty with a little man at the next table. I could see he was really terrified and nobody was doing anything. Then Reg got up and put a stop to it.' Greaves looked up at her. 'He had his own wife and children there, a perfect excuse not to get involved, but he just walked over and ordered them to behave.'

'Was there a fight?'

Greaves shook his head. 'There was no more trouble. They just quietened down. When he got back to us I asked him why he'd acted in such a way, and he said, "You've got to take sides in life." Then I realised which side he'd chosen.' Greaves leaned forward. 'I saw that it was all straightforward – good and bad existed as positive forces, tangible realities that affect our lives, not just as abstract ideas, but most people feel helpless when they're faced with the power and certainty of a bully. They want someone else to deal with it, someone who has chosen sides.' He shrugged. 'What Reg had done made sense to me – it seemed worthwhile.'

'Do you still feel the same way?' Sarah asked.

Greaves sat back in his chair, his hands in the pockets of his raincoat. 'Yes,' he said slowly, 'I think there are things in life worth defending. Someone has to keep the polar bears from eating the seals.'

Sarah looked down at her hands that were folded in her lap. 'That's a rather high-minded ideal. Hard to live up to.'

'That's what my wife used to say,' he answered. Then, 'Tell me, why did you want to become a journalist?'

She thought about his question, 'I didn't want to,' she said finally, 'I just sort of drifted into it.'

'How?'

'My father expected me to become a doctor. I tried hard because I wanted to please him, but I just couldn't make it. Writing always came easily, but I didn't consider it proper work. When my A levels weren't good enough to get into medical school I didn't know what to do. Then one of the nuns at my convent sent a short story I'd written to the old Consolidated Press and they offered me a junior's job on *Standard* magazine. I didn't even know about it until the letter arrived.'

'What was *Standard* magazine?'

Sarah smiled. 'It was a very strait-laced publication for young girls,' she explained. 'When I was there they still had the original motto under the masthead: "For Daughters of the Empire". I worked there for two years. Then I sold a couple of features to the *Gazette*. They gave me some holiday relief shifts as a reporter . . .' she shrugged, 'and now I'm back where I started.'

'Was your father very disappointed?'

'He thought being a reporter was a pretty worthless occupation, so I didn't hold it in much regard, until I met Jack. He taught me that the job could have real value.'

They did not speak for a time. He watched her while she drank the last of her tea and then said, 'I didn't think I would ever feel this way about someone I met halfway through my life.'

'What do you mean?'

He held up a hand. 'Love – infatuation, I'm not sure. All I know is I think about you constantly. I see things, objects, situations and I say to myself, "What would Sarah Keane think of that?" A few days ago I didn't know you existed. Now you seem to be with me all the time.'

Sarah remembered the warning she had given George Conway. It seemed only fair to state it again.

'Be careful what you say,' she said, 'I come with a lot of responsibilities.'

He smiled, 'I've seen them. I'm not a boy, Sarah. Although I must sound like one now.'

She shook her head and suddenly felt elated; a glowing sensation, as if she were filled with a substance that made her lightheaded. In a rush, the problems that had bowed her down with concern that morning passed through her mind, and each one now seemed insignificant. It was a moment of pure joy and she thought: I didn't ever expect it to happen again, but this man loves me.

Greaves stood up. 'Let's go for a walk,' he said. 'Then I can hold your hand.'

CHAPTER
SIXTEEN

T HERE was no news of an arrest that afternoon, or the following morning. Just before Sarah went shopping with Claire, George Conway rang to tell her he'd heard on the grapevine that Fanny had apologised to Meadows for her television performance and assured him that the chairman had told her that no action would be taken against any of the staff members.

When she returned to her desk after the break, the room was empty. She ate two pieces of the fruit she had bought in the market and finally began to read the cuttings from the *Gazette* on Sir Gavin Temple.

At first it seemed a complicated story; each article she read in the heap of photocopies implied more than it revealed. Clearly the *Gazette*'s lawyers had been wary of libel, and each piece was hedged with a thick undergrowth of qualifications and disclaimers. But the story that gradually unfolded proved simple in the end.

Sir Gavin Temple had bought an old and once respectable company called Anglo-Baltic Marine Insurance. By high-pressure advertising techniques that offered cut-price premiums he had persuaded millions of people to take out motor insurance policies with him. For a time the company had boomed and Temple had become something of a blue-eyed boy in the City. Then rumblings began. Stories circulated about unpaid claims and insufficient funds to meet commitments. Eventually the Fraud Squad began an inquiry and their investigations proved the rumours to be correct. Temple had gambled heavily with the reserves of the company on foreign exchanges and had lost the lot.

It wasn't a big story as City frauds go. Everyone paid compliments to the charm of Sir Gavin but no one would bail him out, and eventually charges were brought. Usually such cases were extraordinarily complex and took months of unravelling, but Temple had kept immaculate records of all his dealings so the police had little to do. None of the events were familiar to Sarah, but the reason why became obvious when she consulted the dates. It had all taken place when she was close to giving birth to Emily, so she had been concerned with other things.

She had almost reached the bottom of the pile and had just read the headline: THREE-YEAR SENTENCE FOR SIR GAVIN TEMPLE when the telephone beside her rang. She picked it up and the tape recorder clicked on. She was about to push the override button when a familiar voice said, in almost gentle tones, 'Castor here.'

Sarah felt her throat constrict with fear. There was the same feeling that she was literally being touched by something.

'What do you want?' she managed to say.

Castor chuckled, 'Revenge, of course. It's a lovely day, somebody's last.'

'Will you repeat that?' Sarah said.

'Don't try and be clever, Mrs Keane. I know exactly how long these conversations must be timed before a trace can be made.'

Sarah felt her flesh crawl when he used her name. It was like a physical violation.

'How can you be sure it's me?' she asked, her breath catching as she spoke.

Castor laughed again, 'Oh, I feel we're old friends now. After all, we have something in common. Like actor and critic. I give the performance and you write the review.'

Sarah could not speak again. She wanted to scream her rage and fear at the faceless voice, but it seemed that the power of speech had been taken from her.

Castor continued. 'Tell Superintendent Greaves that he'll be working late again tonight. Oh, and remember, sixteen is sweet, but so is revenge.'

He hung up and Sarah sat with the receiver clutched so tightly in her hand that the flimsy plastic began to creak in protest. Slowly she replaced it in the cradle and the tape recorder clicked off.

The room was completely silent. She looked down at the desk top: there was a neat pile of orange peel and the litter of photocopies. As if trying to re-establish normality, she swept the orange peel into a wastepaper basket and carefully placed the cuttings in her holdall. Each movement was slow and deliberate. It was as if she were at the bottom of the sea, with every gesture made cumbersome by the deep, cold water. It was the effect of evil, she told herself. Castor was not a human being, but a living embodiment of wickedness, the Devil's work. The nuns at her convent had been right: there were forces that went beyond the rational world.

Castor had reached out to her when he spoke and touched her with his own depravity. She began to say the prayer of her childhood. The canvas bag gaped open on the table and she saw a photograph of Emily and the boys that she carried with her among the other clutter of possessions. She looked at their faces while she spoke and gradually her breathing returned to normal.

Then she picked up the telephone and called Conway.

It took them some time to track down Greaves. Eventually a call reached him on a car telephone.

'Where are you?' she asked.

'Close to King's Cross,' he answered. 'I'll be passing your office in a few minutes, judging from the traffic.'

'Castor has just called,' she said.

'Can you play me the recording in the car?'

'Yes, I can.'

'Wait outside your offices,' he instructed. 'I'll pick you up.'

Hurriedly she collected her belongings and by the time she reached the roadway, Greaves was pulling to a halt. He was in the front passenger seat next to the driver. Sarah got into the back of the car and leaned forward to pass him the cassette. He played the recording twice before he handed it to her again.

'He still sounds confident,' Greaves said.

Sarah nodded. Then she looked through the car window. 'Where are we going?'

'To watch Detective-Sergeant Holland make an arrest, I hope.'

'You think you've got him?'

'It looks like it, everything matches.'

159

'Where?'

'King Street, Covent Garden.'

The traffic was so heavy that in Bow Street Greaves decided to abandon the car. Sarah had to walk fast to keep up with his long stride.

'We traced the company this morning,' he said, as they weaved their way through the crowded market. 'There's no doubt he was the one people saw. The work sheets confirm it. He called in an hour ago to say where he was taking his lunch break. These boys have various places around town where they congregate for their breaks.'

As they crossed the last few yards of cobblestones, Greaves slowed down, and Sarah saw a cluster of motorbikes at the deadend of King Street, where a row of bollards blocked cars from driving into the pedestrian areas of the market. The leather-clad riders gathered about their machines and talked to each other or gazed with bored hostility at passers-by, like soldiers of a victorious army looking with contempt on the conquered civilians who surrounded them.

Greaves stopped a few yards from the bollards and held out a hand to restrain Sarah.

'How will you recognise him?' she asked.

'We've got his name and the number of his bike, and he should be wearing a jacket with the name "Mercury" written on it.'

Sarah searched for a face that she could put to a voice, but they all looked very much alike. Then she saw the word 'Mercury' written on the back of a youth who sprawled across one of the machines. Is that the object of my horror? she wondered, and as she watched, two other young men in motorcycle leathers approached him.

'Are they policemen?' Sarah whispered, although they were still some distance from the group.

Greaves nodded. 'If he were to get away it would be impossible to catch him in a car. We've had bikes on the streets all over town.'

Suddenly, as if sensing danger, the sprawling figure swung himself upright before the two policemen reached him. They darted forward, but moving with surprising agility he stood up on his machine and, using the seats of the other motorbikes as stepping stones, seemed to dance the distance to the black metal bollards and leap into the pedestrian-way beyond. Head down, his arms pumping like pistons, he sprinted towards Greaves and Sarah.

Greaves pushed Sarah aside, so that she staggered and sprawled against a passing couple. With a weaving movement, he feigned towards the running figure, making him swerve in another direction. It looked to Sarah as if they had avoided contact, but Greaves had caught the running figure with a sweep of his body that forced him to tumble on to the cobblestones. Recovering instantly from the fall, the biker launched himself at Greaves from a half crouch. Greaves caught one of the flailing arms and twisted it in a jerking motion. The youth screamed in pain. By now the two other policemen were upon him. It took both of them to hold him down while he was handcuffed.

In the few minutes in which the event had taken place, a small crowd of spectators had gathered in the corner of the market. Sarah noticed that one of the tourists she'd blundered into had been taking photographs of the scene with a very professional-looking camera. 'Do you speak English?' she asked him.

'Certainly,' he replied with a trace of a German accent.

'I am a journalist,' she said in a clear voice. 'Will you sell me the film in your camera?'

'For how much?' he asked, after a rapid consultation with his partner.

Sarah guessed an amount. 'Five hundred pounds,' she said.

The man considered for a moment. 'I wish to retain the syndication rights,' he said quickly.

Sarah nodded and scribbled out a note on a sheet of paper, which she handed to him.

'What about my five hundred pounds?' the man asked as she took the film he had unloaded from the camera.

'Take a taxi to the address I have given you and ask for Mr Conway. I have written his name on the piece of paper. He will pay for the taxi and give you your money.'

'How do I know this?'

'You have my word of honour,' Sarah said.

'Ah,' the man said, 'the word of honour of an English gentlewoman.' It seemed to satisfy him.

Sarah turned away and saw that a police car with flashing light and blaring siren was forcing its way through the crowd in King Street. The leather-clad figure was bundled into the back and he turned to look out of the window. For a moment she saw his face, and it remained, printed on the retina of her eye as an after-image. She could still see it when Greaves walked over to her. Small eyes, close together, set in pale, blemished flesh and hair cropped short enough to reveal the contours of his skull: a banal face, not the ultimate image of evil that she had imagined.

161

'Are you all right?' Greaves asked.

'I think so.'

'Did I hurt you?'

'No, I'm fine.'

'I'd better go,' he said. 'Can you make your own way?'

Sarah nodded.

'I'll call you later,' he said. Then he smiled. 'It looks as if I might be free on Sunday.'

She watched him walk swiftly to one of the other police cars.

Later in the day, Peter Kerr came into the little office and slumped down opposite Sarah, who had been writing her story of the arrest.

'I've got good news and bad news,' he said. 'The bad news is, the lawyers say we can't use the pictures of the arrest.'

'Why?'

'They show Castor's face, it would be prejudicial to a fair trial. In fact we can't say anything except the usual "A man has been detained who is helping the police with their inquiries." Trottwood says we'll have to save all the background stuff until after the trial.'

Sinclair sat on the edge of Sarah's desk. 'That means the other papers will get everything we've got when it comes up in evidence.'

'That's right.'

'That's a pity,' Bradley said. 'A lot of good work is going down the tubes.'

'I don't know why you're worried,' Kerr said scathingly. 'The only thing you've written on this job is your expenses.'

'Be fair,' Bradley answered. 'You had me trying to talk to the bloody parents all the time.'

Kerr gestured towards Sarah. 'Yeah, but she was the one who actually got an interview.'

Sarah did not like Bradley, but she felt the accusation was unjust. 'I didn't get that,' she said flatly, 'George Conway handed it to me on a plate.'

'There, you see,' Bradley said. 'I'm just a battledore in a game of office politics.'

Kerr looked at him with contempt. 'You mean shuttlecock, you prick. It's a bloody good job you didn't write anything.'

'What's the good news?' Sinclair asked.

'The editor is giving the team drinks at 6.30 to celebrate.'

'Do I have to go?' Sarah asked. She would have preferred an early night.

'He wants everyone there. Greaves says he might be able to get along for a bit,' Kerr told her. Sarah saw that his gaze lingered on her as he spoke.

He knows, she thought. He must have noticed something when we were at the London Apprentice. The realisation was disturbing.

When they gathered in Meadows's office, she kept to the other side of the room when Greaves entered, and began a long conversation with Trottwood, who revealed to her that he was a passionate gardener. Eventually Meadows rapped a glass on his desk to gain silence an then made a short speech of praise for a splendid job.

'And I would also like to extend our thanks to Superintendent Greaves and New Scotland Yard for their part in working with the *Gazette*.' He continued, 'From time to time relations are strained between the police and the press. This case only goes to show what can be achieved in a spirit of trust and co-operation.'

They all looked at Greaves, who was clearly expected to reply. 'I'm glad it worked out,' he said quietly, 'I hope we all learned something.'

There was a pause while they waited for him to say more but it was clear to Sarah that he wasn't going to make a speech. Conversation resumed and after a bit, Sarah saw that Fanny Hunter had entered the room. She came and stood next to her and raised her glass. 'Round one to you,' she said, without smiling.

'Are there going to be other rounds?' Sarah replied.

Fanny nodded. 'I haven't heard the fat lady sing yet,' she paused. 'You did use to be fat, didn't you?'

'Why don't we end this?' Sarah said.

Fanny shook her head and looked away. 'You're on my patch, sweetie. That little girl act may work with men, but not with me.'

Sarah moved away and found herself standing in a group close to Greaves. She smiled quickly, but did not look into his eyes.

'I must say I had my doubts when I heard that he was a motor-cyclist,' Meadows said. 'The voice on the tapes sounded very middle class to me, more of a Rover man.'

Greaves shook his head. 'Don't let appearances deceive you. He comes from a pretty comfortable background. His father is the creative director of an advertising agency.'

163

'What sort of people are the parents?' Meadows asked.

'The beads and Indian cotton variety, sixties flower-power genera-tion. His mother is successful too, she designs fabrics.'

'Do you think they're partly to blame?' Stiles asked.

Greaves looked at him without expression. 'I don't know,' he replied. 'They said they encouraged him to find his own freedom from the beginning, but he dropped out of their kind of life and even joined the army for a time.'

'The army?' Meadows repeated as he offered more champagne.

'Yes, I spoke to his commanding officer. It seems he deserted when they were on NATO exercises in Norway.'

'Ah,' Stiles interjected, 'Scandinavia. Could that be where he picked up that runic symbol thing?'

Meadows raised his eyebrows to Conway. 'The thought did occur to us,' he said lightly, 'and to Superintendent Greaves, I'm sure.'

Greaves studied his champagne glass. He had hardly touched the contents. 'It was certainly where he picked up his drug habit.'

'Does he have any other form?' George Conway asked.

Greaves nodded. 'Assault with a deadly weapon; he's a member of a soccer gang. He served six months a couple of years ago.'

'Anything else?'

'He was named in a rape case but the charges were dropped. We think the girl may have been paid off.'

'None of the victims was raped.'

'That's right, but we found a hammer and a Stanley knife clotted with dried blood in his room.'

'Did the blood group match any of the girls'?'

'Some were the same – there were traces of several types.'

There was silence and then George asked when the biker would be charged.

'It's hard to say. Maybe never.'

'Why?' George asked.

'Because he's in a padded cell now, wearing a straitjacket. The first psychiatric report says he could be unfit to stand trial.'

'Doctor Carlyle?' Meadows asked.

Greaves nodded. 'He's very excited by him. He told me there are weeks of work to be done. He even wants to write a book: My Search for Castor.'

'Do you think he's mad?' Stiles asked Greaves.

'I've no medical qualifications, but yes, I do. He's the ultimate kind of drop-out, the sort who's decided to drop out of the human race.'

'You say his parents are sixties people,' Meadows mused, then he turned to Conway. 'There could be a good series in that, George. "Children of the Lost Generation", that sort of thing.'

Sarah could see the endless newspaper process beginning again. The time of the murdered girls was passing; minds were seeking other stories.

Greaves put down his glass and turned to Meadows. 'Thank you for the drink, I must be going now.'

Meadows shook hands. 'Would you be so kind as to see Superintendent Greaves out?' he asked Sarah.

She noticed Kerr watching them from the other side of the room as they left.

They walked slowly down the wide staircase and Greaves paused on the landing. 'Is there something the matter?' he asked.

'No,' Sarah said quickly, then: 'Well . . . I think Peter Kerr has guessed there's something between us.'

'Does it matter?'

She thought for a moment, and then realised with a little shock of surprise that it didn't: she was a free agent, not a married woman. She smiled at him. 'No, it doesn't.'

'So how about Sunday?'

'I'm free.'

'I'll come and pick you up about ten.'

Sarah thought again and he watched her face. 'Would you mind if I drove to your house?' she asked.

He smiled gently. 'Your children?'

Sarah reached out for his hand. 'It's not that I'm ashamed of you or anything. . . .'

'But you don't want them to see you being taken off by a virtual stranger.'

'Something like that.'

He laughed. 'It's a good job I don't care what my neighbours think.' Then he leaned forward and the kiss was so gentle she hardly felt his lips touch her.

CHAPTER
SEVENTEEN

EARLY on Sunday, Sarah stood at the french windows and breathed the morning air. The sky was tinged with pink, and the weather forecast promised a day of tropical heat. The grass needs cutting, she thought, noticing how the garden was showing signs of neglect. The boys could manage the lawn, but she would have to get somebody more professional to work on the vegetable garden and the flowerbeds.

More staff. Only yesterday she had finally accepted Claire's advice and engaged a woman to come each day to do the housework. 'You're killing yourself,' Claire had said, 'Besides, you'll need someone in the house during the day.'

At other times such responsibilities would have worried her, but now she felt a sense of peace and contentment. She sipped coffee from her mug and watched a squirrel dart from the garden wall into the lower branches of the cherry tree. Suddenly she felt a cold touch on her bare leg, beneath the hem of her dressing gown. She looked down into the dark, liquid eyes of the puppy Claire had bought Emily for a birthday present the day before.

'Hello,' she said softly. The creature squirmed with pleasure. She knelt down and stroked his fat little body and the dog shivered joyfully. Sarah trusted labradors. Her father had always had them when she was a child, but Jack had not cared for dogs so they had never owned one. Another sign of his fading influence, she thought.

'Come on,' she whispered to the puppy, and she led him out on to the lawn, where his passage through the grass left trails in the dew. The squirrel froze at the intrusion, and then leaped from branch to branch until it reached the safety of a neighbouring garden.

Enjoying the feeling of wet grass on her bare feet, she walked slowly after the puppy until it began to explore the undergrowth in darker corners of the garden, where the wide branches of an ancient cedar tree cast shadows over a plantation of ferns.

Sarah turned away and stood in the sunshine to look down at the place where she had knelt and wept those weeks before. The cause of her grief lay before her. 'Glistening like coral,' she said softly, as she reached out to touch the Japonica bush.

It was the first plant she and Jack had ever bought together. The garden had been a wilderness when they moved into the house. The solicitor's widow who sold them the property had been too frail to care for it, but she had told them of its glories when her husband had been alive.

Jack had not shown much interest at first. He had always lived in flats as a boy, the only child of a couple who had devoted their lives to the family business of importing leather goods. His parents had travelled a good deal; there had been no time in their lives for pets or growing flowers. They had been killed in a car crash when he was in his early twenties and he had continued his life as a flat dweller until he married.

But Sarah's father had been a keen gardener and she had worked with him during her holidays. So, under her supervision, they had slowly reclaimed the flowerbeds, the lawns and a stagnant pond, which they restocked with fish. To his astonishment, Jack had discovered that he was good with his hands. At the far end of the garden was a conservatory, overgrown with brambles and rank weeds when they had moved in. Gradually Jack replaced the broken glass and rotting floorboards until it was fit to use again. During summer evenings they would sit out there with friends, listening to Jack's collection of dance band records.

Sarah thought of those times and it was as if she could still hear laughter and the lyrics of old love songs. Jack had been everything to her then. Now she was going to make love with another man. It was such a profound change, so different from anything she had expected from life that she still felt waves of concern. Physically, she knew that she wanted Colin Greaves, but there was still part of her mind that considered such an act to be unfaithful. Finally she grew exasperated with her indecision, and turned her mind to the events of yesterday. Emily had appreciated the presents given by the rest of the family, but when Claire had arrived with the puppy she had been overwhelmed, and was reluctant to leave when Ric came to take her to the theatre. His present turned out to be two-fold. The first, an obscure record of chamber music; the second – and more dramatic – a new voice. Overnight, nature had bestowed on him a constant and pleasing baritone, which caused Sarah and Claire to exchange glances.

As soon as Emily left the boys descended on the puppy and spent the rest of the evening crawling behind curtains and sofas in an endless game of pursuit. The puppy eventually tired of the game and found refuge between Claire and Sarah, where it passed into a deep sleep. The boys withdrew to their bedroom and the two women relaxed in the peace that ensued.

Claire fetched them glasses of wine and when she passed Sarah her drink, clinked her own glass against it.

'Relax, honey, even if they wanted to, they don't have the opportunity.'

'How do you know what I'm thinking about?' Sarah asked.

Claire smiled, 'Because a big light bulb is hanging over your head with the name "Emily" written on it.'

Sarah sighed. 'Sometimes I wish we could manage without sex.'

'Well, we can't!' Claire replied. 'The goddamn snake's been around since Adam and Eve.'

She held out a restraining hand and gestured towards the television set. ' This is the movie we want to watch.'

The puppy blinked awake momentarily, then buried his head in Sarah's lap.

She watched him now, as he emerged from the flowerbeds and nosed towards the Japonica. Sarah looked down at the delicate flowers on the bush once more. All was tranquil.

'A new life, puppy, like you,' she said, but the dog ignored her. She heard a soft sound, and turned to see that Emily had joined her. There was concern on her daughter's face, and Sarah realised she was standing where Emily had found her that time before.

Sarah put her arm about her and gestured towards the puppy: 'He likes the garden.'

They stood in silence for a while and then Emily said, 'Was dad the only man you ever loved?'

'Yes,' she replied without hesitation.

'Didn't you even fancy anybody else?'

Sarah smiled. 'Oh yes, I had a big crush on another man when I first met your father. We were going to be engaged.'

'Who was that?'

Sarah indicated that they should walk. They moved to beneath the cedar tree and sat down on a bench.

'His name was Frank Ashby,' Sarah said. 'He was a commodity dealer in the City.'

'What happened to him?'

Sarah looked down at her bare feet before she answered, 'The last I heard, he owned a television station in Australia.'

'So he became rich?'

'That's right.'

'Was he upset?'

Sarah thought again. 'I think he was more annoyed than upset. He kept saying, "Look what I can give you!"'

'I bet dad was better looking.'

Sarah laughed and shook her head. 'Frank was very handsome.'

'What was it, then? Why did you choose dad?'

Sarah reached down and scratched the puppy, who continued to circle their feet. 'I suppose it was because your father liked women,' she replied eventually.

The answer puzzled Emily. 'Didn't Frank Ashby like women?'

Sarah looked at her daughter. Her long hair was coiled on top of her head and she wore no make-up. This morning she looked very young again.

'He liked women in one sense, but it didn't suit me.' She could tell from Emily's expression that her words had been too enigmatic. 'Some men want women,' she continued, 'but they don't really like them. They want to make love, but sometimes they don't know how to be friends.'

'Dad wasn't like that?'

'No, he wasn't, he taught me all sorts of things, but mostly how to have fun.'

'I hope it happens to me. I think I love Ric, but I worry sometimes.'

'It will,' Sarah said, silently praying that she would be right.

They walked back to the house and found the kitchen filled with blue smoke from the boys' efforts to make breakfast. Sarah turned on the extractor fan and then sat down, as instructed by Paul.

'Sorry about the black bits in the egg,' Martin said when he ladled the last item on to her plate. Sarah thanked him and began to crunch her way through the food with simulated relish. When Claire arrived she took the opportunity to slide the remains of her food into the rubbish bin, but Martin saw what she was doing.

'Why don't you give what you don't want to the dog?' he said. Sarah shook her head. 'It'll be a long time before he's ready for fry-ups.'

'OK, you guys, let's get this show moving,' Claire said in her sergeant's voice. 'There's a two hour drive ahead, so visit the can now. I want to hit the motorway and go non-stop until we get to the air base.'

'I'll just call Ric,' Emily said. They were to be separated for a few days while he visited relations.

'Make it snappy!' Claire barked. 'Hello, I love you. Goodbye should do it!'

Sarah noticed that Claire's harrying commands really worked. It must be the American accent, she told herself. When she tried something similar it sounded like nagging and only produced a sullen, lethargic response.

'You two,' Claire snarled at the boys, 'what's the drill with the dog?'

'We keep him on the plastic cover at all times, in case he's sick or he disgraces himself.'

'You've got it, Mister. One drop of pee or poop on my upholstery and the pooch walks home – and you two with him.'

'May we take him with us to Clifton's house later?' Paul asked. The boys were to spend the night at a friend's when they returned from the softball match.

'Negative!' Claire snapped. 'The pooch comes back here. Emily and I want a display of dog devotion this evening. There's nothing like a bit of puppy fawning when you've been breaking ass all day.' She slapped her hands together. 'Now let's move it, team. In five minutes I want to be two miles from here, and halfway through the first verse of "On Top of Old Smoky".'

Sarah waved them off, cleaned the kitchen then she had a bath. She thought about what to wear, and settled for jeans, a blue blazer and sports shoes. No one could accuse her of being a vamp, she thought, when she inspected the result. Then she took two packages from the back of her wardrobe. They contained new underwear and a silk nightdress, which she carefully placed in her canvas bag.

171

CHAPTER
EIGHTEEN

THE roads were quiet but Sarah drove slowly to Notting Hill, always giving way to other cars and keeping within the speed limit. A battered white Cortina hooted her angrily at a roundabout and she caught a glimpse of a contorted face mouthing obscenities as the driver accelerated past her in a cloud of exhaust fumes.

When she arrived at the house, Greaves opened the door before she had walked the length of the path. He looked different without a collar and tie: younger. The roll-neck sweater and dark sports jacket suited him. He wore clothes well, she thought, slim people usually do. They smiled shyly at one another and he leaned forward to kiss her on the cheek. She could smell shaving soap and the peppermint from his toothpaste.

'You changed your scent,' he said as they stood looking at each other.

'Yes,' she replied, and raised a hand to her throat.

'It suits you, what's it called?'

'Paloma.'

'Made by Picasso's daughter.'

'That's right!' she said.

He noticed the surprise in her voice and smiled. 'I read newspapers. Insomniacs must have a hobby.'

'I read them as well.'

He took her arm and they walked along the street. 'No, I mean every word, even the small ads. Most people don't know the price of a loaf of bread these days – I can tell you the value of a two-year-old reconditioned washing machine, or a time-share flat in Majorca.'

'I must get you to do my shopping,' she said. She looked about her. 'Where are we going?'

'Not far, the garage is just behind these houses.'

He opened the doors and she saw a shape shrouded with dust covers. He pulled them back to reveal a beautiful old car that looked as if it had just come from the showroom. Deep blue paintwork and chrome glittered in a shaft of sunlight.

'It's a Riley,' she said.

'That's right. This is my other hobby.'

Sarah slid into the soft seat and inhaled the comforting scent of leather, wood and petrol.

'It's lovely,' she said. 'Do you come down here and polish it at night?'

'I take it for drives sometimes,' he replied, as they turned into Holland Park Avenue.

'Where do you go?'

'Usually somewhere along the Thames valley. I like the river at night.'

'So there you are, hurtling along the motorways after midnight.'

He smiled at her. 'No, I go by the old roads. We know our proper place.'

Sarah reached out and touched the dashboard. 'My dad had one of these, it smelt just like this. Cars aren't like cars any more.'

On the M40 Sarah noticed how he drove on a fast road. She had been a nervous passenger since an accident when she was young, but Greaves did not cause her any worry. He drove fast but without bravado; there was no attempt to impress. The regular rhythm of the engine and the warmth of the car made her feel drowsy. She had slept fitfully the night before. Now the comfort of the seat overcame her, and she fell asleep.

She came to with a start, unaware for a moment where she was.

'Woodstock,' Greaves said. 'Not far now.'

Soon they left the arterial road and travelled down narrow lanes lined with hedgerows, until a final turn took them down a short path beside a little river that fed into a reed-fringed lake. Greaves drove through an open gate and on to a gravel drive that was shadowed by outbuildings. A lawn rose steeply to a fine Cotswoldstone house set back against a hill. Vines grew about the mullioned windows.

He searched above the door lintel and withdrew a large key while Sarah looked at the landscaped gardens about her.

'I thought you said this was a cottage,' she said. Greaves unlocked the heavy oak door. 'My sister calls it a cottage,' he answered easily. 'I suppose it is, compared to her house in London. That has a ballroom.'

'What does her husband do?' Sarah asked as he led her into a stone-flagged kitchen.

'Guy runs the family business.'

'Your family business?'

Greaves nodded.

'You're rich, aren't you?' she said, realising her words sounded like an accusation.

'Yes.'

'I thought your father was a civil servant?'

'He was. My great-grandfather made all the money.' Greaves turned away and opened the refrigerator. 'Would you care for a drink?'

He produced two beers. While he was pouring them, Sarah looked about her. Suddenly she saw a movement in the shadows and two Siamese cats leaped on to the long kitchen table, making a peculiar mewling cry.

'Hello,' she said. 'Who looks after you?'

'My sister is here most of the time,' Greaves explained, 'and Jack, their handyman, comes every day when no one is here.'

He put down his beer and circled her with his arms. 'Are you glad you came?' he asked. She nodded. As he was about to kiss her the bleeper attached to his belt began to sound. He activated the message panel and then picked up a telephone extension, but the line was dead. He groaned with sudden frustration. 'My sister is a sweet person but at times infuriating,' he said, as he replaced the receiver.

'What's the matter?'

'She keeps forgetting to pay the telephone bill. They've cut her off again.' He sighed. 'I'd better go to the pub. I won't be long.' He looked at his watch. 'Just make yourself at home. I'll be about fifteen minutes.'

Listening to the car driving away, Sarah unzipped her canvas bag to look at her nightdress again. It was beautiful, she reassured herself. As she was about to replace it she noticed some sheets of white paper in the depths of the holdall. Pulling them out, she saw they were the photocopies of the cuttings on the Baltic-Marine case. The last two she had not read fluttered from her hand and as she bent down to retrieve them she noticed the headline: TRAGIC SUICIDE OF TEMPLE'S DAUGHTER 16. The story was short. It reported that the day after Temple's sentence his daughter, Gillian, killed herself. It was her sixteenth birthday.

Sarah had an ominous feeling of foreboding. Wanting something to do, she began to search the kitchen for utensils to make a pot of tea.

Greaves took longer than fifteen minutes. When he returned his forehead was creased into a frown. He sat down next to her and accepted a mug of tea.

'He's escaped,' he said bleakly.

Sarah felt suddenly cold, as if his words had chilled the air around them. 'How?' she asked softly.

Greaves shook his head. 'What a bloody cock-up! They'd transferred him to a psychiatric ward. They'd taken the straitjacket off and he managed to get hold of a syringe. He filled it with his own blood and when the nurse returned he held it against the man's throat. . . .'

Sarah guessed what he was about to add, 'He's HIV positive, isn't he?'

Greaves nodded. 'The drug taking.'

He drank some tea. 'There's something else. It turns out those people I saw aren't his parents at all. He went to live with them when he came back to England from Scandinavia.'

'Why did they lie?'

He shook his head wearily. 'God knows. They use a lot of drugs, it makes a strange fraternity. Addicts will tell you anything, but now we don't even know his real identity.'

'Is there any connection between them and the Lindsay family?'

'The man who claimed to be his father was a friend of Lindsay. We discovered they were both cocaine addicts and did a bit of dealing on the side. We think Castor ran drugs about town for them. That's why Lindsay let him into the house. The neighbours had seen him call before.'

'Will you catch him again?'

He rubbed his face with his hands. 'Oh yes, but it's anyone's guess what he'll do in the mean time.'

'Do you have to go back?'

He shook his head again. 'No, they can manage this part without me.'

Sarah sat down at the table again and remembered the cuttings. 'By the way,' she said, 'I think you should look at this.' She handed them to him, showing him the picture with the symbol first. He studied them for some time and as he read he began to tap the table. Finally he looked up. 'We must find out how this girl killed herself.'

This time Sarah accompanied him to the public house in the village. It was a curious place, pleasant enough from the outside, but so refurbished that the interior appeared to be made entirely of plastic. The friction of Sarah's shoes on the nylon carpet caused a charge of static electricity to build as they walked to the bar and a little blue flame darted between them when she brushed against Greaves's hand.

He paid with a ten-pound note and asked for the change in coins, then they took their drinks to the public telephone in the cramped little lobby. Greaves began a long series of calls, trying to track down the policeman who had worked on the case.

While he continued, a blonde woman came from the bar and sighed audibly when she saw that the telephone was engaged. Sarah turned and gazed at her so hard she retreated into the bar again. Eventually Greaves found a contact who had some memory of the events. After a few minutes' conversation he hung up.

'Clive Tremaine, one of the commanders at the Yard, was in charge of the case, but he's on his way back from some bloody conference in California and won't get into Heathrow until the morning,' he said, and then he shrugged. 'We might as well have another drink and then go back to the cottage. There's nothing more we can do tonight.'

The wind had changed direction and the sultry heat of the morning had given way to a cool breeze coming from the north.

'Smells like rain,' Greaves said as they walked to the car.

By the time they reached the cottage, the wind had grown stronger and was whipping the tops of the willow trees that stood on the far bank of the lake.

'I'm a poor host,' he said when they entered the house. 'I haven't offered you lunch yet.'

They found some cold chicken in the refrigerator and sat at a long table in the stone-flagged kitchen to eat. 'I thought we could go out for a meal this evening,' Greaves said. 'There's a decent restaurant about twenty minutes away.' He thought for a minute. 'At least that's what my sister always says; actually it's nearer forty-five – if you drive like a normal human being.'

The journey to the pub had some how altered the romantic feelings they had both experienced when they had first entered the house, but Greaves' preoccupation did not bother Sarah.

She looked around her at the lavishly appointed kitchen. She had already noticed that the refrigerator and deep-freeze were stuffed with food.

'I could easily cook something,' she suggested.

'What do you have in mind?'

Sarah remembered that he had been to an English boarding school: 'Potted shrimps, steak and kidney pie, a sherry trifle and Stilton – if you can manage it.'

'You can do all that?'

She nodded, 'Just watch me.'

While Sarah set about her preparations, Greaves went down to the cellar and returned some time later with three dusty bottles. He opened the first two and left them to breathe and then carefully decanted the port.

'That'll teach them not to pay the bloody telephone bill!' he said with satisfaction. 'Guy behaves like Ebenezer Scrooge with that cellar. You have to climb over crates of Spanish rubbish to get to this stuff.'

While she made pastry, Sarah gave him other tasks to perform and as they became preoccupied with the pleasant, mundane work she slowly realised a new sense of intimacy between them. It was different from the time they'd spent at the zoo. Then their conversation had been hedged with reserve: each had wanted to learn more about the other, but, anxious to preserve the fragile attraction, their conversation had been as brittle as glass. This was more like two friends secure in their need not to impress each other.

'That should do it,' she said finally, when she had set the saucepan of steak and kidney on the stove. 'We've got a couple of hours before the pie goes in the oven.'

Greaves looked out of the kitchen window. The wind was still high and the sky thick with dark clouds but the rain had held off. 'We could go for a walk?' He found coats and a row of Wellington boots in the washroom and they set off, skirting the lake and stopping to watch a pair of swans that glided about a small island in the centre of the wind-ruffled waters.

Sarah noticed a jetty where a small boat was moored. 'If the weather had been better I would have taken you for a row,' he said.

'Can you swim in the lake?' Sarah asked.

'Oh, yes, the water's quite clean. It's fed by the stream. Mind you, there are pike.'

'The boys would love it here,' Sarah said as they entered a coppice, thick with ash, hawthorn and oak.

'We could bring them next time,' Greaves said easily. Sarah felt a happy moment of reassurance at the thought. For all her enjoyment of the day, she still harboured a lingering guilt that she had somehow abandoned her children to go off and satisfy her own pleasures. As if he guessed her thoughts, he added, 'Emily might like it too, she could bring her boyfriend.'

They had left the little wood, and now Greaves led her to the foot of the steep hill behind the house. At the summit they stopped to look across a patchwork of fields and hedgerows, towards a line of trees that fringed the rooftops of a village.

'Once round the steeple,' he said, pointing to the distant spire, 'and then home for tea.'

The wind dropped, and when the rain began it fell like a soft mist, seeping into their surroundings and fading the view before them into a soft obscurity. Eventually, they reached the grey stone church. The only sound was the melancholy cry of rooks in the elms about them. Sarah shivered for a moment and Greaves put his arm about her shoulder. 'Cold?' he asked.

'A bit,' she answered, but it was other thoughts that had caused her to shiver.

They walked back along a lane that was sunk between banks of high hedges and turned on to a bridle path that led to the cottage. When they entered, the kitchen was filled with the scent of steak and kidney.

'I'm going to make a fire in the living room,' he said, and when she brought him the large whiskey he had asked for, kindling flames already crackled beneath the logs.

Sarah returned to the kitchen to make the final preparations for the meal. Later, when she got back to the living room, Greaves was asleep before the fire, half lying in the depths of a deep sofa, his feet stretched out on a footstool, the whiskey untouched beside him. She searched among the books on the shelves each side of the fireplace until she found a beautifully bound copy of *Persuasion*

179

then settled down in an armchair with a feeling of perfect contentment.

Greaves slept for nearly three hours. Twice Sarah got up from her chair when he uttered clear, disjointed phrases. The second time she found a patchwork quilt in one of the bedrooms and covered his restless form. The food was almost ready when he finally woke up. He was filled with apologies, but Sarah reassured him, holding up the book she had been reading.

The meal was a success. Of course the food did not surprise her, but Greaves's obvious enjoyment and the selection from his brother-in-law's cellar exceeded her expectations. Sarah enjoyed wine, but she knew very little about it. Even so, she could tell this was something special.

'What is it?' she asked, holding up the glass.

'Château Latour,' he replied, 'a much prized vintage and a proper accompaniment to this wonderful pie.' He paused and said, 'You know, I used to dream of food like this once upon a time.'

They talked about their schooldays. Sarah learned that he had played the drums in the orchestra, excelled at woodwork, and loved cricket, a game that had always represented terminal boredom to her. Sarah's favoured sports had been quick and nervous in their performance.

'How could you bear to lounge around for an entire day?' she mocked. 'No other game in the world has intervals for two meal breaks.'

'It livens up when you've got someone bouncing a ball towards you at ninety miles an hour,' he said drily.

'Who is your favourite drummer?' she asked, deciding it would be wiser to change the subject.

'Gene Krupa,' he answered without hesitation.

'I wonder if I've heard him?' she replied.

'He played with Benny Goodman,' Greaves said, 'you probably have.' He held up the decanter: 'More port?'

'Yes,' she said, 'when I've cleared away.'

She loaded the dishwasher and returned to the living room. Greaves had drawn the curtains and was just putting a record on the turntable. The room was warm and scented with woodsmoke.

'This is the Goodman orchestra,' he said, and the room filled with soft dance music. 'Later on there's a drum break by Gene Krupa.'

Sarah sat down on the sofa, remembering that they had this number at home, among Jack's collection of old dance band records, but she didn't say anything.

For more than an hour they listened to music, and the fire turned to embers in the hearth. Greaves stirred the remains before placing more wood on to the sparkling coals, then he turned and leaned down to kiss her.

At first their embrace was gentle, but gradually Sarah felt a growing urgency, which he responded to with equal hunger. They clasped one another in the depths of the wide sofa, and feeling his hand upon her breast she remembered the unwelcome attentions of Patrick Stone. Pulling away, she began to remove her clothes, but when she was naked, sudden shyness overcame her and she sat with her eyes cast down at the hands she'd clasped together in her lap. Greaves undressed more slowly and then, kneeling beside her, gently ran his hand across her shoulder. She felt as taut as a bowstring and shuddered slightly at his touch. Reaching out, he cupped his hand under her chin and she raised her head to look at him. When he spoke his voice was caught with emotion.

'I didn't know you would be so lovely.'

Sarah looked down at herself, and thought her slim body looked almost youthful in the soft glow of firelight.

'I'm not a girl any more,' she said softly, 'my hair is going grey now.'

He did not answer, but instead kissed the top of her head, then each of her eyelids. Taking her shoulders he gently laid her back and stretched out beside her. His touch was firm and sure and the feel of his hands on her body caused tiny shocks as he brushed over her belly and slid his fingers in her pubic hair. Already wet with anticipation, she reached out and took hold of his erection. With her body arched against his, she guided him into her. He made three deep thrusts and then, with a convulsive shudder, lost control, and she felt him flooding into her.

'I'm sorry,' he said softly, and raised himself so he could look down on her. 'It's been a long time.'

They lay wrapped in each other's arms for a while, then Sarah reached out to touch his face, pulled his head down, and whispered in a low voice what she wanted him to do. The words triggered a current of energy between them and she felt the rushing blood engorge him once more.

This time he began more slowly, building an insistent rhythm that gradually increased in tempo. Sarah moved her pelvis in the same time until his wiry frame pounded against her with maximum force, and she responded with equal ferocity, matching his efforts and power. She lost all awareness of the external world about her.

Thoughts, emotions and physical being all blended into one driving, primeval need, a concentration so elemental, they both exerted strengths that bruised their flesh. Release came in a series of volcanic shocks that drained the energy from their bodies and left them clinging to each other, exhausted.

When Sarah gradually regained possession of herself, she was aware that she had undergone a change. The guilt she had felt since the night of their first meeting had now passed away. It was as if she were complete again, the painful wounds she had inflicted on herself suddenly allowed to heal.

When they had rested for some time they began again. They never got to the bedroom; like famished waifs presented with a banquet, they feasted upon one another in the deep splendour of the sofa throughout the night, exploring each other's bodies with carnal desire and careful tenderness. When at last they slept, strained and battered bodies entwined, the hunger both of them had endured for so long was finally ended.

The crash of the iron door knocker woke them at seven o'clock, and they sat up like guilty children in the cold dawn light. Greaves pulled on his clothes and went to answer, while Sarah, wrapped in the patchwork quilt, sat and listened.

A motorcycle policeman saluted Greaves when he opened the door. Sarah could hear their conversation quite clearly from the living room while she pulled on her jeans and shirt.

'Superintendent Greaves?'

'Yes.'

'Sorry to disturb you so early, sir. Did you know your telephone is out of order?'

'Is that what you came to tell me, constable?'

'No, sir, actually it's not you I'm after. Do you have a Mrs Keane staying with you?'

Sarah's heart began to race with fear. 'Oh God!' she thought, 'something has happened to the children!' she hurried to the door. The young policeman disguised his thoughts at the sight of her disarray, and looked at a space above her head when she spoke. 'I'm Mrs Keane, what is it?' she asked urgently.

'We got a message from a colleague of yours, madam. We don't usually do this, but seeing you were with the Superintendent. . . .'

'What is it?'

'Fanny Hunter says will you ring her at once, it's very important.'

'Fanny Hunter?'

'That's right.'

Greaves thanked him and watched his face for any sign of amusement, but the young man maintained his impassive expression until he turned away.

'What on earth can Fanny want?' Sarah mused when they returned to the living room, 'and how did she trace me here?'

'Probably through Peter Kerr, if your hunch that he knows about us is correct.'

Sarah nodded. 'I suppose I'd better get dressed properly,' she said.

'In a few minutes,' Greaves said, unbuttoning his shirt.

'Again?' Sarah said as he reached out to remove her clothes.

She winced as he entered her. He noticed and said, 'Am I hurting you?'

'No, it's all right,' she said quickly, 'I'm just a bit tender.'

'Shall I stop?'

'Don't you dare,' she replied, and circled his neck with her arms.

'Hello, sweetie,' Fanny Hunter said briskly. 'Sorry to drag you away from your policeman.'

Sarah had a sudden impulse to dash the telephone in her hand against the window of the booth she stood in.

'No you're not, Fanny,' Sarah answered.

'You're right,' she said flatly. 'This is about work. I'd call you if you were having an audience with the fucking Pope if it were necessary.'

Sarah resented her deliberate coarseness. 'I'm sure you would,' she said icily.

'Don't condescend to me, you snotty little cow!' she fired back. 'You work for me now. Edward Carter was sacked yesterday and I've taken over as assistant Editor in charge of features. Meadows has agreed that you'll join my team. So get yourself out of bed and in here, I'm holding a conference at 10.30.'

'Bad news?' Greaves asked, when she rejoined him in the car. She nodded. 'It seems I now work for Fanny Hunter.'

He could feel her dejection. They sat for a few moments, looking out at the single narrow street of the village that was wet from the seeping rain.

'You don't have to go back there if you don't want to,' Greaves said eventually.

She looked at him questioningly and then shook her head. 'I want to see it through,' she answered with sudden resolution.

He started the car. 'I must go to Heathrow to meet Clive Tremaine's flight.'

Sarah looked at her watch. It was still before eight. 'You can drop me there,' she answered, 'I'll get the train into town from the airport.'

With the exception of Cat Abbot, Fanny Hunter's outer office was crowded with people Sarah didn't know. Three young men and two women made spasmodic remarks but there was no attempt at conversation. She could feel the tension among them. At last the door was opened by Pauline Kaznovitch, who ushered them in. A semicircle of chairs had been arranged before Fanny's desk. Pauline gestured for them to sit while Fanny continued to make notes on a pad without looking up. When she did, there was no preliminary greeting. She announced that the editor had agreed to strengthen her team with the inclusion of Abbot and Sarah, and then gave each of them an assignment in turn. The only two not included on the job list were Abbot and Sarah.

'That's it,' she said, looking up. 'I'd like Sarah Keane to stay, and if you wouldn't mind waiting outside for a few minutes, Cat.'

When the others had filed out, Fanny sat in silence, studying her. 'I don't like trousers in the office,' she said.

'I wasn't expecting to come in today,' Sarah replied.

'It's best to be prepared for the unexpected,' Fanny continued. 'Take Cat Abbot, for instance, he's got all his old notebooks. He showed me yesterday. One of them covers the time of the Oaklands job we worked on, a full record of the interview we had with the widow.' She leaned back in her chair. 'What have you got? The word of some batty old woman.'

She looked down at her list again. 'I want you to write a series called "The Housewife's Diet" – tell the readers how to get the fat off with old-fashioned work in the home.'

'I'm not very good at that sort of thing,' Sarah said.

Fanny smiled. 'That's not what I heard; still, if you can't, you won't get past the trial period, will you?'

'I was hired as a reporter,' Sarah said, keeping her voice even, despite Fanny's efforts to provoke her. 'Isn't it against the union house agreement to change my role without consultation?'

'What union?' Fanny said contemptuously. 'This isn't the seventies. Don't you know what's happened in Fleet Street?'

'Yes, Fanny, sadly, I do. Is that all?'

'Copy by Friday,' Fanny ordered, returning her gaze to the list of assignments.

Cat Abbot was leaning against a wall in the outer office. He began to sing as she crossed the room: 'You can't trust a Special like an old-time copper when you can't find your way home. . . .'

Sarah wanted to leave the building now but she had agreed to wait for a call from Colin Greaves. She sat alone in the operations room, feeling low, and called Claire. 'How did it all go?' she asked.

'Fine,' Sarah replied, 'but I've got trouble with Fanny.'

'I heard the rumours.'

'How's Emily?' Sarah said quickly.

'She's got orchestra practice tonight, she said will you pick her up at eight o'clock from school?'

'Thanks, Claire. I don't feel like talking now. I'll tell you everything later.'

She hung up and after a few minutes the telephone rang. She expected it to be Greaves, but instead it was Osbert Hannay. 'Sarah?' he said, 'I'm downstairs in the entrance hall. I wonder if you could spare me a few minutes?'

When she joined him, he led her away from the commissionaires, and said, 'Is there somewhere we could talk in private?'

Sarah thought for a moment. 'There's a sandwich bar along the road.'

A few minutes later they were seated with cups of coffee, and Hannay looked out of the window at the traffic, then turned to her. 'This is very difficult,' he began, 'but I feel I must warn you that Fanny harbours deep feelings of resentment towards you.'

Sarah smiled wryly. 'I know that.'

He drank a little of his coffee and then pushed the cup aside. 'I don't think you appreciate how strong those feelings are . . .' he held his fingertips to his forehead for a moment. 'When I first married her, she was – another type of person; quieter.'

He looked down at the table and Sarah sensed how hard it was for him to speak.

'How did you meet?' she asked.

'I taught her at Cambridge, medieval German history,' he shrugged, 'a long way from Fleet Street. We met again when my first wife died. At first she seemed happy, then, quite suddenly, she changed. I remember the time clearly, she had just returned from a visit to America. It was as if she deliberately set out to make herself more vulgar.'

He glanced away again and Sarah could see the pain in his eyes. Then he continued. 'She'd changed in other ways as well. Previously, when she couldn't get her own way she would become sullen. After America she would erupt in violent rages. When it happens she loses all self-control.'

'Is there nothing you can do?' Sarah asked.

Hannay shrugged. 'In the Middle Ages I would have called for an exorcist. I tried to get her to see a psychiatrist – pleaded with her – but there was no way I could compel her to go, and now she goes missing at erratic times and lies to me about who she's been with.'

'It sounds as if she's having an affair.'

'She's always told me of anyone in the past.' He reached his coffee again but changed his mind and pushed the cup even further away.

'There's something else,' he said finally. 'Recently she has begun to talk about your family incessantly.' He paused again. 'I understood that your husband and she were friends at one time.'

'I know about it.'

Hannay laced his hands together so tightly the knuckles showed white. 'She wasn't particularly coherent, but I do remember her saying that your children should really be hers. I only tell you this because I worry about her influence over others. Obsession and power are a destructive combination in people.' He looked out of the window again and sighed. 'This has been a painful business, but I felt it was my duty to tell you.'

'Thank you,' Sarah replied. 'I realise how difficult it must have been.'

They left the sandwich bar and Hannay caught a taxi. Sarah began to return to the office and saw Greaves standing on the pavement before the *Gazette* building.

'I've traced the man who worked on the Temple girl's suicide. An ex-chief superintendent called Arthur Capstock. I need to make a call,' he said. Sarah took him to the public telephone in the entrance hall and listened when he dialled the number.

'Mr Capstock? We haven't actually met, but we have friends in common. My name is Colin Greaves. Yes, that's right. I wonder if I might come and see you today with a friend. It concerns a case you worked on some years ago. . . . Fine, I'll see you quite soon.'

'Where to?' Sarah asked.

'Pinner,' Greaves replied triumphantly.

CHAPTER
NINETEEN

T HE journey took longer than expected; chains of plastic cones funnelled them into stretches of single-line traffic on the Western Avenue. When they finally reached Pinner, Sarah guided them to the address with the street map.

It was a quiet road of semi-detached houses. They rang the bell of Number 12 and a middle-aged woman answered the door. The smell of cooking drifted to Sarah.

'Good-day,' Greaves said, 'We've come to see Mr Capstock. He is expecting us.'

'Dad?' the woman said, 'Oh yes, he's in the back garden. Would you like to come through.'

She led them past an open door, where a nondescript man sat before a television set. Then into a kitchen where a youth in a brightly coloured track suit was peering into a refrigerator. Neither paid them any attention. 'Don't you eat anything, Roger!' the woman said. 'You'll spoil your dinner.' She turned to them. 'Out there,' she said, pointing to the door. 'He's down the end somewhere.'

'Thank you, we'll find him.' Greaves spoke with such gratitude that the woman smiled as if he had paid her a compliment.

The long, narrow garden of the modest house was extraordinary. A winding path led them through different sections, each divided from the other by a variety of shrubs and hedges. Carefully tended lawns and flowerbeds unfolded before them, until they arrived at a greenhouse concealed by a high, dense hedge. Inside they could see a heavy-set man, who wore half-spectacles and a baggy red cardigan. He looked up with sharp blue eyes when Greaves rapped on the glass door. Arthur Capstock's hair was iron grey, and his complexion had a dark flushed tone that often signals high blood pressure. His voice was mild when he greeted them. There was the slightest trace of a country accent, but Sarah did not recognise the region.

'Sit down,' he invited them after the introductions, indicating two old kitchen chairs. 'I'll be finished in just a moment.'

He placed more flags in a tray of seedlings and then turned to them with a smile. Sarah liked the greenhouse. The warm air smelt of pipe tobacco and the sharp acid scent of tomatoes.

Capstock sat down and took a pipe with a charred bowl from the pocket of his cardigan.

'You have a wonderful garden,' Sarah said.

He looked at her with shrewd eyes while he packed the bowl of the pipe with a stubby finger. 'You like gardening, Mrs Keane?'

'Very much.'

'Which of my plants do you favour?'

She thought he might be testing her to see if her comments were genuine, but Sarah was up to the challenge. She gave her assessment of his achievements with an expertise that confounded Greaves.

'Blue monks,' Capstock chuckled. 'I haven't heard them called that since I was a boy.'

'Where was that?' she asked.

The old man nodded over his shoulder. 'Just past Uxbridge.' He lit his pipe and pointed it at Sarah. 'I'm sorry you couldn't have met my wife, Mary, she loved to work in the garden. She had greener fingers than me. I swear we used to sow alternate rows and hers would always be the stronger plants. Funny that people don't believe in magic any more.'

He put another match to his pipe and more fragrant smoke filled the air about them.

'You live with your daughter's family now?' Sarah asked.

'They live with me,' he answered easily.

'Aren't they interested in gardening?'

He smiled and gestured towards the house. 'When they moved in, I said to Reg, "You look after the front and I'll take care of this end." You saw what he did. Put bloody pavement down so that he wouldn't have to mow the grass.' He pulled twice more on his pipe and then pointed the stem towards Sarah. 'You're not a police-woman, but you're used to asking questions. What are you, a social worker or a reporter?'

Sarah laughed. 'A reporter, Mr Capstock.'

He looked towards Greaves and raised his eyebrows.

Greaves answered the unstated question. 'She's doing this with my permission. Her paper is co-operating with us.'

Capstock nodded. 'Tell me about it.'

But before Greaves could speak, the youth in the track suit appeared in the doorway. 'Mum says will you come for your dinner now, and are your friends staying, because there's plenty for everyone?'

Capstock stood up. 'Tell your mother they'll be staying, and to lay the table in the dining room. We want to have a private conver-sation.'

'We don't want to impose on you,' Greaves said.

He shook his head and smiled. 'Reg isn't much of a gardener, but my daughter is a good cook, better than her mother was.'

Capstock led them back to the house, pausing to discuss various plants and flowers. By the time they had reached the dining room preparations had been made and the table was set as he had instructed. It was clear that the room was not used very often. There were few ornaments on the sideboard and Sarah could smell that air-freshener had just been used. She sat down facing the pure-white net curtains and noticed the car parked on the paved forecourt. It was indeed a contrast to the back garden.

While they ate, Greaves outlined the case with such clarity there was no need for Capstock to ask any questions. After the meal the old man reached for his pipe again. He made sure it was well lit and began to speak with equal precision.

'I was called to Temple's house at approximately five o'clock in the afternoon. His sister was waiting. She led me through the prem-ises to a large room at the rear. Temple's daughter lay on a large, silk-covered sofa before the fireplace. She was naked, and lying on her side. She'd been dead for some time.'

He paused and put another match to the charred bowl of his pipe.

'How had she been killed?' Greaves asked quietly.

Capstock hesitated and glanced towards Sarah, then continued in a lower voice. 'She'd eviscerated herself with some sort of ceremonial knife, a little thing, sharp as a cut-throat razor. It had fallen from her hand on to the carpet.' He looked up at the ceiling while he continued. 'The cut ran from vagina to breast bone. The contents of her stomach cavity had spilt on to the floor beside the sofa.'

Sarah could see that Greaves had clenched his fists as Capstock spoke; she could feel her own tension in the knot of muscle between her shoulder blades.

Capstock raked the bowl of his pipe in the silence that followed. The only sound was the rasp of his penknife on the blackened wood.

'You say there was a sister,' Greaves said.

Capstock looked up, his blue eyes half-hooded. 'That's right, Sylvia Temple, a curious woman.'

'In which way do you mean?' Sarah asked.

Capstock glanced towards Greaves and then turned to Sarah.

'Policemen aren't allowed to include feelings in evidence – just those things that can be proved, material proof that can be produced in court. Feelings don't come into it.'

'I understand that,' Sarah said.

Capstock sat back in his chair. 'People often behave strangely when they talk to a policeman; even the innocent can act as if they're guilty of something.' He paused, then went on, 'You know in forty years, I met perhaps half a dozen people I thought were completely good.' He stopped again and looked towards Greaves, who half nodded in confirmation. Then he turned to Sarah again. 'There's more of the bad ones.'

'Bad?' she said. 'You mean criminals?'

Capstock shook his head. 'Criminals are usually just stupid, a lot of them are too dim to do anything else. But now and again you meet someone who is bad, really bad. Once upon a time people would have called them evil, before they were taught to think no one is really to blame for their own actions.'

Sarah looked towards Greaves. 'Have you met anyone like that?'

He looked up. 'Oh yes.'

She turned back to Capstock. 'Are you saying that Temple's sister was evil?'

'I thought so. She had no more feeling for that child lying there than I would have for a weed.' He nodded, as if to himself. 'She said the right things, mind, but there was no real emotion. I got the idea she was more annoyed by the mess on the carpet.'

Greaves took out a notebook. 'What was the address?'

Capstock told him without hesitation.

'You have a good memory,' Sarah said.

The old man began to refill his pipe. 'I won't ever forget that house,' he said.

The door opened and Capstock's daughter entered the room. From somewhere up above, they could hear music playing. A steady discordant thump, but it was reassuring to Sarah, after the grimness of Capstock's story.

'All finished?' the daughter asked brightly. 'Can I clear away now?'

CHAPTER
TWENTY

I T started to rain again when they were in the Riley. The sky was filled with rolling grey clouds. Greaves turned on the heater but Sarah still felt a coldness within her, and as they drove on the storm thickened into a deeper gloom. They stopped briefly at a public callbox so that Sarah could ring Claire.

'I'm caught up in a story,' she explained. 'I'm not sure how late I'll be. Would you mind picking Emily up from orchestra practice?'

'That's fine,' Claire replied. 'Don't worry.'

The house was on a hill, facing tall trees that edged Richmond Park. Set back from the narrow road, behind tall iron railings, the ground floor was obscured from view by thick laurels, their fleshy leaves made slick by the falling rain. Greaves stopped the car opposite and looked up at the drab, brick exterior. There was an air of seediness about the building, as if it had seen better days.

'Flats,' he said. 'I wonder if she still lives here.'

They crossed the road and entered a gravel drive where four cars were parked. Sarah noticed that the ground-floor windows to the left of the porticoed doorway were blanked by heavy shutters. When they stood in the sheltered doorway, gusts of rain blew against them while Greaves examined the row of nameplates next to the bells. The last one said 'Temple'. He pushed it and they could hear distant ringing but no one came to answer. He tried the bell above and this time there was a response.

They could hear a dog barking and a few moments later a woman opened the door. Sarah could see part of a dark panelled hallway. The young woman who looked out seemed rather cross. She reached down with one hand to hold the collar of a growling terrier. 'Yes?' she said impatiently.

'We're sorry to trouble you,' Greaves said and he reached out to let the straining dog smell his scent.

'Be careful,' the woman warned, but the dog licked the hand he offered and the woman, seeing the reaction of the terrier, released a chain and opened the door wider.

'You shouldn't do that,' Greaves said quickly. 'Intruders will put things on their hands that dogs like.'

'Who are you?' the woman said, puzzled by Greaves's instruction. He produced his identification.

'Police,' she said, 'Well, at least you're not Jehovah's Witnesses!'

'We want to speak to Miss Temple,' Greaves said. 'Do you know where we might find her?'

Before the woman could answer another voice spoke from the dark interior. 'It's all right, Mrs Hooper.'

The woman pulled the dog away and another figure, who remained in the shadows, looked out at them.

At first glance Sarah was deceived by her appearance. A black, close-fitting dress showed a youthful figure and her shoulder-length hair was the colour of brass. She wore dark eyeshadow and bright lipstick, but then Sarah realised that the face watching was like a plaster cast, smoothed with heavy make-up.

'My name is Superintendent Greaves and this is Mrs Keane. May we speak to you?'

Sylvia Temple stepped back further. 'Come in,' she said, in a throaty, theatrical voice. She turned and led them across the hallway, her stiletto heels clicking on the marble floor. The shuttered room they entered was even darker than the hallway. Two dim lamps shed just enough light to reveal the vague outlines of furniture. There was a heavy scent of incense that could not quite disguise the muskiness of decay.

Sylvia Temple sat down on a sofa next to the fireplace. 'Come and sit next to me,' she instructed Greaves. Sarah was ignored.

While Greaves told Sylvia Temple the purpose of their visit, Sarah looked about the room. As her eyes became accustomed to the darkness, shapes began to take on form and detail: heavy pieces of rosewood furniture, carved with flowers and mythical beasts. Slowly she began to recognise objects from the photograph of Temple.

'You appear to be admiring my furniture, Mrs Keane,' Sylvia Temple said suddenly, interrupting Greaves.

'You have a wonderful collection,' Sarah answered.

'Thank you. It's been in my family for generations.'

When Greaves spoke again Sarah could tell he was selecting his words with care.

'We really would like to talk about your niece, Miss Temple, if the experience is not too painful for you.'

Sylvia Temple sighed and raised a hand that resembled a chicken claw to her cheek. 'The child was driven to her death.' She let the hand fall to her lap. 'My brother was quite innocent. . . .' She looked away into the dark recesses of the room as she spoke.

'He was a perfect gentleman. To accuse him of fraud was absurd. Those people would have got their money, every penny, if the newspapers hadn't begun their vendetta.' She gripped the arm of the sofa. 'My niece worshipped her father. When he was sentenced to prison it turned her mind; she killed herself in this room.'

Sarah began to feel the darkness of the surroundings pressing in on her and the stifling atmosphere caused a feeling of dizziness.

Sylvia Temple continued to extol the virtues of her brother until Greaves said, 'You talk about Sir Gavin in the past tense, Miss Temple?'

She stood up and rested a hand on the high mantelshelf. 'My brother is dead, didn't you know that? He died abroad, some years ago, broken by his persecutors.'

Sarah and Greaves exchanged glances in the gloom. 'Are there any other members of your family left alive?'

She shook her head. 'I am the last of the Temples.' She gestured about her in her theatrical manner. 'We once lived in a mansion, with a dozen servants, when I was a child. Now I have two rooms in this house.'

As if to signal the end of her performance, the doorbell sounded.

'Now, I must ask you to leave; another guest has arrived,' she announced grandly.

They followed her from the room. When she opened the door Sarah saw two men waiting in the shelter of the portico. One was young, powerful and dressed immaculately in a dark suit of some shiny material. He carried an umbrella to shelter his companion, who was very old and seemed as fragile as porcelain. A long coat hung from his emaciated frame and he carried an old-fashioned doctor's bag. Sylvia Temple did not introduce them. She ignored Sarah and after wishing Greaves goodbye, ushered the new callers into the house.

After hurrying back to the Riley through the pelting rain, they sat for a time thinking.

'There *must* be a connection between Castor and that woman – what the hell can it be?' Greaves said. He pointed to the car that was parked in front of the house. 'I assume that belongs to the doctor. I think we'll follow it and have a word.'

Twilight was fading into darkness when the two men left the house and made their way to their car. It was easy for Greaves to keep them in sight, for the young man drove slowly.

'It's almost as if they expect you to follow them,' Sarah said when the car ahead did not take the opportunity to cross a set of changing traffic lights.

'I think you're right,' Greaves replied, and he began to whistle a curious tune that sounded oriental to Sarah.

The car made its way to the West End and then along Shaftesbury Avenue, eventually turning into a side road near Wardour Street. Garish neon signs and bright restaurant windows reflected in the wet roadway that was piled each side with black plastic bags and boxes filled with rubbish. Like all Chinatowns, the street seemed to pulsate with life. Even in the heavy rain, figures hurried past or stood huddled in doorways.

The car they followed stopped in front of a restaurant window that was filled with the carcasses of wind-dried ducks and the young man helped his elderly companion from the passenger's seat. 'There's nowhere to stop here,' Greaves muttered, and, as if sensing his problem, the young man looked towards them and pointed to the doorway before he entered.

'An invitation,' Sarah said.

A few minutes later they were walking back through the crowded streets until they found the restaurant once again.

The staircase they climbed was uncarpeted and the walls crusted with grime and crumbling with age. On the first landing they saw into a smoke-filled room where men sat playing a board game. The

196

table was piled with banknotes and the men shouted excitedly at each other.

'I thought orientals were supposed to be inscrutable,' Sarah said, as they continued to climb.

Greaves laughed but did not answer.

They reached a door at the top of the stairs, which bore the nameplate: Doctor Civik. It was opened before Greaves could knock and the young man stood waiting for them.

'I would like to speak to Miss Temple's doctor. My name is Superintendent Greaves.'

'Doctor Civik has been expecting you,' the young man said softly, and he pushed the door open further.

The room was crowded with tall wooden cabinets, each labelled with a Latin name-tag so there was barely room for some chairs and a desk covered with papers, where the old man sat watching as they entered. The only light came from an Anglepoise lamp that shone on the desk. He gestured for them to sit down and the young man whispered so softly that Sarah did not hear the words. The old man replied just as softly and then looked up at Greaves, revealing large yellow teeth. 'My name is Doctor Civik, how may I be of service to the police?'

'I wish to know about Sylvia Temple's family.'

'What do you know already?'

Greaves shrugged. 'Very little. She lied to me.'

'How do you know?'

'Call it a policeman's intuition.'

The old man smiled again. 'Poor Sylvia.'

'Have you known her for long?'

'All her life. I delivered her.'

'So you knew the family. Will you tell me about them?'

Doctor Civik inhaled deeply on his cigarette before he spoke. 'Her grandfather came to my homeland, Estonia, before the Russian Revolution. He made a fortune in the import business. My mother worked as their housekeeper. He paid for me to go to medical school; eventually I became their personal doctor. They were a family of peculiar tastes – shall we say it suited them to have a member of the medical profession close to them. When the war began they returned to England. I came with them.' He smoked some more of the cigarette. 'They did not thrive in their own country, their fortune declined. Sylvia's grandfather and father died quickly, but there was enough money left to care for Sylvia and her brother. They did not go away to school as is customary. They could

197

not bear to be parted as they had formed a special relationship. It was a pattern that was to be repeated in the family.'

'But Sir Gavin married?'

'Yes,' Doctor Civik replied slowly, 'but Pamela did not wish to share their vices. It was not a union made in heaven.' He smiled. 'Such a pleasant phrase, don't you think?' He looked at the cigarette for a moment, then went on, 'His wife stayed with him until after the children were born, but she resented the closeness of Sylvia. Eventually she left him and the children and went abroad. Australia, the city of Melbourne, I think. I heard that she remarried, to a man called James Brinkley.'

'Children?' Greaves said quickly. 'I thought there was only the girl who committed suicide?'

Doctor Civik raised his eyebrows. 'Didn't you know there were twins? The girl had a brother.'

Sarah and Greaves exchanged glances. 'What happened to him?' Greaves asked.

Civik shrugged. 'I believe he went to live with his mother in Australia.'

'Sylvia Temple told us she was the last member of the family alive.'

Doctor Civik slowly stubbed out his cigarette. 'Sylvia is unwell, the truth is sometimes . . . difficult for her.'

'Thank you, Doctor, you've been a great help,' Greaves paused, 'and I must commend you on your loyalty to Miss Temple.' The old man nodded his head once more. 'Estonians are a loyal race, Superintendent.'

Greaves got up. Standing by the doorway, he turned again, and asked. 'Tell me, how often do you visit her?'

'Once a week.'

'Why?'

'She is a registered drug addict. I call to supply her prescribed dosage.'

'What drug?'

'Heroin,' he replied through the blue smoke that filled the room.

Greaves paused once more. 'Is the restaurant downstairs a good one?'

The old man smiled again, 'When circumstances caused me to first live in Soho it was a cosmopolitan area, but there were few Chinese. Now we older residents can do nothing about the invasion, except resist the cuisine.'

They walked down the staircase, past the room full of shouting men and stood for a moment in the cool air of the doorway. The rain still fell in bouncing patterns on the black plastic bags that almost covered the pavement. Greaves said, 'Let's go into the restaurant, I want to call Arthur Capstock.'

He spoke Chinese to the waiter who greeted them, and they were shown to a table. Greaves ordered a meal and went to a telephone at the little bar by the entrance. He was some time. When he returned the waiter was serving the food. Greaves watched him walk away and then said, 'Capstock has no recollection of a twin boy but he remembers Doctor Civik. He also said the local people in Richmond were unhappy with what used to go on in that house. There were rumours, but nothing that could be proved.'

'What sort of rumours?'

'Capstock says some sort of sex rituals involving children.'

'Does he think the girl was murdered, then?'

Greaves shook his head. 'He says he was certain it was suicide.'

Sarah did not have much appetite for the food. She thought for a moment. 'Do you think the motorcyclist could be the missing brother?' Greaves glanced around the restaurant before he answered.

'He must be about the right age, it would make sense. The father is exposed by the *Gazette* alone, his sister commits suicide because of the disgrace. That would appear to provide a motive.'

'But why would he kill the other girls? They have no connection with the paper. The only thing they have in common is their age. It still doesn't make sense.'

Greaves ate some more of the food before he answered, 'Sometimes things don't make complete sense – there are loose ends in any case.'

'What will you do now?'

'Get on to the police in Melbourne and see if they can trace the family. It should only take a day or so.'

He was about to order more beer when the bleeper at his waist sounded. Sarah looked at her watch: it was 9.30. Greaves returned to the telephone, made a call and then beckoned to Sarah. By the time she had reached him he had placed two ten-pound notes on the counter and spoken to the waiter. 'They've found him!' he said in a low voice.

'Where?'

They were already on the pavement when he answered, 'Greek Street. Come on, it'll be quicker to walk.'

Ignoring the rain, they hurried through the crowded streets while he spoke rapidly to her. 'Castor was in a club, two men from the Drug Squad were there, they recognised him.'

By now they were weaving their way through the traffic in Shaftesbury Avenue. When they crossed into Soho the streets were completely solid with stationary cars. They could hear the sound of angry horns from all around them.

The police lines had caused the chaos. Greaves waved Sarah through a checkpoint and they found Detective-Sergeant Holland outside the entrance to a club that was decorated with illuminated photographs of strippers. They joined him under the awning.

'Best stay under here, sir,' he said with a nod to Sarah.

'Are you sure he's still up there?' Greaves asked.

'Certain,' Holland replied. 'He's prising tiles off the roof and chucking them down on anything that moves.'

Greaves looked around the deserted street. 'Are any of our boys armed?'

'Yes,' Holland replied. 'We've got snipers on the roof opposite, he's an easy target.'

Greaves took hold of his arm. 'I don't want anyone picking him off. "AIDS victim shot dead by police" would *not* make a good headline.'

'He's still got the syringe of blood,' Holland told him. 'Surely that constitutes a deadly weapon? Two of the sniper positions can see him quite clearly.'

Greaves did not answer immediately.

'Have they got searchlights?' he asked.

'They don't need them, the rifles have night sights.'

'Get some mobile searchlights up there, as many as you can. But don't turn them on until I signal. Then hit him with them at exactly the same moment.'

'What's the signal?'

'Get me a handgun. I'll fire one shot in the air.'

'Why don't you make it his head?'

Greaves pushed him gently. 'Go and get me a gun, and get those bloody lights moving.'

As he spoke, two splintering crashes came from across the street as slates shattered the windows of parked cars. Sarah looked at Greaves, who smiled. 'Take care,' she said softly.

'I think you'd better move back,' he answered. 'Stand over there. Those policemen will cover you and you should be able to see everything.'

She watched him enter the building, then, worked her way to

where a group of policemen formed a protective shelter with their riot shields. Through the clear plastic held above her head, Sarah looked up at the rooftop and could make out a shadowy figure standing on a narrow parapet set against a mansard roof. As she watched, Greaves emerged on to the same ledge and began to work his way forward. The figure turned and crouched towards him, holding out his left hand. She had no doubt what he held. When the gap between them had closed to about five feet Greaves raised the revolver and fired into the night sky. Six mobile searchlights lanced through the darkness and illuminated the figure, who, blinded by the lights, nonetheless thrust out his arm further, as if threatening Greaves with a dagger. Now Sarah could see the syringe quite clearly as he lunged forward and brought it up in a stabbing motion. At the same time Greaves swung the revolver and struck the youth's wrist. The syringe flew from his hand and curved through the air to land in the street, where it rolled beneath a parked car. The two figures grappled with each other and Sarah could see Castor making snake like movements with his head as he attempted to bite Greaves. For a moment they teetered on the edge of the parapet and then both began to fall. Greaves was luckier: he hit the awning of the strip club before tumbling awkwardly to the pavement. The youth made a wider arc. With arms flailing, his falling figure missed the awning and his head struck a parking meter. It made an ugly sound, like a watermelon bursting.

Greaves was still lying on the wet pavement when Sarah reached him. He was conscious, but clearly in some pain. 'My arm is broken,' he said. He moved his head to look towards the other figure.

'He's dead,' Holland said.

Greaves blinked with the pain and then looked up at Sarah, who knelt beside him.

'It's better this way,' he said. Then he closed his eyes as a spasm of pain swept over him. A stretcher crew arrived but before they could lift him he slowly reached into his pocket with his good hand. He took out some keys and handed them to her. 'Look after the Riley,' he said and she watched as they lifted him into the ambulance.

She turned to where the body of Castor had lain, and in the blurred light of the headlamps, saw that the rain had already washed his blood into the gutter.

CHAPTER
TWENTY-ONE

SARAH looked at her watch. Just after ten o'clock. It seemed as if a week had passed since they had sat in the restaurant. Time was running out: she had to decide whether to file the story by telephone or make her way to the office and write it there.

She pushed open the doors of the strip club, and after a few brief words with the manager persuaded him that valuable amounts of publicity would ensue if he allowed her to use the telephone in his office.

George Conway was on the desk when she got through. 'What are you still doing there?' she asked.

'I stayed for a drink. I was just on my way out.'

'Don't go, George!' she said urgently, 'I've got a great story.'

'How great?'

Sarah took a deep breath. 'I've just witnessed Superintendent Colin Greaves fall from the roof of a Soho strip club holding on to Castor. Greaves is alive. Castor is dead.'

'You're kidding!'

'The gospel truth, George.'

'Just where are you now?'

'The Candy Club in Greek Street.'

'Come into the office and write it here, you've still got time for the main edition.'

Sarah thought for a moment. 'Do we know anyone in Melbourne?'

'Yes, Mark Preston. He's on the *Tribune*, used to be an agency man in London.'

'Mark Preston? I remember Mark, he was a friend of Jack's in Vietnam. Get on to him, will you? See if he can find out anything about a family called Brinkley. Husband's name: James. The wife's previous name was Lady Pamela Temple. They shouldn't be too hard to track down.'

'What do you want on them?'

'Everything he's got.'

'Is it important?'

'Really important. It could be the key to Castor's identity.'

Sarah hurried from the club, and half ran through the rain to Lisle Street where Greaves had parked the car. It took her a little time to get used to the old-fashioned controls, but soon she was heading east, through the thin traffic in Holborn, and as she drove she began to form the story in her mind. The legal problems were the most pressing, they would affect the entire shape of her piece.

Now that the youth was dead, would she be able to say that he was Castor? She couldn't see any reason why not. The police believed he was the one, and if Preston could pin down his identity they had it in the bag; they would even be able to use the arrest pictures taken in Covent Garden.

Sarah felt suddenly liberated, as if tight ropes that had bound her were now cut away. At last, he's dead, she thought, and suddenly she was filled with exaltation. Even the memory of her interview with Fanny Hunter now seemed insignificant. And there was something else: a sense of pride. She had this story, no one could take it away from her, no matter what Fanny Hunter tried to do with the rest of her life.

When she had parked and entered the building, she ran up the stairs two at a time and burst on to the editorial floor, waving to George. She headed down the brightly lit room towards the reporters' desks: It was 10.25 by the newsroom clock and most of the staff had gone home, but there was still a sprinkling of people on the late shift.

She sat down at one of the empty desks and logged her catchline on to the terminal. There was no time for careful prose. She wrote in short, staccato sentences and George came and stood behind her so that he could read her words from the screen. After a time she noticed that he had been joined by Meadows, who was wearing a dinner jacket. George gestured for her to continue and without speaking she turned back to the terminal. When she had finally finished he leaned forward and squeezed her shoulders. 'This is sensational stuff!' he said. 'Meadows wants to see us in his office.'

Sarah stretched before looking up at him. 'Did you get hold of Mark Preston?' she asked.

'Just now, he's going to ring back. We can do an update on the next edition.' He patted her shoulder. 'Come on, Meadows wants to buy you champagne.'

It was only white wine when they got to his office, and Fanny Hunter was there, wearing a long dress.

'We've been upstairs,' Meadows explained, 'dining with the chairman.' He turned to Fanny. 'Of course, you know of Sarah's triumph, don't you?'

Before she could answer, his hot line rang. He listened for a few moments and then said, 'I'll be right up.'

He looked at the others. 'There seems to be some problem at the print-works, I'm just going up to see the chairman for a few minutes.' Then he looked at Fanny, and when he spoke Sarah thought she could detect a slight edge to his voice. 'Why don't you pour them a drink?'

As he got up to leave, George followed him to the door. 'There's something I want to tell you,' he said. 'I'll walk with you to the lift.'

Now they were alone, Fanny nodded towards Meadow's open cabinet and said, 'Help yourself.' Then she swept from the room.

Sarah felt like a drink now. She took a brandy and sat down on the sofa. After a time, Meadows returned alone and picked up his drink from the desk. 'Fanny gone?' he said breezily. 'Oh well, it really hasn't been her day.'

'Have they sorted out the printing?' Sarah asked. She was anxious that her story should appear in the paper.

Meadows seemed slightly preoccupied. 'Yes, that's fine, just a bit of a delay. The chairman is very pleased with your story, it seems that the Home Secretary has been moaning to him of press harassment of the police. Fanny had started another of her diatribes when

George rang with news of your story. I just left Sir Robert boasting to the Home Secretary on the telephone about the job you've done. He was saying that tomorrow the *Gazette* would tell the world what heroes the police were.'

Sarah looked up. 'He still doesn't understand, does he? It isn't a plug we're putting in the paper because of pressure from above. It really happened. Colin Greaves was truly brave.'

Meadows shrugged. 'Don't object to blessings, no matter where they tumble from. And at least you weren't writing about diets.'

She glanced up quickly and he smiled. 'Oh yes, I know all about that.'

Sarah had made a decision. 'I won't be able to work for Fanny,' she said. 'I don't want to be difficult, it just wouldn't work out.' 'Don't worry,' he said, 'you won't have to.' He drank some more of his whisky and loosened the bow tie. 'Do you know why she hates you so much?'

Sarah nodded. 'She had an affair with my husband. It still rankles.'

'There was another incident actually, didn't you know?' he said.

Puzzled, Sarah shook her head.

Meadows sat down in his chair. 'It happened in New York. I know, I was there. It was before I joined the *Gazette*.' He drummed with his fingers on the table top for a moment. 'During the 1982 Democratic Convention I was staying at the Algonquin Hotel; a lot of us were. Jack was making a documentary for television and Fanny was covering for the *Gazette*. She was having a lot of difficulty writing her stuff and begged Jack to help her with the big piece she had to do on the last night. I don't think he wanted to, but, well, you know how good-hearted he was?'

Sarah nodded but did not speak.

'There was a great deal of celebrating going on.'

'I can imagine.'

Meadows looked at his glass for a moment and then continued: 'Fanny had had a skinful, more than anyone else. She was telling us all that Jack had proved how he really felt about her, that he really still cared. At first we made jokes, but then it got embarrassing; she started reciting a poem to him, it was something she'd written herself – a declaration of her love. He tried to leave, and she just went berserk, she lost complete control of herself. The staff of the hotel got her upstairs eventually.'

He stopped and Sarah looked up, waiting for him to continue. 'When she reappeared the following day Jack had already gone.

There was a certain amount of embarrassment, but she acted as if nothing had happened. In fact she had changed profoundly. It was as though her previous personality had been stripped away – all of the mannerisms and speech patterns she'd acquired had gone, like a snake sloughing off an old skin. Suddenly she was tough, crude, aggressive – in fact the Fanny we know today.'

'And the change was that sudden . . . ? It hardly seems possible.'

Meadows clasped his hands behind his head and glanced up at the ceiling. 'Oh, I don't know. The constant pressure of presenting a manufactured personality to the world – the trauma of a big emotional shock, people have been tipped over the edge by less.'

Sarah studied Meadows for a moment. 'Do you think she's unbalanced?'

'Barmy, you mean?' he said lightly. 'Oh, yes, but then I think all excessively ambitious people are. Beware of anyone who has a sense of destiny. Frustrate them and they believe you're defying the will of God.'

Sarah was about to speak again but George re-entered the room accompanied by the night editor and the duty picture-desk assistant. Meadows waved towards them. 'I've invited other colleagues to raise a glass as well.'

Both men congratulated her. 'Pity there were no photographs,' the picture-desk assistant said. 'It must have been fantastic when he fell from the roof.' He turned to Conway. 'One day everyone will carry a little camera the size of a cigarette packet that will transmit pictures straight back to the office as they happen.'

Conway nodded wearily at the man's enthusiasm. 'Yes, and they'll call it television.'

The telephone rang, Meadows listened for a moment and then handed it to George. 'Mark Preston calling from Melbourne.'

'Shall I speak to him?' Sarah asked.

George nodded. 'I'll transfer it to the secretary's extension.'

Sarah went outside and as she waited she glanced down at her crumpled jacket. It had looked smarter in the morning.

The line from Melbourne was clear; nonetheless, she raised her voice slightly. 'Hello, Mark, it's me, Sarah Keane. How are you?'

'Sarah!' the familiar voice answered, 'it's good to hear you. This story George called me about. . . .'

'Yes, I'm working on it. Do you have anything on the Brinkley family?'

'Plenty. I don't remember it myself, I was in Europe at the time, but the old hands around here do. The supermarket papers really went to town. James Brinkley had a crazy stepson. He chopped up both his parents. They say he might have had an accomplice, a neighbour swears he saw a woman leaving the house.'

'Did they sentence him for long?'

Sarah heard a brief consultation taking place, then Preston came back on the line. 'They never caught him.'

'Do you have any pictures of the son?' As they talked, Sarah had begun to feel a slight sensation of unease, but she put it aside.

'We think yes, we're looking now,' Preston answered.

'If you get one, fax it to me first, will you, Mark?'

She gave him the number in the operations room and they said their goodbyes.

She sat and thought for a time and listened to the sound of laughter coming from next door. It was curious how much a room could change, depending on the time of day. From ten in the morning until six o'clock at night, this little office was a vital part of the newspaper. Meadows's secretary sat in command, like the operator of a railway junction, pulling the switches that allowed the staff to come and go, always controlling the flow of people who streamed through the editor's office. Now the room seemed dead, simply an extension of the corridor outside. Suddenly she felt hungry and thought regretfully of the meal she had hardly touched earlier.

George came out of the editor's office and held his arms wide. 'Meadows thinks you're a genius, the chairman thinks you're a genius, and they both think I'm a genius for hiring you! There are bonuses to be distributed. Name whatever you want and it shall be yours.'

Sarah considered his words. 'I'd settle for a meat pie in the Red Lion,' she said finally.

George smiled. 'Then I shall escort you there in triumph,' he said grandly.

The rain continued as they crossed Gray's Inn Road, soaking into her expensive jacket, but she was no longer cold. The street was so free of traffic that they could hear their own footsteps as they approached the Red Lion.

Harry Porter was still in the bar with a group of reporters. There was some sort of celebration going on; the counter was lined with champagne bottles.

'Tony Prior's wife has just had a baby,' George explained. They joined the group and were both handed glasses. Sarah toasted the new father and then caught the attention of the barmaid, who brought her a meat pie that was luke warm from the heated display counter. She had begun to eat when a fragment of conversation from the group came to her. It was Prior speaking with the slow deliberation of the very drunk. 'The boy is called Alexander James Prior and the world will see his name for the first time the day after tomorrow, when it will appear in the birth columns of *The Times* and the *Daily Telegraph*.'

'Why not tomorrow?' one of the other reporters asked.

Prior squinted at him. 'Because it takes at least forty-eight hours. Christ, it's not going on a news page, you know.' His words cut into Sarah's thoughts – the birth column! She remembered that the *Gazette* used to have one before it went tabloid. She pushed away the awful pie and, calling an excuse to George, hurried from the pub, across the wet street, back to the office.

The library was bright with lights and the duty assistant sat at a desk near the counter watching a portable television set.

'Do you still have the old bound copies of the paper here?' she asked urgently.

'Out the back,' the man answered, without taking his eyes from the screen.

'I'll help myself.' She hurried through the high rows of filing cabinets until she reached a wall of shelves that ran the entire width of the room. It only took a moment to find what she wanted. A few minutes later she carried the heavy bound volume of old broadsheet newspapers into the operations room and, laying the book on her desk, began to search through the pages.

There they were: the names of Castor's victims, in the birth columns of the old broadsheet *Gazette*. He had murdered them on the anniversary of their births being printed in the newspaper. 'The children of the *Gazette*,' she said softly. But why? Where was the logic? Sir Gavin Temple had been exposed by the newspaper and his daughter had killed herself because of the disgrace, according to Temple's sister – was that the reason? The *Gazette* killed the child of Temple, therefore Castor would take revenge on the children of the newspaper?

'That must be it,' she said aloud. Slowly she turned the pages, seeking Emily's name. The anniversary of the announcement was tomorrow. Then she looked at a clock on the wall – it was after midnight – tomorrow had already come.

Sarah thought back. She remembered now: Jack hadn't been able to get the name into the *Gazette* until three days after Emily's birth. He had brought it to her in the nursing home. She recalled how proud he had been when he showed the copy to the nurses.

No wonder they hadn't traced the connection. The old *Gazette* had been considered a quality newspaper; the families of the murdered girls must have given up taking the paper years ago, when it had become a tabloid.

Sarah reached for the telephone but it rang before she could touch it. She picked up the receiver and the voice that spoke chilled her like a winter wind. Her blood seemed like ice and she could feel the hair rising on her neck, as though an unwelcome hand had brushed her body. It was Castor. 'I'm looking forward to the next edition of the *Gazette*,' he said in the same chiding voice. 'I intend to get to the heart of the paper today.'

Sarah forced herself to fight the panic that threatened to engulf her: the blind fear that she was confronted with some supernatural force that could brush aside human captors. Her rational mind told her that she was dealing with a human being.

'I know how you choose your victims,' she said quickly. 'You won't be able to kill any more children, Castor. They'll be too well guarded. Now they'll catch you, because you won't be able to stop trying, will you?'

He laughed. 'You really are pathetic, Mrs Keane. I won't have a problem. None of you is able to stop me. It could be any one of a dozen. Even your own daughter. Goodbye for now.'

The line went dead. Sarah swiftly punched her own telephone number and after a moment heard the ringing tone – but no one answered. She tore the page of names from the file and raced downstairs to the newsroom.

Alan Stiles was sitting at the desk. He stood up in alarm as Sarah bore down on him.

'Get the police incident room on the line,' she shouted.

Stiles held out his hands, as if to placate her.

'Now just calm down, love, don't panic,' he said in a patronising voice.

Sarah did not try to explain, instead, she hit him with her shoulder so that he cannoned away from the desk and fell over a wastepaper basket. She snatched up the hotline telephone and a voice answered after a wait that seemed to last for ever.

'You're lucky to catch us,' he said lightly. 'This operation is standing down.'

'This is Sarah Keane,' she said, forcing herself to speak with calm precision. 'You haven't caught Castor yet. He just called with another threat.'

'Christ!' the voice answered, 'are you sure?'

'Of course I'm bloody sure!' she said, her voice rising with sudden rage. 'Now listen, I know how he chooses his victims. It's from an old list of birth announcements in the *Gazette*. Take these down.' She dictated the names, then said, 'My own daughter is on that list, she's either at my home or that of a Claire Trevor.' She gave him the addresses. 'I want a guard on her right now, and a call when you locate her.'

She hung up and turned to Stiles, who stood beside her.

'Are you going to write this?' he asked.

She shook her head, 'Give it to somebody else,' she answered, walking away. Slowly she climbed the stairs to the operations room, feeling as if her whole body was numb. She wanted to go home, but logic told her to stay by her telephone until she knew where Emily and Claire were.

Seated at her desk, after a few minutes she reached out and ran her fingertips against the ragged edge of newsprint, where she had torn the pages from the bound volume. She felt a moment of regret for the act; she hated defacing books. As a child she had looked after her own so carefully that they were in perfect condition when she handed them on to Emily.

The thought caused her to bow her head. 'Please God,' she prayed silently, 'protect my child, see that no harm comes to her.' Minutes ticked by, and the wait seemed interminable, then the telephone rang. It was Castor. 'I understand the paper is late,' he said. 'I'm so excited, like a child expecting a special present.'

'You can't win, Castor,' Sarah replied, but her voice lacked conviction.

'But I already have,' he replied.

Sarah wanted to hit out. 'You vile creature,' she said, her voice rising. 'You murdered your own sister. It wasn't suicide.'

'She was killed by your paper,' he replied and suddenly his voice had lost its taunting edge. 'I loved her and you drove her to her death.'

As he spoke a soft ring told Sarah that the fax machine before her had been activated.

'You caused her to kill herself,' Sarah continued. 'Doctor Civik told us what happened in that house, what you did to her.'

As she spoke a face began to print out on the fax machine. Sarah watched as the features were revealed. In the first moments she did not want to believe what she saw, and then the full horror came to her. The face was unmistakably that of Claire Trevor.

'Oh God!' she cried, before she could check herself.

Castor detected the changed tone in her voice.

'Has something disturbed you?' he asked tauntingly.

Sarah tried to think but her mind was clouded by the same dense fog she had known when Jack died . . . it pressed in upon her claustrophobically. Suddenly, without knowing why, she said, 'Castor, let me talk to Claire.'

There was a long pause and she could hear his breathing, then he said, 'What makes you think she's here?'

'I know she is,' Sarah answered. 'You're holding her, just as you are my daughter.'

There was another pause and then Claire's voice answered. 'It's me, Sarah,' she said, but there was no strength in the words. It sounded as though she were far away.

Sarah felt her own desperation. 'Can't you look after Emily, Claire? She loves you.'

'I've tried,' she answered. 'I love her too, but he's too strong for me, Sarah. He's killed me before.' There was another pause and then Claire said, 'Goodbye, pray that God has mercy on my soul.'

The line went dead.

Sarah began to cry. She let the telephone fall from her hand. 'My child,' she said in despair. 'How can I save my child?'

Then the words that Castor had spoken seemed to echo in her mind. 'I intend to go to the heart of the paper.'

They seemed familiar. She repeated them – and then remembered the old printer who had talked to them. The machine room, the heart of the paper. She started to run for the stairs.

Taking them three at a time she hurtled down the wide stairwell and almost collided with a messenger in the entrance hall. He was carrying a bundle of papers and had stopped to exchange words with the doorman on duty.

'Just arrived,' she heard him say. 'There would have been bloody hell to pay in the old days.'

'Has anyone taken one of those?' she shouted to him.

The man looked up and blinked at her through the thick lenses of his spectacles. 'Only that woman who does the computers,' he answered, 'she stopped me outside.'

Sarah ran on into the vanway, splashing through the puddles in the yard. The door leading to the basement was still open. She pounded down the metal staircase, and momentarily thought she could hear footsteps ahead of her. But it was only her own echo.

She raced across the vast, empty paper store and paused before entering the machine hall, where a single strip of neon shone down on the presses.

Sarah looked around for a weapon. There was a metal table near her, where tools were laid out in neat rows. Almost without breaking step she snatched up a hammer and began to run towards the light. Her sports shoes made no sound on the metal flooring. As she got closer she could see, through a service gap in the machines, a figure dressed in a man's clothes crouching over Emily's still body.

Sarah launched herself through the narrow space and the hammer she carried struck a piece of the machinery. Castor looked up at the sound, and Sarah saw that he was holding the stone with which he had been stamping the Nordic symbol on to the copy of the newspaper.

'Get away from my child!' she shouted, her voice charged with rage.

Castor straightened up and Sarah felt a sudden shock when she saw the face turned towards her. It was like a brutal caricature of Claire's, the hair pulled away so that the usual features now appeared hard and savage.

Moving with sudden speed, Castor drew back his arm and threw the stone at her with all his strength. His aim was not true: the heavy object struck one of the metal rollers and deflected on to the starter button of the machine.

Sarah moved forward. The press began to turn, slowly at first, until it gained greater momentum. She stood facing Castor and now she could feel the vibration from the thunderous machine in the whole of her body. He reached up and Sarah saw the glittering butcher's knife in his hand. Acting instinctively, she swung the hammer at his head, but he raised the knife like a sword and the two weapons clashed with a ringing sound that Sarah could hear above the roar of the machine. Like gladiators, they began to circle about Emily's unmoving body, each seeking the advantage. Five times more their weapons clashed together. Sarah began to gain confidence, realising she could match his agility. Like the image of dancers, their shadows played over Emily. Suddenly he made a wide sweeping motion with the knife and as the weapon reached the full width of its arc Sarah lunged forward. Her foot touched the copy of the newspaper Castor had prepared for his ritual and it slid beneath her weight on the greasy metal floor. She went down, but quickly twisted to cover Emily with her body, then turned to look up.

Castor now raised the butcher's knife with both hands and Sarah looked into his face. He smiled again and it was as if she gazed into a devil's mask; but there was still some grotesque remnant of the friend she had known.

'Claire!' Sarah called out in desperation, not sure if her voice could be heard above the roar of the machine. 'For God's sake, help us!'

The knife was still poised above them, but, as if responding to her words, Castor's devil mask began to contort. First there was an expression of surprise, and then it changed, as though he were now suffering a sudden, overwhelming agony. Sarah began to see two images: Claire's face, but superimposed upon the mask of Castor, like a photograph that has been double-exposed. The image flickered as each now fought for supremacy. The terrible smile seemed to dominate, but then changed to an expression of puzzled surprise and his body began to jerk backwards, stiff-legged, like a marionette being pulled by invisible strings. He gave a long, moaning scream and as he lurched further away from her, Sarah saw the machinery catch at his clothing so that he became entangled with the whirling presses. The great rollers snatched up the writhing figure for a moment and then cast his half-mangled body aside. He fell to the ground, torn apart by the power of the machinery.

Sarah turned her face from the dreadful sight. She knelt beside Emily, and slowly lifted her slender body.

It was easy to carry her from the basement. She could see a dark bruise on her temple, but her daughter still breathed. As they came out into the vanway once again she was overcome by a wave of fatigue. She laid Emily down on the wet ground, and began to stroke her face, her tears mingling with the falling rain.

Slowly her daughter's eyes opened and she gradually came to, blinking at her strange surroundings. Then she saw Sarah.

'What happened?' she asked faintly, 'Where's Claire?'

Sarah stroked her bruised forehead. She was vaguely aware of figures running towards her.

'She's gone now, darling,' Sarah said gently, 'but she saved our lives.'

CHAPTER
TWENTY-TWO

PAULINE KAZNOVITCH stopped her car before Sarah's house. Unsure if she was at the correct address, she checked again with the one written in her notebook. It all looked so different on this sunny afternoon. During the previous week, when the story of Castor's death still dominated the headlines, she had become used to seeing the house as a backdrop to earnest television reporters speaking their datelines from the tree-lined street. But cameras tell only part of the truth.

Even the stormy weather that followed the death of Castor contributed its own distortions to reality. Now the absence of reporters, photographers, television lights, police guards and spectators huddled from the lashing rain changed everything utterly. The mantle of normality had once more descended, and Sarah's house looked similar to thousands of others that ringed the cities of England.

Carrying an enormous bouquet, Pauline rang the bell. It was a long time before Sarah answered, 'I'm sorry,' she said when she had accepted the flowers and led Pauline into the living room, 'I was in the garden.'

'Those are from everybody in the newsroom,' Pauline said, indicating the roses, Then she turned to look through the open french windows, where she could see moving figures and hear a shouted conversation. An image from *Alice in Wonderland* came to her, and immediately Sarah confirmed it.

'A friend is teaching them croquet,' she said, following her gaze, and she closed the doors to cut off the sound of sudden laughter.

Pauline looked around the room for a moment. 'Did Castor ever come in here?' she asked.

'Claire Trevor did, quite often,' Sarah answered, then said, 'Forgive me – would you like a cup of tea or coffee?'

'Coffee would be lovely.'

'Let's go in the kitchen,' Sarah suggested. Pauline followed her to sit at the table while Sarah prepared the percolator.

'You know Brian Meadows and George Conway asked me to come?' Pauline said finally.

Sarah laughed. 'I guessed as much when you rang. In the old days it always used to be the managing editor who turned up as the official emissary. I'm glad to see a bunch of flowers is still obligatory.'

Pauline grinned; she was relieved that Sarah was so relaxed. From the grave concern the editor had shown when he instructed her to make the visit, she'd half expected Sarah to be lying on a chaise longue with the curtains drawn. The robust figure before her was clearly not prostrate with shock.

Pauline continued, 'They say you're not to come back to the office until you're absolutely ready.'

'Tell them thank you, and I'll be in on Monday,' Sarah replied as she set two mugs of coffee before them. 'So where has the story got to?'

'How much have you caught up with?' Pauline replied.

'Very little. We haven't watched television or seen the papers for the last few days. Just tell me everything you know.'

Pauline nodded. 'I think it's just about wrapped up now. A lot of early stuff about Castor's life came out from Doctor Civik. He gave one exclusive interview to the *Daily Telegraph* and then disappeared.

'It seems that Sir Gavin Temple and his sister Sylvia ran some kind of sex ring from that house in Richmond. The pair of them had an incestuous relationship that went back to their childhood, and they encouraged one to develop between Temple's twin children. It involved a lot of supposedly Nordic ritual, which Temple invented. In reality they were just a crowd of degenerates. The boy was captivated by it all, but Temple's daughter was horrified. Eventually it turned her mind, and that was the reason she killed herself.

'The boy wouldn't accept that; he blamed her death on the *Gazette*'s exposure, which ruined his father. Aunt Sylvia made the boy take an oath on the Revenge Stone that he would swear to avenge the family. Then she got him away to his mother in Australia.

'According to school records in Melbourne, he was quite brilliant. He must have been: it appears he managed to transfer most of his stepfather's considerable fortune to California by a combination of forgery and computer hacking. Then he murdered his mother and stepfather and vanished.

'The Los Angeles police department picked up the story then. They say a Claire Trevor suddenly appeared in Malibu two years later. An ex-patient from a private hospital confirmed that she remembered her having undergone surgery and hormonal treatment to become a woman.'

Sarah interrupted. 'Was there ever any indication that the boy had a desire to change sexes?'

Pauline shook her head. 'Doctor Carlyle's theory is that part of the boy's psyche was in conflict with his actions and actually wanted to assume the personality of his dead sister as an act of redemption. In fact, to become both twins: boy and girl. Even the choice of name – Claire Trevor – was an indication.'

'But the boy kept emerging?'

'That's right,' Pauline continued. 'But not for some time. Claire Trevor went to university and tried to find a new life. She got a job with the Rainbow Division computer section in California but when the *Gazette*'s parent company bought the British rights to the system, Doctor Carlyle believes Castor felt that fate was dealing the hand. Claire Trevor applied for the job of systems editor and the *Gazette* was delighted to hire her.'

The door to the kitchen opened and Martin came in for a glass of water.

'How's it going?' Sarah asked.

'We're winning,' he answered, and with a smile in their direction slammed the door behind him.

Pauline looked up again. 'You know, the night of the Kerris Road murder Claire Trevor actually slipped away from your daughter's school concert to murder the girl.'

'I'd worked that out,' Sarah replied. 'What about the motorcyclist

217

– did they find out why he was at the home in Barnes when the family was killed?'

'He was delivering cocaine to the girl's father. The police think he must have arrived just after Castor had left, leaving the door still open. When he found the bodies he ran, and that's when the neighbours saw him.'

There was the sound of more laughter from the garden. Pauline glanced towards the window. 'How are your children now? It must be . . . extraordinary for them. Have they coped with the truth?'

Sarah poured herself some more coffee before she answered. 'The boys seem fine,' she said. 'But then they never saw Castor – just Claire Trevor. Only Emily and I met him.'

Pauline paused and then asked 'Do you think it will harm her?'

Sarah thought for a time. 'I'm not sure,' she said slowly. 'But I don't think so.'

'Why? Have you talked about it?'

Sarah shook her head and smiled. 'Not yet, but Emily's a very logical girl, she likes to work things out for herself. Claire bought her a puppy called Sam, and she really loves it. Last night, when we were taking him for a walk, she said to me: "If Sam ever went mad and attacked me, I think I'd still love him for how he used to be."' Sarah paused again. 'I think she was telling me something about Claire.'

'And you, how do you feel?'

Sarah shrugged. 'Time will tell.' She hesitated briefly and then said, 'Does Fanny Hunter know you're here?'

'No, I work for Edward Carter now. He's been reinstated, didn't you hear?'

'I've been out of touch with the office.'

'Fanny's gone on holiday to the south of France – actually I think the big romance is over and this trip is a payoff.'

'Big romance?'

'With our revered chairman, Sir Robert Hall. It was all supposed to be a secret – he was worried about his peerage. But I found out the moment she took me into her department. Jackie, her secretary told me.' Pauline stood up and held out her hand. 'Well I'd better be getting back. I'm glad I can report that all is well.'

Sarah saw her to the door and then stood in the quiet of the living room. She felt at peace; nothing had disturbed the tranquillity of her home. Then she opened the french windows and went in to the garden, where Colin Greaves had spent the day instructing them all

218

in the mysteries of croquet. Sarah's father was about to make the winning stroke of the match in play.

'Your whole family cheats,' Greaves protested to her.

'Another game!' the boys shouted.

'You play your grandfather and Emily,' Greaves replied. 'I'm supposed to rest my arm.'

He made for the seat under the apple tree and Sarah joined him, sitting so that he could place his good arm around her shoulder. They watched Emily make the first strike, and slowly Sarah lowered her head on to Colin Greaves's shoulder.